praise for
chris lombardi

I Ain't Marching Anymore (The New Press, 2020)

"A highly original book, at once scholarly and intimate, exposing the clash between personal conviction and social expectation whose significance stretches far exposing beyond the battlefield."

Eric Jaffe, author of *A Curious Madness: An American Combat Psychiatrist, a Japanese War Crimes Suspect, and an Unsolved Mystery from World War II*

blue: season (Mumblers Press, 2022)

"A richly textured and deeply felt tale of life tragedy turned into art."

Kirkus Reviews (starred review)

"As it traces a brilliant young woman's path into psychosis, *blue: season*'s supple prose mixes poetry with delirium, finding truth in delusion. The novel as it intensifies carries you deep into madness and then back out."

Louis B. Jones, author of *Radiance* and *Particles and Luck*

jehanne darc, book one

jehanne darc, book one

From Domrémy to Orléans

Chris Lombardi

This is a work of fiction. Names, characters, places and incidents either are the product of the author's imagination or are used fictitiously and any resemblance to actual persons, living or dead, businesses, companies, events or locales is entirely coincidental.

Cover design by Mike Karpa

Cover art: Joan of Arc at the Porte Saint-Honoré during the siege of Paris in 1429. Miniature from the Martial d'Auvergne manuscript, *Les Vigiles de Charles VII*, circa 1484.

Author photo © Kyle Cassidy, @kylecassidy, kylecassidy.com

Published by Mumblers Press LLC, San Francisco CA USA

ISBN 978-1-963221-07-7 (paperback) | 978-1-963221-08-4 (e-book)

LCCN Pending

To Frederic Tuten—who started it all by asking me to write a ghost story

prologue: la chapelle camp, outskirts of paris

September 1429

The bridge is burnt, the horse watered, the city lost before sunrise.

At first, awakened by the smell of the horse nosing at his tent, Father Jehan Pasquerel wonders if he dreamed the burning. The horse smells of the Seine, outhouse to a city. "Where's your master?" asks the priest. He's not good at talking to animals, and tries to evoke his order's founder, St. Francis. "Did he really carry out the king's command?"

A gasp behind him: rushing past the horse a young squire, sweat plastering his hair to his cheeks. "Good morning, father. Is she awake?"

"She hasn't slept, so far as I know." The priest looks at the boy, thirteen years old when they met six months ago. Now years of care are in the boy's eyes. "Just like you." He sighs and makes himself stand, giving up the effort to sleep, to let dreams uncurl for a brief moment. It is anyway too hot. He offers the squire a draught from his winesap. "Of course, she has been praying the night."

The boy smiles wanly. "If there was ever a time we needed the voice of God . . . May her voice give her a path to conquest."

"Like in Orléans," Pasquerel says absently. Three months past, a lifetime ago.

"The men, they're coming behind me, father," says the squire. "They will hope to hear from her—to learn how we will do this, now."

"Have you come from Alençon?" The voice behind him sharp, unmistakable.

Daulon, the Maid's squire, straightens automatically, like a well-trained sentry. "Good morning, *mademoiselle La Pucelle.* Yes."

His questioner, barely taller than he, speaks so quietly that they have to strain to hear. Her color is high in both cheeks. "Did he burn the bridge?"

"As the king did order," Pasquerel supplements the boy's nervous nod.

"Yet there are widows begging him to enter Paris. Begging *me.*" Her voice grows even lower, threatening a whisper. Behind her, the sun rises over the city, as if she has beckoned its arrival.

The spires of Notre Dame, once visible above the city's squat homes even from this distance, are now obscured by barricades redoubled: English and Burgundian troops both at twice their normal mass. Still the cathedral's highest points rise over the rabble.

"I said I wanted to see Paris from much closer," Jehanne Darc says more gently, as if trying a joke.

"How is your wound?" Pasquerel half-kneels as if to examine it; her doublet is still ripped near her thigh, from the crossbow. The poultice has dried overnight to a crusty shield. "Are you in much pain?"

She waves dismissively. "Don't be one of those doctoring fools. Come and help me with my armor." She stops the squire in mid-grin. "I meant the Father, *fair homme.* I need his counsel."

She lets the crestfallen boy lay down for a nap and leads Pasquerel to her tent, where her white armor lies in a corner like an unwelcome guardian. It looks twice her size. "He *is* a coward," she says as she steps into a leg harness, Pasquerel holding it still. "I should have waited to crown him." She winces at the next harness, her swollen thigh tight against the armor.

"What does your voice say?" Pasquerel asks gently.

Jehanne looks up at her confessor, tears on the edge of her eyelashes. "Too much to tell you. The roar is deafening. Take Paris, not take Paris. King's betrayal? No matter but. The noise. Make it stop. Instead it's getting worse." The words rush out in a tumble, a battlefield confession of sorts. She reaches up and tightens the cord that binds her black hair, which has grown again past her collarbone. "The smell of siege makes me sick." She stares then, till he knows what she means.

Pasquerel bows, not wanting to witness her oldest injury yet again. He reaches for her breastplate, carrying it with both hands. "Can you turn this to a victory?" lifting the plate onto her chest and beginning to lace the sides. "Like Orléans?"

"That's the wrong question," says Jehanne. She reaches for the arm harnesses, white iron barely battered, and hands them to Pasquerel. "The question you should ask is, *Do I want to?*"

Pasquerel starts. His head starts to hurt. Why drag them here then? He swallows and slides the left harness over Jehanne Darc's elbow, choosing his words carefully. "What do you want to do now?"

"Find Alençon," Jehanne snaps. Her hands, emerging from the armor, seem tiny, even in mail. She bows for the gorget, which Pasquerel slips around her neck, but waves away both the capeline and the sallet, preferring an uncovered head. Her hood falls back behind. "And reassure them that I am still alive."

Pasquerel has seen this transformation many times since her

armor was beaten into her shape: but he can't help but bow to it now, peasant girl in boy-doublet now royalty in blazing white iron. He calls to Daulon, who's ready with the black horse Alençon gave her, the one she calls Le Lune Trois. She barely needs the squire's assistance to mount the horse, whisper into its neck.

By the time Pasquerel, on foot, reaches the edge of the camp, the crowds have already gathered around her. Footmen and infantrymen and archers, nurses heavy with bandage and cooks, assorted priests humbler than the Augustinian. Jehanne's whisper gone, she issues her words in a strangled shout.

"We fought bravely and well yesterday!" half-smiling. "That crossbow could not silence the voice of God!" She swallows, hard. "The King has ordered that we pause before we renew our assault on Paris—"

The shouts match her then, troops denying the king's power, demanding the blood of Burgundians. She waves her lance, furious. "*Silence!*" She waits for the roar to subside, but it doesn't. The noise escalates. Then she realizes what they are all saying. "*La Pucelle! La Pucelle! La Pucelle é victoire! La Pucelle é victoire de Dieu!*" Some have sunk to their knees and hold their hands together, in half-prayer. Others wave their weapons. The clanking of armor and screaming of steel.

She looks over the crowd and beyond them, at the sleepy barricades, the whisper of Notre Dame. Her face is unreadable. The sun rises further, heating their armor. As he has all summer, Pasquerel wonders that the lot of them don't faint of it.

one

Domrémy, 1424

BY THE TIME the fourth soldier pulls her legs open, she can't feel anything below her throat. Her eyes watering in the July sun. Drops of sweat, salt already crystallizing. A sharp pull on her scalp, her long hair wrapped around a strange gloved fist. Stay with the drops of salt. Her hands don't exist, each in the custody of a different soldier. Her legs don't exist. The smell of their horses fills her nose. It competes with the smell of sheep dung, of blood. She turns her head. The sky past their faces. She fills her eyes with sky, with sunlight. Her hair then pulled tighter, till she has to attend to it, to that pain alone.

The sound of another horse is startling, then, followed by clashing sentences, those flat loud angles: English words. The fourth soldier stands up and pulls up his trousers. The others pull away from the group, fear in their boy-faces.

An older man, now, bends to her face, speaks to her in slow, awkward French. "Is it possible . . . can you walk?"

Rage in her fingertips: "*Je suis mort.*" *Merde*, she should have played dead from the beginning.

He turns to the soldiers, issues more sharp English words. Gestures, sounds of horses being mounted and ridden away. The older man stays a second more, looking down at her, shaking his head. Then he, too, pulls her legs apart. She fears he may split her in two.

Domrémy: a border town emptying slowly, relentlessly. Every fortnight a family leaves, the house then inhabited only by the small animals left behind. Over the nine years since France's huge defeat at Azincort (renamed Agincourt by the victors), fewer and fewer villages in these parts are loyal to France, Domrémy among them. Father Guillaime, the local confessor, has been watching the village wilt as surely as the grapes. He picks his way down a ridge into the village, breathing heavily from the heat.

The valley protects the smell of old fires. He's breathing the dead. He doesn't wear a pin of either side, though if he could it would be a dolphin—sign of the Dauphin, France's not-quite-king. In this civil war, wear the wrong pin and you may die, none at all and you fear: the enemy is now your cousin. Looks like you. Wears your clothes. No way to know for sure who is who. Until.

It has been like this forever, he thinks. Or almost. Or at least since the emperor 300 years ago erected his magnificent rough-hewn castles, chattel kissing the feet of priests. Then, as now, the grasses were in multiple shades of green, then as now the oaks and deep pines and shy pale beeches intersected to create grove-temples. Then, as now, knights and vassals beat each other to pulp, extorted their blood money from tenant farmers.

But the rules they fought by then are all shattered now; crusades and inquisitions and assassinations have made useless music of the word *chevalerie*. Now, here is only a thatched roof, broken in places, clay stone worn down by time and the hammering of metal, now given way to wildflowers and weeds.

A few of the houses bear signs of fire, their cattle chased off or stolen. Silence, instead of children, or cow sounds, or heavy wheels approaching the road. The Darcs should have left too, he thinks now. So should he. But Jacquot Darc, the village *doyen,* the richest of its tenant farmers, said things were getting better. Until.

The Darc house looks not built but sculpted: clay facade, stone walls, a sloping roof creating a pale ghost triangle. Inside, the house is narrow, dark. He can barely make out the plump form of Jacquot's wife, Isabelle Romée—she was his star pupil, her last name a tribute to her pilgrimages to holy places. He holds her hands a moment as she whispers her apologies for Jacquot's absence, gesturing upstairs.

He climbs the narrow staircase carefully. "When did it happen?"

"Three weeks ago, father." Isabelle's whisper is more like a hiss. "Twelve years old and never a drop of trouble, and now—" she stops mid-sentence as they enter the tiny side room. Affixed to one wall is a rough-crafted crucifix; below it, a thin pallet for sleep with red-brown stains: blood, vomit?

The girl shifts her weight and tightens her arms around her knees. Scratches from her own nails down her slender legs. Her hair, black spun silk, is uncombed, twined with wild grasses from the sheep's grazing fields. She looks at nothing, past the priest, and holds her breath. She takes a handful of hair in one palm and twists it, harder and harder, till tears leak out of her eyes.

"Jehanne?" the priest says softly. She turns her head, as if hearing a bird sing through the window, her eyes blank. She doesn't answer, rolling her hair tighter and tighter. Then she curls on her side, burying her face in her folded arms.

The priest sighs and kneels beside her. He's seen this before, in other girls, other villages, though not other wars. He doesn't want to know the details. He watches her shudder, her arms convulsing, her chest in a hard spasm as if her heart's about to make an exit.

"Jehanne, it's me. Father Guillaime. Do you remember me?"

"Of course she does," Isabelle says, unhelpfully. "She loves going to Mass. She's my best little church girl, eh *petite soeur?*"

Father Guillaime waves to silence the mother, draws closer to the silenced daughter. "Jehanne, I know these are hard times," an absurd sentence the moment he says it. "I've missed you in church these last weeks."

The girl's eyes close, as if in sleep. Only her fist, still wrapped around her hair, stays tight and betrays her.

He doesn't know how long they all remain there, only that the room is darkening, the small window granting sunset in full orange glory. Finally he reaches into his pocket and brings out a circlet of small dark stones with a crucifix attached. "Jehanne, this is for you."

Her eyes open, she stares at the rosary, her mouth softening. Her words when they come out are hoarse, as if her voice were unused. "Thank you, father." She sits up and extends her hand, receives the stones on her scratched palm. "I will say my rosary tonight."

"Very good, then," the priest tries to hide his surprise. He places the stones in her hands. "Try not to frighten your mother so much, eh?"

"Oh, I knew you would help her," Isabelle's voice too sharp, wavering, a half-desperate tremolo. "Will you have supper with us tonight, Father? It's a long walk back to St. Rémy."

"You are very kind." The old man's words are uneasy, looking over at the girl again. He knows what is being asked of him, now, and joins the silence. "I admire the peace of your house," he says, hoping that's clear enough.

"Merci, pére." Isabelle's eyes still anxious, as she nods her thanks, before turning to the girl beginning to lower herself from the pallet. "Jehanne, you will come down and help me with supper?"

The girl straightens, exhaling, her feet unsteady as they slide to the floor. "Yes, ma mére."

The priest's astonishment is undeserved: Jehanne has gotten this far many times over the past three weeks, only to sink back. Still, Isabelle thanks him for the rosary. "I will say it with her, tomorrow morning." Daughter of pious men and women, Isabelle Romée has taught all her children saints' days, holidays, the holy year: the crosses at her throat testify to her pilgrimages. "I have said the rosary with them every morning, ever since they could say the words." Jehanne was her greatest hope, for the convent she herself never chose.

It's after the priest has left that it happens again, as if rehearsed: a heavy plate crashing to the floor after Jehanne throws it from the table. Her brother Jacquemin lifts the girl and carries her up the stairs, while Isabelle sweeps the shards out from under the table. They all try to ignore the now-familiar screams, followed by the sudden silence that frightened them the first time.

Pierre, the youngest brother, who's only a year older than Jehanne, looks down at his plate as if he has just eaten soured meat. Isabelle and Jacquot look at each other. "Not a child anymore," Jacquot tells his son.

As children Pierre and Jehanne, a mere year apart, were inseparable, harassing sheep and trying to poison the cows' water, giggling. Now Pierre follows Jacquemin and takes care of the apple trees. He barely ever sees her. But still. He leaves the table, escaping into the early-evening air.

Upstairs Jehanne curls tight on her bed, then the floor. She is back in the sheep meadow now, no dark but blazing sun, the smell not of candles, or even sheep, but horses. Unlike when it happened she feels everything, the push and the blood and the tearing inside.

She crawled home, that day three weeks ago. Made her way home on her belly. Her dress was green with grass, covering the blood. Isabelle afraid to wash me. I couldn't speak. Yes, they'd been by. Her mother's rage: I'd run off from spinning to mind the sheep. The nunnery now obvious. Three days later the flood started.

Whispers fill her head, whispered voices of other girls, other boys, all pushed to the ground by soldiers and discarded in pieces. Some of the voices are not speaking French, the words thicker, more glottal, odd music of tones and angles. Her headaches. She wishes they would go away. She's terrified they will, and leave her alone with the soldiers. She can't tell Isabelle about them: she knows her mother would collapse and quote the Book of Revelations, and ask Father Guillaime for an exorcism. Are these whispers devils? Do they have tails like scorpions? No, they're children. They're boys with broken wrists and girls with bleeding cunts. Like hers.

A few days later they came back, all of them, in the middle of dinner. Then the other stuff pushing in: these other soldiers talking other languages. Her own dreams? The stuff of dreams? Weeks and weeks of wondering. Maybe they're devils and she does need an exorcism. How would an exorcism feel? Would it wash her skin clean of them, empty her filled ears, calm her vibrating skin? Perhaps she could sleep, then. With the new rosary, maybe she can do it herself.

She forces herself sitting and picks up the rosary, begins to sing its attached words slowly, like at Mass. *"Credo de unum Deum . . ."*

Her voice holds the sky open, rises, taking her with it. Far down below, she can see the clump of soldiers, half-hidden by trees. She looks away, toward the orchard half a mile away, past the meadow where soldiers push open a young girl. She can't feel a thing. She says the next prayer. The stones glow in the dark of her room. No exorcism, this.

She begins to laugh, liberated by the rush of blood to her head. "*Ave Maria*," she begins with a fit of giggles.

These are her days, for three years:

Wake up past midnight, terrified: sweat from the past cements fabric to her skin: back to the meadow with her. Sunlight hurting her eyes, scream like she never did for real. The captain the heaviest. The scared younger one staying limp, pushing and cursing, until the others' insults, their catcalls, his rage turned him hard and cold.

Sit up at sunrise. Slowly, against dizziness, against being pushed down. Pull off damp nightclothes, sweat mixed with blood where she scratched herself. Then farming clothes, layers of rough-cotton skirts, heavy boots: time to milk the cows. Teats flush milk, semen, smell of blood, soldier's fingers squeeze her nipple sometimes. Milk cool on her hands. The soldier who spat when he was finished. When she stops and lets the milk run through her hands, her father pushes her aside, as if he could catch the milk she dropped.

Her head hurts. Voices clash with memories, obscure what's in front of her. *Merde merde merde* why now why not a day of peace? What is peace? She doesn't want to work. She doesn't even want to pray. She wants to sleep. But too many weeks like this have passed already, and no one will tolerate it.

She should be better by now. She's not the only one, not even the first, says her mother. But Isabelle doesn't know how the girls and boys push at her, force her to feel their pain too. Huge men of many races and colors of armor pushing into them, into her. Cold-burned skin shuddering to a stop. She doesn't just have the soldiers in the meadow. When will they tell her what they want? They must want something.

She wishes Pierre were here too, helping. Helping *her*. Instead Jacquot has assigned him to manage a small plot of his own, to plough and prepare for harvest: "He's fifteen, after all, he'll be married in just a few years."

When Pierre looks at her, it's as if he wants to vomit. No trace of the boy who whispered "Come see!" to a giggling seven-year-old Jehanne, taught her how to hunt down field mice, showed her a pair of woodchucks mating behind the maple tree. Jacquot had put an end to *that* when Jehanne was nine, sending ten-year-old Pierre to Larzicourt to help their cousin with the planting for a season, telling Jehanne flatly "You're not a boy. With your brother gone maybe you'll remember that, and help your mother with the spinning and sewing instead." Jehanne bowed to the inevitable and learned to spin, now a faster spinner than Isabelle: *yes, a girl,* like a taunt.

Then the sheep meadow slapped that truth in her face. And drove Pierre away. Again. Just when she needs him, needs *someone* to talk to about these voices, these faces.

She tries again with the cows, reaching with practiced hands to refill the jug again and again. The cows' bellies relax as she releases them. The one who sent them all away before he turned to her. Then next, fast, another one, armor not metal but thickly woven cloth, high-pitched warrior wail: Zheng He. She slips again, lets milk wet her feet, then redirects it to the proper container.

Maybe she's not the first in her village, as Isabelle says. But the others weren't chased this way, drowned in stories. Are they just dreams forced on her? Because she's so often awake during night's deepest velvet dark, the dream-home? Is she merely insane?

No, they say, no. She feels them on her skin, terrified. *In* her skin, like some itching insect. They roar so, she can't hear her father's voice. Finally he bellows: "Jehanne, you're going to run off my cattle. Go help your mother with the spinning."

These are her days, for three years.

After spinning, or doing whatever else Isabelle wants, Isabelle sends her to church. She no longer rebels. St.-Rémy is small but sturdy, built of old stone and dark wood, dark inside even in winter's bright-cold. This is a safe place, where she can stare and tremble to her heart's content. Here it's not madness but God. Her nameless boys and girls not devils but angels.

They kneel with her at the altar-tableau, a wooden diorama with tiny wooden figures embedded, representing the life of Jesus from birth to resurrection. Jehanne moves closer to it, fascinated. The rough-hewn bodies like small birds, like dolls she could hold in her hand. Chipped red paint for the crucifixion scene. Jesus wept. The girls and boys in her head cry with him.

"I hear them all the time," she tells Father Guillame, every day.

He has heard it all, now, and is still trying to decide what he thinks about it. He prays to see if he should believe her, believe she hears martyrs' cries.

He tells her more of the lives of her saints. First, of course, Margaret of Antioch, whose story she knows, whose statue smiles gently from a corner of this church: rejecting a conqueror's rape, she survived the mobs that tried to burn her and drown her. Jehanne stares at the statue's smooth gray stone, its calm arms. She feels a little smile tremble on her lips. The roar inside her approves. The girls and boys love martyr-stories: she comes back every day for more.

Jehanne Darc's addiction to the small church becomes near-notorious. Unnaturally thin, "she prays instead of eating," the old women whisper. Every Sunday, she comes early to help set up the church. As the year progresses the old priest is ever more grateful. His altarboys have all been pressed into soldier's garb.

One Sunday morning, the priest's robes are lined with thick

wool, and like everyone else he wears a cap to shelter him from the chill. Tall tapers on either side of the altar keep blowing out, from the wind that sneaks through the closed door.

A younger priest from Avignon, sent by the bishop to help the old man, looks suspiciously at the skinny girl who moves through the sanctuary with such authority. He tells himself that it's just a trick of light from the candles that makes her rosary glow. She stands before the statue of St. Margaret for what seems like hours, her lips moving.

Throughout Mass, she bows her head and doesn't move. She's not alone, she's never alone. Not with these girls and boys. A new girl pushing at her: deep ridges on black skin, scar tissue bubbles. Lips tight with rage. Jehanne's stomach twists. She blinks, and again, tries to look only at St. Margaret. If she blinks enough will they go away? Her cheeks are burning.

Look at the young priest instead, the sweat on his neck: vein popping, he could be the fat one, flesh popping out between armor. Steel singing against flesh. The noise escalates. Not the hymns but the jammed voices filling her ears. Not screams. something closer to death. Jehanne presses the rosary to her lips, trying not to vomit. She murmurs prayers instead: rosary-words, meaningless, comforting. Priest-words: the veins on his neck, on the other. A tired boy with a weapon bigger than him and a frozen face. Tears jam against her throat, hers, theirs? She can hardly breathe, and her prayers come out faint, inaudible.

Until her blood heats and she's above them all, higher than the church's low ceiling. She watches the huddled parishioners staying close together for warmth, kneeling and rising at the priests' words, while the girl with the glowing rosary stays still, shudders, tears streaming, her lips moving. She sees the villagers stare as her eyes open, as she laughs, her face damp with tears and sweat. Her mother's face pale and anxious, her father and brother stolid, looking at the priest, ignoring the girl.

When the tapers blow out for the tenth time, Jehanne stands

and stares at them. her gaze soft suddenly, until each one has lit of their own accord. The villagers gasp. Jehanne laughs, looks over at the old priest, who knows. At Isabelle, who has been dousing candles all over the house for years. She holds her rosary to the unseen sky.

After mass, Isabelle approaches Jehanne quietly. "Will you come home now? Or will you stay?"

Jehanne looks over at her mother. Don't look so scared, *maman*, she thinks. You're not nearly as scared as I am. I still can't feel my knees. "I'll come."

She looks to the church door, to her brothers with their restless feet, her sister with her babies, to Jacquot uncomfortable in his rough church coat. He hasn't been able to look her in the eye for three years.

As they leave the church, Jehanne walks a little ahead, falls in with her father. She breathes soft, and walks as slow as he. Her feet sink into the softening earth, the morning-dampness making mud of the road. Before, *papa*, I was your *petit fleur*. I was your helper, you took me with you to collect taxes, taught me to ride a horse and milk cows and prepare ground for planting. Now, when my head is drowned with voices and I can't feel half my body, you turn from me as if from a bitter taste. She doesn't say any of it. Instead, "Is it time to harrow, soon?" She knows that before seeds can be planted, they'll need to pull the large grid over the fields, puncture the frost and mud.

Jacquot turns, startled at that little voice saying not just prayers but questions about farming. "Next week or so, I think."

"I think Maman can lend me to you then," she says carefully, watching his eyes. She reaches for his hand, a gesture that was commonplace in the days he taught her to ride. Jacquot's hand stiffens as if burned. He's given her over to Isabelle, to his wife's dream of a convent, of the glory of a Christ-bride daughter. He's been having nightmares about her, in which she becomes a soldier. He doesn't want to talk to her at all. But he swallows, closes his rough-furred hand around hers.

Papa, don't leave me alone with them. She doesn't say it. They arrive at the little house, door left open by Isabelle, and leave mud-footprints on the kitchen floor. She looks up at him: "Tell her you need me, papa?"

Jacquot sighs. Her stare reminds him of her infant self, not the mischievous seven-year-old but the wailing infant yelling for its mother's nipple. He ran from her then, handing her to Isabelle and retreating to his fields. Now, he wonders about the convent, if she's asking to harrow. "I'll tell her, I promise. In the meantime—" a test, to see that she doesn't break down—"you can go dig the beet and rose beds, up in the garden."

That afternoon she climbs up the ridge to the garden, at the entrance to Jacquot's orchards and groves. The bag of spades and shears feels heavier than she is.

Louder, living voices float down to her from uphill: she looks up the long, meandering bridge and sees Joubert, the carter, and his wife. They have avoided her this past year, they looked away when she cried in church. She calls up anyway: "Monsieur Joubert! Madame!"

Madame Joubert smiles in a wolflike baring of teeth, eyes bright, staring; her husband shelters behind her thick cloak. "Good day, Jehanne Darc," she says. "What are you on about, on a Sunday?"

"Up to my father's garden," she says. "Before planting."

"Good for you," Joubert concurs from behind his wife. "We all need to be doing that, soon enough."

Madame Joubert shoots a look of fire at her husband. Jehanne swallows, as Madame's eyes flash at her skirt, her lips bare her teeth again.

Deep flush, not her skin but internal. There are no secrets in her village, despite priests' promises. If she wanted it quiet, forgotten, she should have melted into the background. Not put on such a show. But it wasn't my show, it was theirs. She straightens her back stares Madame down, addresses her husband. "Will you be planting soon, then, Monsieur?"

Joubert ignores his wife, again. "I just hope it stays peaceful long enough for us to be getting some benefit of it."

Jehanne's skin chills, her blush forgotten. "You think more fighting? Here?"

Madame Joubert usurps his reply then, with a vague "Your father's garden is the pride of Domrémy."

Jehanne bows her father's thanks, willing her voices to stay back, not to confuse her while she's trying to talk. "My papa says he thinks, he hopes, the worst is over. You don't think so, Monsieur?"

Joubert, now directly addressed, summons up the courage to tell a sliver of the truth. "Mademoiselle Darc, my grandpapa was sliced open in Tours, nearly a hundred years ago. I don't know if it'll ever be over. Especially now, everyone round us bowed to Burgundy—only little Domrémy left to hail the Dauphin!" He grins and taps the little dolphin on his surcoat.

"Domrémy will survive," Madame Joubert asserts, her smile —already a weapon—turned a beacon. "Jehanne, I hope we can all enjoy your garden."

She reaches the crest of the ridge just as sun is turning every-thing to rose: the wildflowers, the stone marking the road, the shy beech tree. Now it seems to bow, to welcome her to another church. A sharp intake of breath: she kneels. The beet-beds are fringed by flowers the color of her hair.

On her own her arms feel weak, her fingers half-numb in the cold. But the girls and boys make her stronger, help guide her fingers in the cold soil,. Her elbows push the spade-blade further, further. Her own grave, their graves. Not devils but angels. But they smell real. The girls have menstrual blood. Half the boys have bleeding rectums.

She starts addressing them as if in a some live crowd. Her voice trembles when she tries it aloud, her breath a white cloud.

"This war is old, they say. And they only know about France." She hammers at the spade, splits rocks that seem to have grow up from the soil. "What the hell am I supposed to do about it?" She looks down and sees that her hands are bleeding. She couldn't feel it happening. She tells the girls and boys to help her or go away.

"What do you want?" she asks, to sudden silence. She looks into the garden, but sees only her bloody fingers.

After the harvest is over, Isabelle takes Jehanne to the miller's "so we can get enough flour for four hands." She lets Jehanne carry the bag with the money, which is far heavier than the flour will be.

She notices her daughter's thickening arms as she hands Jehanne a pile of sacks: ploughing and planting have widened the girl's shoulders, ballooned her calves, no wonder she eats as much as her brothers. The nuns at St.-Urbain's convent will approve of Jehanne's industry when they receive her. Isabelle reminds herself to plead with Jacquot. It's time, now.

They wait patiently in the group of women counting their sackfuls of money. Jehanne, knowing nothing of Isabelle's plans, looks into hers, its piles of *derniers* and *ecu*. The crosses sit in the center of the battered coins like unkept promises. She stares at the other side's insignia of Lorraine, the duke who keeps dancing between Burgundy and the Dauphin. It makes her uneasy, with odd flash-images of women being dragged into the streets. The images make her squeeze her eyes shut, so her mother won't see.

"My Claud, he went last week," one of the women ahead of her is saying. "He said *maman*, don't worry, I'll be back with a sackful of gold and blessings from de Baudricort." She's easily twice Jehanne's size, and her son is even bigger.

"De Baudricort, who is that?" Her friend is short, with red hair like Hauviette's and a few freckles that have gone nasty with the last fever.

"The captain of Vaucouleurs, *non*? He saw my boy at games, and was impressed how strong he is. He invited him to go there, to learn how to use a bombard."

"Well that's a trade, isn't it?" the shorter woman giggles, stopping quickly when her friend doesn't join in.

"Better that than he fall in with Burgundy, like half the people here."

"*Pardon, madame*—how far is it to Vaucouleurs?" She'd swear she hadn't said it if she couldn't see her reflection in the pool of standing water by the door: faithless, it shows her lips moving. Isabelle grips her shoulder, as if the gesture could recall her words.

The two women walk away from her in backward steps, while the miller's wife keeps her head down, filling sacks.

Finally a tall, lanky man at the doorway answers her: "About a day's ride."

She bows her head to the man, again ignoring her mother. They may be trying to avoid her but they do look at her, in obvious curiosity: what the hell is the mad Darc girl up to, now?

It's Isabelle who blushes now. "Don't you remember?" she asks her daughter, in a voice meant to public consumption. "When we went to visit my cousins, Jenelle and Durand? You rode right by there. Pierre was so excited, he wanted to crawl over the walls and raise a lance right there!"

Jehanne laughs suddenly, a five-year-old memory clear: Pierre, at ten years old, waving a twig and shouting *"Vive Lorraine!"* She tries remembering Durand, then. and comes up blurry: a slender young man, blowing his nose over and over.

"Durand? The boy with the broken down horse and the bad cold?"

Isabelle's giggle turns to a full-fledged howl. "He'd rail at that picture, my girl. He's 28, thinks he's some big soldier now."

Finally the miller hands over their sacks; Jehanne waves away the errand-boy who offers to help and hoists three of the bags over her slim shoulders. The mothers behind them, waiting for flour, stare hard. Almost four years and they're still checking her for pregnancy.

On the way home, Isabelle's tone of voice doesn't change much from her public question. "Have you started preparing to marry Our Lord?"

Jehanne swallows, though she knew this was coming. Whenever Isabelle has to endure their stares she retaliates against her, using her oldest weapon. She wanted a daughter who chose the nunnery, asked for it, didn't want to have to prescribe it against her will. Until.

"I pray every day," Jehanne tells her mother a truth. "Voices fill my blood." She wonders if she will ever be able to describe the flood. She wonders if her mother will care. "Every day I learn about more saints, and take their stories to me."

Before she goes to the church that day, she slips over to the river for a swim. A child-pastime. She wishes Mengette, her child-friend, could join her.

She walks to the riverbank as quickly as she can, her muscles stiff from carrying, and peels off her clothes shyly, ducking behind reeds. She's fifteen, but thinness has delayed her woman-blood and her chest is nearly as flat as the day she was raped.

She slides under water, submerging quickly: the river is another shelter from sunlight. It mutes the voices, water filling her ears. Under water, she watches the lichen peel off the sides of the river. She remembers pointing it out to Mengette, her best friend, over and over. When Jacquot and Isabelle sent little Pierre away, at ten years old she clung even more to Mengette.

She and Mengette would practice holding their breath, breathing under water, giggling too much to accomplish much. They held hands under water and when they were done, lay with their bodies touching in the shallow creek-beds. Hands twined in each other's hair.

Now the water-darkness submerges that memory too. She lets her head above water, to take in air; she pushes hard to chase off the flood of voices that wants to follow, and looks now only for silence.

Each night that year, she climbs the ridge to walk in her father's groves, leading into the orchards' green bounty. Their thickness makes it feel dark in there, the green now jeweled. The apple and beech trees sing deep in the throat, like a blessed cough. The aging trees lean in to protect the younger, the sheaves brushing her ankles as tiny wildflowers defy darkness.

As she walks, the voices, her own personal bleeding angels, whisper at her, lay their bodies across her feet. Which will follow her this time? The old whore with too many soldiers to count? The dark girl with no words left? She's afraid to know and has to know. They're all that seems real: they're the only ones who know. The one who pulled at her hair.

The same groves are invaded, every spring, for the festival by the Lady-Tree, the hugest beech of all. She'd forgotten this festival, one she adored as a child in Isabelle's arms. This year it's Jacquot who urges her there, hoping her dance will find her a husband, regardless of Isabelle's convent dreams.

Even in daylight, the grove-trees shelter her from direct sunlight, from the sheep meadows, almost as well as river-water. The grove is crammed now with girls, women, not her angels but girls from surrounding villages, glad to take a day away from spinning and cooking. Mariel, a young healer who once delivered

Jehanne from fever, joins hands with Jehanne and her child-friends, Mengette and Hauviette.

Jehanne relaxes, finally: she can almost feel her feet, her hips, when she dances. She's astonished that her body will still dance with them, surrounded by daffodils and hortensia's pale purple flowers; this is where the healers have danced for centuries.

Mariel dances with her derriere to the stars, like she's harvesting midnight. Mengette and Hauviette urge Jehanne into the circle, but she'll only go when Mariel, when her broken angels, say yes. *Dance, stay strong,* say two waif-like angels, one with only one hand. They join her in the center of the circle.

Laughter bubbles in her throat. She's surprised that her feet will still move at all. She feels less like the nun her mother wants, a little more like the wife Jacquot hopes she'll be. Her shoulders lift and drop, carelessly, first the right then the left, a wavelike motion, lift and drop, until she starts laughing. The voice warmer, approving.

This time of year, men also invade the healers' grove for the beech tree dances: even the village boys break from their sword-fighting lessons. By now, most of Lorraine's villages have tired of the dying and sworn fealty to Burgundy; Domrémy and Vaucouleurs are among the last holdouts. Some of the boys and men watching them are thus allied with the Burgundians and the English. They clap at the girls dancing, whistle too close to Jehanne's ears for comfort. The one who pulled at her hair.

Finally, Jehanne drops away from the dance. She's tired of the anxious boys and wants nothing to do with the boasts of so-called knights. She leaves after a tall, rangy man from Toul, so soaked with mead that she can smell it over the explosive garde-nias of the grove, tries to dance with her, his armor streaked with mud. Too much like the others. The one who sang low-throated songs to the meadow-grass, before he laughed and pushed his way in. She freezes in place, remembering.

Then the flood answers, unfreezing her: making her hands

burn. Her blood feels heated. First it's just voices, the roar by turns comforting and maddening, and then she sees them burst out of the crowd, flesh and bone and color and sound, but hers alone.

The skinny girl with the ripped overshirt and broken teeth, the broken soldier with shield smoldering like a not-dead fire, all come to her in benediction. Laughter bubbles in her throat. The chevalier laughs back, not seeing who she sees.

The angels stop dancing after a little while, pull her closer, into the curve of a tree. *The Dauphin needs you,* they murmur into her ears. One slides over to one of the boys observing, one who still wears a dolphin-pin, one who's not yet learning English. The angel closes her hand around the pin, a small embrace.

Jehanne starts. The dolphin needs her? The king represented by the tiny bronze circle? What could he need from her? And what does that have to do with her? The tallest one counsels patience.

Jehanne smiles as they usher her out of the grove: not enemies but rescuers. No longer frightened but angry. She shelters them under the cloak, pulling it tighter around her as she descends the ridge into her village.

By the time she gets to the house, her sweat has dried and her smile is elusive to her mother and brothers. Isabelle climbs the stairs with her, kneels with her in the narrow bedroom. She notes her daughter's upraised eyes, how her lips already move in prayer, how her hands reach under her cloak and bring out her rosary. "*Ave Maria, mater Deum,*" they say together. Isabelle swallows hard, trying not to be frightened by the body turned away from her, Jehanne's manic grin.

As Isabelle leaves, Jehanne kisses her rosary. Her angels kneel beside her on her thin pallet and pray with her. She asks them what they want her to do. How to stop the noise. A bass voice laughs, reminds her of priest tales. Jesus damaged by soldiers too.

The clanking of armor and screaming of steel. The dark broken soldier makes a dolphin-sign. He'll need you soon.

A herald's voice, announcing first the year, sings like a prayer into the small Darc house. Like a cold prayer, a freezing wind. **1 4 2 7.** It silences her.

1 4 2 7. It's now three years after the sheep meadow. Three years of heavy angels on her neck, under her skin. The year in her ears like a code. **1427.** The messenger announces that the chevalier from Toul, the one soaked in mead and glittering with iron, has ignored her coy-seeming retreat at the Lady-Tree. He swears that she accepted his proposal of marriage, and wants her called before a hearing in the town square.

Jacquot, uncharacteristically at home to hear it, is delighted: "Isabelle, I told you she'd marry!" The prospect of grandchildren batters Isabelle's well-known desire for the convent. A nun-daughter, a raped daughter, no good at all for the *doyen*'s reputation, but "a knight's father-in-law? Don't ask me a second time!"

Jacquot and Isabelle share one of the older horses, whispering plans on the way. "So much for old Madame Joubert saying she's too mad!" Isabelle murmurs in Jacquot's ear, making the best of her own dashed hopes.

"Or the miller wondering if she's gotten too old and stubborn," says Jacquot.

"Still I wish we knew this man."

Her husband grunts. "This may be our last chance." He's thinking about the dowry, stowed away in small boxes under Jehanne's well-worn bed. He prays it will prove adequate. It must be, for the chevalier to be suing this hard.

Toul is quite a distance, and Jacquot leaves his orchards in other hands for a day. He even encourages Pierre to come along and allows Jehanne to ride Le Lune, a half-wild filly she loves.

She rides ahead of them, pushing Le Lune into a gallop, her

eyes focused forward. The young filly jumps a little, hurting her legs. Her sweat softens the horse's rough hair.

The hills of the Meuse Valley are laid out before them in an explosion of color. Jehanne makes them stop repeatedly, so she can nuzzle marigolds and kiss pale yellow roses. Jacquot's impatient: "The hearing is tomorrow!" Jehanne ignores him and rides ahead, drunk on the smell of marigolds.

Jacquot looks over at his son, who seems to grow a half-foot every week and will soon be taller than him. "Can you get her to hurry?" as if the two have spoken since the day Jehanne crawled home from the meadow.

Pierre doesn't say anything. He's watching his sister, slowly. The puddle that disgusted him is stretching into a woman-shape, of whatever mad energy or stream. What sort of a woman? What is she staring at, in the pitiless sky? And will she marry here? His hands fist. "Let her be," he says softly to his father. "If this is a wedding-journey, perhaps she thinks this is a farewell?"

They arrive at the fortress half-way to Toul, rising above the lush landscape in twenty-three stone towers. Black, dead, not towering but thick: each stone is as deep as three men. "Vaucouleurs," Pierre shouts, excited as he was at seven. Jehanne rides ahead, and closer to the building.

Men of all ages, in body armor, line the barricades. The one who first found her, and banished the sheep before he tore her open. Jehanne veers to the side of the road and vomits.

"We can't go through with this," Isabelle says, cleaning her daughter's face and trying to ignore the now-familiar silence, her stare past Isabelle's arm, past the fortress. "What are you seeing, Jehanne? Can you tell me?"

Jehanne shakes her head, still staring, and lets Isabelle help her onto Le Lune's back. From the flash to the heat, again: rage warming her fingers now. She calls to her angels for courage, until one—a doughy boy with dead eyes and a long, silver sword

—slides behind her on her horse. His lips against her ears whisper secrets.

At Toul, the crowds far exceed the usual curious locals: Isabelle keeps her arm around her shaking daughter, ducking the whispers. *Darc's daughter has holy fits, Darc's daughter began to go mad after a raid, Darc's daughter must be easy.* Boys otherwise pledged to the Dauphin howl at her as at the moon. Self-satisfied old women cross themselves. Pierre holds tight to his sword, to avoid drawing it on them all.

The chevalier himself, a graying man in dress armor, looks stricken before her pale, thin silence. He sees it's a lost cause. Still he stands before the court and makes his declarations. "And how we danced, she and I!" His armor glistens in the noonday sun.

She sees the armor and freezes. His face blurs. The noise escalates. The one who waited, limp, until his comrades laughed him hard. Not this one but. Her voice rises above it all, made louder with help from her angels, as she denies him in soprano imprecations and high prayers.

Isabelle and Jacquot bow their heads, ashamed. They wish they were surprised. Their daughter won't stop shouting, her arm upraised as if to pull sunlight down and burn them all.

"What was that?" Jacquot's voice is larger than the small house, as large as when it fills his orchard, bellowing at the field hands to help him trim a tree corroded with rot. Now it's Jehanne's wildness needs trimming. "There was no cause to deny him. She's sixteen, she's a strong girl, she can lift a wash-tub one-third her size. She'd stop all this soon enough with a baby in her belly."

Isabelle leans up and kisses him, her lips wrinkling as his thick graying beard scratches her nose. "That man was scared out of his wits, just now. We'll never get him back." She shrugs, the corners of a laugh hidden in the curve of her lips. "She'll be a nun, Jacquot. I'm sure of it." She lowers her voice, as if someone could be listening. "Just talk to Father Guillaime."

"That old fart? I've been wondering if he's having his way with her." The intentionally crude statement has its desired effect; Isabelle leaves the room, her lips tight.

Darc sighs and leans against the wall. Who will marry her now, indeed? he wonders. Most Domrémy boys, those not dead, are off fighting. He calls into the kitchen, softly. "Perhaps you're right. At least she won't marry a soldier."

His first answer is Isabelle's fist hitting a slab of dough, before she pours more flour on and begins to knead. "Are you having that dream again, Jacq?"

He doesn't answer, holding his lower lip unnaturally still. He brushes the flour off his shoulder, uncovering the tiny dolphin pin, the Dauphin sign he sometimes hides with a heavy scarf. "I told you. Every night this week. When I saw her at Vaucouleurs—" Despair cuts his sentence in half.

"Jehanne turning into a soldier, and running away with a sword in her hand." Isabelle's voice is bruised with frequent repetition of the story. "Our little Jehannette, who won't even touch an arrowhead. And besides, when she thinks of soldiers . . ."

Jacquot comes into the kitchen and puts his arms around Isabelle's waist. His voice is quieter. "Then the dream?" he asks. "Is God telling me that the nunnery is the only place for her, else she *will* open her legs for soldiers? Or is he warning me to marry her off quickly? I swear to you, Isabelle, if I believed that dream would come true, I'd ask you to drown her. Or do it myself."

Isabelle sighs. "She's a good girl, Jacq."

"But all the other daughters are married. Many with child. Look at Mengette."

Isabelle sinks both hands into the floured dough, then reaches backward and smears her husband's cheek with it. "Yes, Mengette's got a new baby, a little boy," she says. "And Pierre will start his own family soon. Don't you think Jehanne is a little lonely? What's the harm then, listening to the voices of angels? Studying the saints?"

In Jehanne's honor she makes saint cakes. St. Margaret brown bread, with clover honey. Saint Catherine sugared, fried dough. St. Michael porridge, thick with butter, bitter with rosemary. They make Isabelle smile, at least.

To make Isabelle's dream true, Jehanne prepares for the convent. A year of studying, of learning catechisms and saint tales, the three orders of Saint Francis and the history of the three popes. Her angels urge the priest-words through her lips. Popes: knights: the commander, crying as he hurt her. She pushes the priest away and drops to the church floor. The tiny bodies on the altar-tableau look ravaged, jammed together tightly like stacked dead birds.

Jesus damaged by soldiers. The story important. The ruined saints. The noise is the same.

At Easter, she holds the crucifix high and sings hosannas to resurrection, under Isabelle and Father Guillaume's approving eyes. She knows resurrection is true enough: the dead hum under her skin. They come out of the woodwork and lean against her side, their bodies heavy, invisible.

Jesus crucified, still bleeding from a soldier's lance. The clanking of armor and screaming of steel. Of steel and of women. A skinny dark woman, half-covered in black cloth, points to the dolphin pin on Jacquot's coat, to the Lorraine trefoil on another. *The noise won't stop till France is whole*, she whispers.

Meaning never. Jehanne raises the cross higher, saying "*Et resurrexit tertia die . . .*" He rose on the third day. *A good story*, a soft angel giggles in her ear.

Father Guillaume watches Jehanne's face, as he tells the rest.

She grows calmer, though a little harder, with each week. Her voices are louder, she says. He's beginning to believe it: that her voices are the multiple faces, names, of God. The voices of the burning bush. A soft breeze opens the church door.

The house of Mengette's husband, Yves, is smaller than the Darc house, but with more light, sacrificing heat for the sun on her kitchen table.

"What do they look like?" Mengette Joyart is a year younger than Jehanne, but time and childbirth have widened her hips and neck; she lifts her newborn closer to her nipple, encourages his questing lips. "Like people?" Jehanne's throat tightens around a true answer. Her angels are damaged, bleeding, angry, beautiful: she cannot tell Mengette any of that. "Like children," she says.

"How fascinating! . . . When you become an angel, you come closer to being a child of God, then!" She looks up from her baby and fixes Jehanne in her uncompromising brown-eyed gaze. "And they visit you in the garden?"

"And the groves," Jehanne says. She doesn't say, *near where we used to swim, you and I.* Mengette now seems too grown up, too much of a mother to remember their swims.

"The same groves where I brought Yves that time?" Mengette chuckles, trying to coax Jehanne with her laughter. "It's a good thing after all you never brought a boy there. Else your saints would never talk to you."

"Why?"

"They want a virgin."

Jehanne's silent, looking at her hands, dirty from the garden. Mengette lifts her child from her breast and adds sternly, "And all that long ago—they don't count that! All that suffering only brings you closer to God, in my humble opinion." Her baby starts to scream, as if in pain; Jehanne's hand under the table tightens. "Oh *cherie*, you're not done yet are you?" Mengette nestles her nose in the baby's spare hair. "Or are you too sleepy to know?"

"I can rock him to sleep," Jehanne offers. "If you have a need."

"Oh why not try? He's been like this all day." Her eyes are heavy with too little sleep. "You can come with me while I wash his clothes, for the fifth time today." She hands Jehanne the tiny screaming body matter of factly, as if handing off another pile of clothes.

The tiniest person she's ever touched: her breath catches at the perfection of him. Xavier's cries escalate with his transfer, though Jehanne rocks him gently, easily, sings softly in his ear. She sings hymns and Christmas songs, she sings songs her angels taught her, her tongue light around other languages. Some are harsh in her mouth, with consonants from deep in the throat. Finally he quiets, his eyes wide, his mouth open in a perfect O.

"You're a miracle worker, Jehanne," Mengette says. "Not that he's given me much trouble, honestly. Not like Solange."

Jehanne grimaces. Her hands still damp, though she put the little girl into bed. "Nothing works, then?"

Mengette shrugs as she scoops water out of the cistern into the washtub. "Not just the fever—she's not running around, not at all. She still points to her belly, says *it hurts, maman*. I don't know what to do."

"Did you ask—" Jehanne stops, more words in her throat. She goes back to rocking Xavier, turns her question into a hymn. Mengette rolls up her sleeves and begins to work on the clothes, her arms reddening from the harsh soap.

"She might not have been able to help," Jehanne finally says.

Mengette's face finally sags at the word "she," its near-mention of the patient woman who left Domrémy last year, taking her herbs and pestles and poultices with her. "Perhaps not," sharply, as she wrings another diaper. She looks like she wants Jehanne to leave.

Jehanne takes refuge in the infant, who stares at her while she sings her whispered songs. The healer's voice has joined the chorus in her head. "I'm sorry," Jehanne finally says

Mengette pours more soap into the wash tub. "It's your Church, Jehanne."

"I never told her to leave!"

"Your priest did. And now she's dead, you tell me." Jehanne nods, wishing she hadn't blurted that truth out weeks ago, when she dreamed it.

After all the diapers have been hung to dry, Mengette drains the wash tub in the creek behind the house and takes her baby back. He burps contentedly, nuzzling into her collarbone, a tiny lover. "I wish you all the best with your angels, my friend, but don't talk to me about prayers and priests any more. Not unless they say Mariel can come back. All the way back."

That night, she takes Mengette's voice to the grove with her.

Jehanne doesn't know how long it has been since the candles were snuffed, how long Jacquot and Isabelle and her brothers have been snoring. She knows she was able to dream a few dreams before she snapped awake. She pulls at her bootlaces, impatient to be out; every crackle of the fireplace makes her start, turn around, looking for danger. She ties the laces, wraps her shoulders in an extra cape. She loves the dark: none of the sunlight that threatens her: no sheep meadow.

The groves cast comforting shadows even muddy and cold, and the mud anchors her, tells her she's not dreaming. The white blooms of the cherry trees glow, teasing the smooth young skin of the beeches, lit by stars under her eyes. Her boots crunch dropped lost cherry branches. Her pace speeds, and she listens.

Then, finally she is not alone. Whispers: *Vaucouleurs* fills her ears, her throat: a *Vaucouleurs* chorus spat louder with each step. *La Pucelle, go to Vaucouleurs.* La Pucelle, *the Maid:* they are giving her back her virginity while they shout blood orders. A virgin is a woman who is not a mother. The word blurs into a howl, wind-like. *Vaucouleurs.*

The noise escalates everywhere. Make it stop. *Vaucouleurs, then the Dauphin. Do not come back until France is whole.* The words now soft in her ear, like her murmurs into baby Xavier's. She listens hard for the component voices. One speaks a harsh, angled language, another sobs curses in between the main demand. Those who can't pronounce the French mash it under tonal vowels, strangled squeaks. *Vaucouleurs.* Her muscles cramp with the force of it. She closes her fist around her rosary. If she goes, English will bleed. She can feel it in her cunt.

Mariel, the village healer, slides down on a vine: her body is tiny, like Xavier's, but wizened, as if she aged when she burned. She curls into Jehanne's hand, pressing heat into her palms, until sparks toss into the soft underbrush. Jehanne's blood heats: it feels like pain. like power. Mariel whispers a recipe for baby Solange through blackened lips.

Jehanne lets herself separate then, watches them all from the highest curve of the same beech tree where she once danced. From that height she sees herself sink into the mud, and kneel, and cry blistered tears.

two

ISABELLE'S COUSIN Durand Laxart has inherited the cottage of his father, which relaxes into the hillside in blond thatches, three rooms, only two windows. The house, in Burey-le-Petit, is halfway between Domrémy and the fortified city.

The morning Pierre Darc comes to see him, the July heat weighs down Durand's skin and his task—chopping wood—creates dizziness. At thirty-five Durand's beginning to grow himself, stretching against his old soldier-tunic. When Pierre arrives, grown impossibly tall at seventeen, Durand's been wondering about his grapes. Will another band or two come barreling through and destroy what he's done? He is growing very, very tired of starting over yet again.

He has to stop every few minutes to wipe his brow, and is happy to stop and greet Isabelle's boy. He's envious of the boy's easy youth, his lack of breathlessness as he swings off his horse. "Good uncle!"

Durand starts to protest, he's too young to be a tall squire's uncle, but swallows it against the boy's happy sweat. He embraces Pierre, searching his face for the toddler who played soldier on this very spot years ago. "Isabelle must be baking your wedding cakes, even now," he grins. "Will you come into the house? J'nelle will want to see you."

His wife, somewhere between their two ages, looks up startled from her mending as they walk in the door. When she sees who it is, her smile fills the tiny room. "My goodness—Isabelle's son?" Nineteen years old, she's about to give birth, but pregnancy doesn't stop her from noting how comely he is. She's seen him once or twice since he came here at seven, but between wars and farming, "there have been fewer peaceful moments than we might like. Look at you!"

Pierre accepts breakfast before he stands up again, a little formally, a little unsure. "My mother sent me with a message."

"For me?" Jehannelle starts a little. "Or both of us?"

He looks at the floor, as if embarrassed, then points toward Durand. "Mostly for you, *monsieur.*"

"*Moi*?" Durand stands up a little straighter, flattered.

"You have served at Vaucouleurs, good sir," Pierre starts, shyly.

"I serve the good captain de Baudricort," Durand says uneasily, "when he needs me."

Pierre shifts from one foot to the other. He's been going over how to say this, in his mind, ever since Isabelle decided to send him. "My sister—"

"Catherine?" Jehannelle asks. Catherine, she knows, also gives birth soon: she hopes the girl doesn't need a healer.

"No no no," he shakes his head. "My youngest sister, who has the same name as you, Madame Laxart."

Durand nods. "The little priest?" he asks. Isabelle has been trying to make a nun of this girl for years, but the last time he saw her, perhaps two years ago, she reminded him more of a priest. A local squire, Bertrand de Poulengy, has called her "le petite prétresse," which still makes him laugh. "Is she finally going to the convent, or starting a church?"

Pierre shakes his head, almost mournfully. "She is going to Vaucouleurs," he says. "She thinks to join the Dauphin's army."

Durand nearly spits out the wine and bread in his mouth, onto the stone floor. "And who is telling her to do this?"

Pierre shakes his head, going on to the next phase of the message. "My mother begs you to help her go safely," he says softly, slowly. "Let her be rebuked there, as she will be, without coming to harm." His eyes meet Durand's. "She is a little mad," his voice is nearly inaudible, "but we love her and want her to return alive."

"There are too many people fighting to get in there now," Durand says, recovering his composure. "They'll spit at her and send her home."

"My mother would like you to guide her on these roads," Pierre completes the message. He's a little shellshocked by what he sees around him, families searching for safety, and not even to Vaucouleurs. He can't imagine his damaged sister, with her temper, doing anything but melting under its pressure like hot lead.

Though what he's seen—"I'll offer to fight in her place," Pierre says. "Not now, not before harvest, but after. I don't know if she'll accept."

"Nor should she," Jehannelle says crossly, the first thing she's said since greeting. "No one as healthy and fertile as you should be offering to dive into that burning pile of *merde*." She looks at her husband, and at Pierre. Boys, soldiers, burning houses. A pestilence. And Durand—she's watching her husband shift and change yet again, now, the larger she grows. She's grown used to how he changes when he comes back from Vaucouleurs, which has long since scraped out the soft-cheeked sweetness she still sees in young Pierre. But the long-sought child's near-arrival has him further at arm's reach, distracted.

Pierre swallows again, avoiding the glances between them. Isabelle wants him back in time to tell her what Durand says.

They fear Jehanne will leave at some random moment, without telling anyone. "Can we tell her —"

"*Ah oui,*" Durand says wearily. Any other answer assists suicide, a mortal sin.

Pierre grins, thrilled to have accomplished his goal. Even this one. He kisses both of them quickly and finds his horse, leaving Jehannelle to sleep and Durand to resume chopping firewood.

Durand watches the youth's carelessly strong back, as he urges his horse north. Then Durand tests the axe, and lays the trunk across the stump gently. His wife has a point, he thinks. Only the young and stupid think there's glory in soldiering. And J'nelle has nursed enough of his nightmares to taste the edge of one or two.

God damn. There's Burgundian and Norman blood already on his fingers. Why offer to soak them again? He's as mad as the girl. As is Isabelle, for not locking her up. As he slams down the axe, he wonders why only one woman in this family seems to have been born with sense.

Jehanne leaves Domrémy at dawn, fog a soft blanket over the valley that lends pale yellow to the center of the fields, blots the terrifying sunlight.

Le Lune, the youngest, whinnies when Jehanne enters the stable. She bows for her, lets Jehanne sling a pair of hastily constructed saddle-bags across her back. She has only ridden her once before, on that trip when her parents thought she'd be married off.

She has packed a spare dress, her rosary, a water sack from the kitchen, and her best red surcoat, a long tunic-like garment a touch too heavy for this time of year. It's the closest she has to priest-clothes, or armor.

The filly waits for her to mount, the soft coat soothing her scarred places. Then Le Lune kicks hard into a gallop, no canter to get her started, headed to the road without mercy. She wraps her arms tight around the filly's neck. Domrémy recedes quickly behind them as they ascend the ridge, cross fields, jump over trees already slashed by some knight's drunken lance.

She knows she's getting closer when she sees the bodies by the side of the road. She smells them first, boys sliced and singed, men robbed of all but their skin. Women broken open. A once-hale man lies across the road, daring Le Lune to jump: instead Jehanne slides off and bends down, lifts what's left of the dead man's face. He sits up slowly, carelessly, his fingers near-crumbling. He tells her that the Burgundians are headed to Vaucouleurs within a fortnight. The words are angled in his mouth, mixed with enemy words: English. She jumps back and lets the horse take her away. The soldier slides back into dust.

More bodies, not on the road but beside it, in shapeless stinking piles barely discernible to her. Maybe some were at the sheep meadow and are dead? Not enough, and she refuses to look. She begins to shake, she holds onto her angels as she prays for them, with them. When she envisions how that Englishman must have died, she feels a smile twist her lips.

Finally sleep begins its insistent demand, long past nightfall. Her shoulders drop. The sky is just beginning the transit to purple when she sees the lights, looking from the road like tiny candles, stars in a low-lying green sky.

She feels as if the forest has made a place for her to rest, in patient thanks for the years of midnight walks. She dismounts and leads the filly through the rocky interior. *"Pardon,."* she begs and keeps moving toward the gentle yellow-gold lights in between the trees. It's grown cooler, finally, and her sweat dries in blotches against the rough surcoat.

One of her angels sits between two of the lights: small, bird-like, a slender child with dead eyes. The lights are small bonfires, not as wide as her waist. Between them are what look like burial mounds. She wonders if she is meant to sleep cradled in the bodies of Englishmen.

Jehanne lets Le Lune sink to the ground, slides her pack of supplies to her feet and lies down. She dreams of Mengette and her sick child. In the dream she is mixing the herbs Mariel whispered to her in the grove, they are together coaxing little Solange to swallow the bitter smear.

When she wakes, her angels have receded. In their place, real children sleep beside her. Real children, women, live flesh, dead only in pieces. One, called Régine, looks like Isabelle but for the marks on her throat. They offer Jehanne breakfast: a piece of *pain* broken into small pieces.

Jehanne wishes she was surprised to see them. "How many are here?"

Régine shakes her head. "Too many to count." Her voice is thick with unspoken consonants. The small black-haired boy has no French at all but smiles incessantly.

"Who feeds you?"

"The popes!" At those words laughter skitters through the forest: only ten years since the schism ended, they may well be fed by clerics loyal to each of three Popes. No one will say now which is true—do the more able ones steal the bread, do they beg in town squares, or do they raid abandoned churches for not-yet-moldy bread and rivers of sacramental wine.

She wonders but doesn't want to ask why they've all come: she knows, she can tell from Régine's throat and the boy's silence. Like her angels, but real to her touch. She could be here for the next year until she has heard their stories, their voices, mixing with that other, multilingual roar, until her head hurts. She wants to stay forever, she wants to flee: she also knows if she does not get out now she will never get to Vaucouleurs, or anywhere else, alive.

Le Lune finds her, kneels to be mounted; Régine pulls

Jehanne's second dress over her. Jehanne tells her she'll be back. She rolls up onto the horse, her face wet.

By the time she arrives at the Laxart home in Burey-le-Petit, she is exhausted, nearly wordless.

Durand and his wife look carefully at the muddy creature leaning into their doorway. Her red surcoat hangs shapelessly on her frame; her eyes are clear and her translucent skin shows high color beside each cheekbone. She begs to sleep, and to be taken once she awakes "to Robert de Baudricort, the Commander, sweet uncle." She staggers a little as Jehanne Laxart leads her to a bed, where she curls into a ball and sleeps instantly.

Durand puts a protective arm on his wife's shoulder. "Are you sure we should leave her there? You may need to rest before she wakes."

"How can I, with all this war about?" She points out the window, free for the moment from torches, random mobs. "And pretty children who want to make it?"

"She's Isabelle's daughter!"

"I know blood-thirst when I see it, Durand." She says it calmly, with less fear than irony.

Their guest rises just as the sun begins to settle, slow, dreamy at first. She kneels before Jehanne Laxart's belly and whispers prayers. "You will have daughters," she says. "Twins. And they will grow up not having to fear Burgundians."

"And why is that?" Durand's voice gentle, answering to her prayers for his child—children? "How do you know they won't fear?"

Jehanne rises, grinning now, her pulse awakening fully and beginning to race. "Because we will have driven out the English!" She laughs, pulls her hair behind her—sloppily, like a young unkempt soldier trying to stand at attention, but believable neither as a soldier nor a prophet. "Shall we go now, or in the morning?"

"*If* I decide to escort you," says Durand, "we will go after supper. But first, I want to hear more of this plan of yours." He watches her face for lies, her hands for avarice. He wishes she were not so winsome, or his wife so bloated.

Jehanne swallows, hard. She sees the disbelief in his eyes. She also sees the way his eye lingers on her collarbone before it's pulled sharply away by its shamed owner. Her memories of him before now are soft: indulgent laughter, deep basso caress-voice, drunken songs late at night with her mother. Pierre had said as much: that she will have to make her case all over again. The thought makes her tired.

She asks her angels for strength and is embraced by one, a red-haired mother in soldier's garb. Her lips on Jehanne's neck are warm as she whispers a prophecy, for Jehanne to serve to Durand with his own black bread. "Dearest uncle, did not Merlin prophesy that France would be saved by a virgin?" She drops it carelessly as she tears a piece of day-old bread.

They all watch Durand as his jaw drops, then snaps shut. He mumbles the word "disaster" around the piece of bread.

"The part about being ruined by a woman is English nonsense,." Jehanne continues. "I can fulfill the rest, but you must take me to de Baudricort." As she slathers butter on the bread, her shaking fingers betray her.

"Your voice tells you this?" The young man's eyes narrow; she feels his longstanding affection for her drop off, as his face begins to harden into that cowardice she's seen in priests' eyes. It's her turn to swallow. Time for the word she hates, the lie, the one that unlocks doors. *Le Dé mentir,* the God lie.

"*Dé,*" she whispers, then corrects her Lorraine accent, "*Dieu.* It is God who tells me, no one else." Sunlight filling her eyes. The forest's damaged women and tiny children drinking sacramental wine.

She looks at Durand's wind-battered face, his tired eyes. The clanking of armor. "I know you are sick of it," she says simply. "It is why . . ." *the braided voice* "God sends me here, today. When France is whole this madness will stop." She doesn't want to ask any more, but leaves her arms open to hear it. Instead silence. She moves over to Jehannelle, and says her next sentence directly to the young mother.

"We are all sick to death of these battles. I may die of it, but it will end."

Durand's eyes meet his wife's. She nods, slowly. He rises and says, "Will your horse support two of us?"

France was not wrecked by a woman. A virgin is a woman who is not a mother: only a broken woman can save France. Women lie in pieces on the side of the road: regenerate in the forest: Hail Mary full of grace. Her skin is loose, light. She is beyond her skin. She has no patience for Durand's muscled words, his arms around her waist as they go forward on her sweet patient horse.

The sunlight, as always, terrifies: she pulls the hood of her surcoat across her face. The one who cleared the hair from her forehead, almost gently. An ugly foreign word murmured, *prih-tee*. The clanking of armor.

Then sundown, blessing, relief. As always her friend, the night, embraces her, tumbles her elsewhere, dissolving Durand's words and their songs.

More dead bodies by the side of the road: "fierce fighting," says Durand. Young boys still clasping useless swords. She's absorbed, watchful, praying under her breath for their voices. Time and water have bloated the arms, blurred the faces, made sores on buttocks. No signs of violation in these bodies, besides the sword's. None sit up and speak for her. Finally Durand lifts her back onto the horse. "We shouldn't tarry," he says. "J'nnelle will fear for my life."

At first, reasons for fear are obscured by the quiet, the night. Then, in the distance they see the fireball: this far away, it looks like the sun has decided to snuggle with the valley, in some sort of demented coupling. She hears Durand take in a short breath: "*Merde.* It's St.-Vincent." She wonders how he can see a church spire from here.

Her next breath, unlike his, is long, deep, begging for the smoke to reach her lungs. "It's not as bad as it looks," Durand tries to reassure her. At that she starts to laugh, then swallows it. Isabelle has already warned him about Jehanne's laugh, but there's no need to pierce his eardrums in this wind. Even if he did earn it, for thinking her frightened.

The road to Vaucouleurs is clogged to stillness, not with soldiers but with farmers, wives, horses, chickens, crying babies and not-crying silenced children. Their fires make twilight of pre-dawn's velvet dark.

She slides off her horse and moves toward the children, while Durand talks to the old man who stokes the fire. "How many of them? How many houses did they burn? How are your fields?"

Jehanne kneels by a girl of perhaps ten years old, laying very still, her eyes hollow. Jehanne thinks to carry her to safety, but the girl, Francine, has other ideas. She screams into Jehanne's ears, joined by the other voices, drowned out by the crowd-noise.

Finally she can separate. Finally she can join the sky, riding on a raincloud. Together she and Francine watch the English storm St.-Vincent, set fire to the meadow, cut open sheep so they can reach in for a bloody breakfast. A man who bars the door is rewarded by a dagger in his throat. The noise escalates. A woman running with her baby sees a soldier take the infant, throw it in the air, and catch it on the point of his lance. The screaming of steel.

Jehanne looks for Francine, who was that day behind the

church, and finds her underneath an English armored back. She stares straight up into the sky, meeting Jehanne's gaze. Under pressure of the flames the church bursts open.

Under the cart Jehanne sobs openly. Francine's face is her face. She leans in and touches her forehead to the little girl's tangled hair. *Make it stop*, the voices tell her. *You can. We can.*

Jehanne sits up, slowly, and lifts Francine, runs fingers through her knotted hair, whispering like a lullaby her string of promises—to make it right, to make France whole, to stop the noise. Her voice soft, singing like a hymn, truer than a prayer. When the girl's eyes close in sleep she hands her back to her mother, a wide-faced woman with eyes flattened by grief.

Then Durand calls roughly; he and Jehanne ride beside the road, Le Lune bravely poking through brambles. By daybreak they are at the gate of the fortified city, its towers above the Meuse less a promise than a tired threat. The fortress dwarfs the small Lorraine families pressing against it.

The troops at the gate have their hands full even before Jehanne's arrival. "In good time, in good time!" shouts a middle-aged man in ill-fitting soldiers' garb to the mob pressing against the walls, their arms outstretched, mute. Not an able-bodied man among them, facing him: only nursing mothers, grandfathers, goats, aging horses. The morning air is ripe with them all.

The gatekeeper looks down at a grandmother carrying a long, empty sack and a handful of gold: bits of prized jewelry as payment or bribe. He looks at her pityingly and waves over a priest, who examines the jewelry critically before he draws back the gate for her family. Three other soldiers, swords drawn, hold off those pressing to follow. "Back now or someone dies!"

As the sun grows more confidently mid-sky, more families keep arriving. The hum of them helps Jehanne think. They'll never get in at this rate. Durand has fallen asleep, waiting. Her angels had promised to help her: how? The armored backs threaten.

She starts to thread her way through the grasping arms and each one she touches burns the same: just a slight singe that makes them step back. "Mademoiselle!" She holds up her rosary, eyes meeting theirs: no witch she. Only La Pucelle. A skinny, freckled boy bows as he retreats.

Deep giggles in her throat: she thanks her angels for this gift, a damn sight more useful than lighting candles. The smell of burnt overshirts and singed flesh makes her laugh harder. Before she knows it she's atop the wall, carried by a confused but compliant fisherman who still smells of his morning catch. She apologizes to him for his burns: "They will heal quickly, I promise." Then she picks her way around to the entrance, asking each soldier in turn "Do I have to burn you too, or will you take me to the Dauphin?" Durand follows below, laughing into his sleeve.

"The Dauphin?" In scorn, they show her their little dolphin-pins, until the fisherman shows them his burnt hands. Most of the soldiers are boys as easily from her village as any other, their helmets ill-fitting; the oldest among them shouts, "Get the Commander! Get de Baudricort!"

Jehanne grins, suddenly exultant. She turns and looks behind her, shouts to Durand, who has followed her progress from below. "I told you!"

The child-soldiers open the south gate for her and for Durand, who rubs his eyes and drags Le Lune, "I won't have this rabble steal our horse." Inside the walls, drunken older soldiers taunt the families they've let in. One urinates in a corner, just missing the grandmother who came bearing the family gold.

Durand draws his dagger, then re-sheathes it when Jehanne looks at him. He's afraid of her, now; what is this burning? Has Isabelle bred a witch after all?

Finally a soldier both older and more sober asks them, "Where do you come from?"

"Domrémy," Jehanne answers, though she knows he expected Durand to reply.

"That far? Domrémy's not fallen, has it? We knew the Vergy brothers were headed your way, but we'd not yet heard they'd got there."

"No, no," Durand reassures him. "Not yet, my friend."

"I thought not! So what brings you here?" He gestures to the human walls surrounding the stone ones. "We are kept busy fighting off all these horses and chickens, when what we need is to go fight." He looks Durand up and down. "You are not in the war?"

"I am," says Jehanne. "He has twin daughters ready to be born. But I've come to join the Dauphin's army—I'm here to drive out the English." She says it matter-of-factly, as casually as she thinks he can stand.

"Now, that's pretty rich—you, little enough for me to carry on my back!" He looks at Durand. "Your daughter?"

Durand starts, unsure whether he even wants to admit they're related. "My cousin. I don't know if I believe her, but she thinks she is the fulfilment of Merlin's prophecy. The woman who will save France."

The wave of laughter comes up first from behind her, a gaggle of younger soldiers fresh with the day's first wine. The soldier who let them in joins their jeering, the laughter another numb wall of noise. Jehanne doesn't flinch.

The huge man that joins them has the biggest laugh of all, laced with the crudest winesap, his uniform dirty and the scent of a camp whore still lingering in his beard. From the nearest cloud Jehanne watches as the others tell de Baudricort what Jehanne has said, watches him lean toward Durand like a doting grandfather. "Take her home and slap her, hard," he tells Durand in a loud laughing whisper. "Then do what else you would like. She deserves it."

Jehanne asks Le Lune to take her out of there, looking deep

in the tired brown eyes. The horse kneels to receive her, then breaks into a full gallop, pushing past soldiers and nearly trying to jump the wall.

By the time Durand catches up with them, Jehanne is nearly crying. He's as shaken as she, he tells her. "Now will you go home and make no more trouble?" *Marry her off now*, he will tell Isabelle, *lest that pulsing energy of hers go to ground.*

Jehanne stares at him hard, as if to silence him. "No, no, I will come back after the new year," she says. "But I must get back to Domrémy—and quickly."

"Why?"

"Didn't you hear him? The de Vergy brothers are coming! Do you want my family to end up one of those poor souls at the wall?"

three

ISABELLE ROMÉE SITS at her daughter's side, turning the muddy rosary over and over. Devout as she is, part of her wants to destroy it. She wonders if the girl will ever wake up, now.

Le Lune nearly battered down the door bringing her there; not the stable but the house itself, the filly's mane matted, her eyes flashing as she rammed against the window. When Isabelle opened the door the horse knelt, offering the sleeping girl wrapped in her own dress.

Too angry to weep, Isabelle thanked the helpful animal and lifted her disobedient daughter into her arms. "How are you helping us now?" she asked Jehanne, or else Jesus, it's hard to know in a house as full of reliquaries, of crucifixes, as hers. She carried her girl upstairs and undressed her, put balms on her skin, cleaned the dusty rosary.

Since then she's bathed her every day. She's had Father Guillaime come upstairs to watch her go through it again, but differently. They stand together in Jehanne's narrow room while the sleeping girls arches her back, cries out, shouts imprecations, laughs. Jacquot refuses to look. Pierre glances once or twice, his face ashen. None of them understands the languages she speaks.

They await word from Durand, but his letters are cryptic and not a little angry. Jacquot's dream was half-true, it seems.

Jehanne sleeps for three days.

The fourth morning after her arrival, Isabelle and Jacquot are eating breakfast when they hear their daughter's heavy boots clomping through the mud to the house. They can see it: she has been up all night. "*Maman*," she smiles and kisses her mother, then turns to Jacquot quietly, like a shy suitor. "*Papa.*"

Jacquot fights his own smile; shouldn't he be holding her off with a finger-cross? "Good morning, Jehanne. I trust you're feeling better?"

She drops her eyes. "I'm sorry I worried you. Both of you."

"And you will drop this nonsense about Vaucouleurs, now?"

She looks at him as if he were a stranger, seeming taller as she raises herself up: a stranger herself, somehow, in her muddy boots. "I will return to Vaucouleurs in the spring," she says. "This time, I learned I must come back to warn everyone. We must pack up the house. Now."

"And why do you say that?"

"The de Vergy brothers are headed to Vaucouleurs." Her smile is gone, her eyes clear as they meet his. "And they will burn Domrémy on the way there—just as they did with St.-Vincent. I've seen it."

Jacquot and Isabelle, irrationally relieved that she's speaking full sentences, wait another hour or so before calling on the priest. "He gave her the rosary," Jacquot's voice nearly silent with rage. "He's the one to account for it all."

Jehanne sees her father's anguish, her mother's confusion: it burns her stomach. She wonders if it will help to say it clear—to tell her parents, as directly as she knows how, about the flood that started the moment she crawled home from the sheep meadow. They deserve the truth, anyway.

She waits until she can work the field alongside her father. She's missed the planting: by the time she returned from Vaucouleurs full-fledged ploughing had begun. Le Lune hates the plough, bucks under the harness, and Jacquot laughs at Jehanne's efforts to control her now. "You bring her to battle, and now she can't handle a little old plough?"

The fields bear dangerous resemblance to the sheep meadow, and the June sun is merciless on her four years after. Still, sweat on her forehead reminds. Swallow hard, till her hands are held by an angel with dusky skin and huge bruises.

"*Papa,* I want to tell you why I went to Vaucouleurs."

"Oh, I know that already." Jacquot, on the old warhorse Le Bonne, drives a heavier plough: the churning of the soil is startling, loud. "It's those saints of yours, right?"

"The saints come with a voice," she says haltingly, a wobble coming from the unsteady movements of the plough and Le Lune, who seems far too curious about a set of gopher holes ahead.

"Watch out!"

Jehanne starts to steer her past, but continues. "This voice, it's so loud sometimes it makes my head hurt, because—"

"Oh yes, my brilliant daughter who hears the voice of God." That super-quiet voice again, the one that means he's truly furious. She can barely hear him over the horses' hooves. Does she try to correct him? Or does she go with this useful fiction that might help the village understand better? But how can she lie to her father? Does she need *le Dé mentir* here, too? *The voice of God* easier for him, for anyone else, to understand than *the braided voices of bruised women and broken boys.*

Le Lune makes one decision for her, by letting her rear foot be snagged by one of the gopher holes. As the filly struggles to right herself she shrugs off Jehanne, who lands in a deep ridge rich with barley rows

"*Merde*" Jacquot's exclamation is involuntary, but applies

perfectly well as his daughter rises slowly from the ridge and holds her palms out toward him. The scraps of grass and young barley are aflame, then smoking. She bends, lifts another handful, lets him watch agape as she does it again, from warm palm to infant flame. She shakes her head, bewildered.

"Believe it or don't," she tells him, her voice shaking. "Just don't say I never told you."

The old church is filled to capacity, which in this heat means it smells of drunken farts and menstrual cloths.

"Slow and easy," Jacquot whispers to Isabelle as they take their seats. "Remember we're the ones who paid for that stained glass." The single panel he refers to, a simple rose window with a wide-bodied Madonna, casts red on their seating area. He steels himself against their whispers, even the good ones:

"Look at her! The Maid! She's going into France to save us!"

"No, it's just the Darc girl, the camp whore."

"I hear she met the Dauphin."

"I hear she swallowed a holy sword."

"I hear she swallowed a sword, all right," the nudge and the wink making laughter.

Beside Jacquot and Isabelle their only other child not married off: Pierre, who's now graduated to active distaste of his sister since she went to Vaucouleurs. He can't believe the priest is letting her do this.

Anxious to see the Maid whore, crowds have pressed in from surrounding villages, testing the capacity of the small stone building. Isabelle keeps herself occupied with Mengette's little Solange. The girl, recovered nicely from her bout of fever, is having trouble staying still, till Isabelle gets her to help with her knitting. She stands very still in front of Isabelle, wool around both hands. "She's such a good girl," Isabelle tells Mengette. "We all thought her lost, with fever."

"Not any more," Mengette leans forward and kisses her four-year-old's forehead. Solange shakes her off, concentrating on her task.

"Feel better now?" Isabelle asks her little helper.

Solange nods, her lips pursing as if swallowing a giggle. "Mamma and La Pucelle fixed it."

Mengette's eyes flash to the altar, to where Jehanne stands close to the statue of St. Margaret.

Father Guillaume, who seems to age further every hour, has conceded this time for Jehanne—her one chance to talk to everyone at once, since girls her age are proscribed from public houses. By now he's near-certain what she doesn't believe herself: she's hearing God, in manifestations more merciless than he himself has been allowed.

Jehanne has been there since dawn, movements jerky, her color high in her cheeks. She wears the same dress she wore to Vaucouleurs, her priest-vestment, as stained and muddy as it is. She wishes she weren't frightened. That there wasn't so much anger in people's faces.

On the altar-tableau on the wall behind her, the tiny Three Wise Men with their thumb-sized gifts seem to smile at her, instead of at the infant Jesus no bigger than her toenail. The Virgin Mary's birch halo-circle is new, a repair done while Jehanne watched.

Mengette sits up front next to Isabelle, baby Xavier in her lap. She meets Jehanne's eyes and nods, *it'll be all right*. But across the room is Hauviette, with whom Jehanne once danced by the Lady-Tree: fifteen now, married to an older cousin, she looks down when Jehanne tries to meet her eyes.

Behind the altar she's conscious of sacrilege, but wants to be sure everyone hears her. "The de Vergy brothers are coming to Domrémy!"

How do you know? She stumbles a little in the telling, the testimony of a drunkard and a dead man hardly enough to justify pulling up stakes and moving. "I hear the voice of God," she lies, then follows up with the truth. "My Voice tells me. So did one of Robert di Baudricort's men."

"I've heard these rumours too," says Joubert, the carter. "We should get ready to go."

"The Burgundians told her! They want us to believe this!" a sharp voice from the back. "As we sit here, the English are deep in France, pushing at Orléans. They're not coming here this second. If we pack up and evacuate our cattle will die, and our crops—"

"What crops?" a stolid woman, her widow's black its own statement.

Another widow, this one older, holding a grandchild's hand: "I came here ten years ago from Rouen. Before the siege. Three of my daughters died when the English came. They threw all the poor women and children out of the city, but the soldiers didn't let them flee, and so they all died right there. I want to get out before we're besieged like that."

The first speaker slams his pew. "We're not a city, we're not important enough to besiege, or even attack. While we pack up and go, de Vergy will have bypassed us and hit in the north, while the bandits rob us blind. This rumor-mongering does no good at all. And the girl telling us—forgive me, Jacquot Darc, but your daughter is cursed." Choruses of agreement from both men and women, including Madame Joubert, who bares her teeth again with seeming pleasure.

"She is not cursed!" Mengette stands up, suddenly stalwart. "She was told by God!"

Jehanne looks at Father Guillaime, who shrugs. He knew this would happen.

The arguments grow louder, a hymnlike chorus not unlike the families at the walls of Vaucouleurs. Jehanne retreats inside them. She can see Domrémy burning, until it becomes a fireball like St.-Vincent, little Solange on the tip of a soldier's lance. The one who cut her open. The screaming of steel. The noise escalates. Make it stop.

She has to go back to Vaucouleurs.

But not yet, she thinks. She needs a louder voice. She needs to know how to use a sword. She needs the Church words to dress her angels more securely in the brocade of the church. Jesus damaged by soldiers. The screaming of steel.

As the crowd disperses she looks over at Father Guillaume, who seems smaller than before the meeting began. "Latin," she says gently. Not in the tone of a request.

He starts, as if awakened from a nap or dying. "No language for a woman, for a girl," he says slowly, without force.

She reaches up and kisses him, lightly. Then she hurries to catch up with Mengette.

Amo, amas, amat. She's mesmerized by the words, not only church words but real words, I love you love he loves. *Amare* to love. *Legere* to read. Father Guillaime whispered the words for her, got her to repeat them back. He cannot teach her to read, but he can tell her how these words work, what they mean.

Jehanne caresses the scroll, reciting it back. Unlock the words, you unlock the scripture. She is not supposed to be learning this, it is not for peasants and women, but with a new pope just installed and priests being killed on the side of the road, who knows the rules? Today a skinny Galician Jew with broken wrists, licks her neck while she recites. They sing the Church song, glittering with new meanings.

Cool words. Her scratched hands slide along the sides of the scroll, try not to disturb the illustrations. The words are on here, though she doesn't know which shapes make the sounds on her lips. She thinks she knows what sounds are the big letters, that start the sentences. *Ideo precor beatum Mariam semper Virginem, beautum Michaelem Archangelum,* words she already knows from Mass. She starts to look and speak along as best she can.

The Gospel is a tale of woe. Jesus wept. She feels every one of the thirty-nine lashes. When she cries, Father Guillaime reaches over to comfort her, but she can't feel him at Calvary.

When the lesson is over, she kneels on the cold floor. She pushes her angels away. The one who pulled at her hair.

Jesus is another angel. The soldiers' lash stings on her back. She lies on the cold church floor and recites the Gospel she has just learned. She will need it, after Vaucouleurs.

First she will go to the camp, where broken women live on borrowed hosts and sacramental wine: they will help her prepare to go back. In her mind Régine kisses her mouth. She falls asleep with the force of it.

The de Vergy brothers wait another month to come, busy burning others' crops ready for harvest. By then, a series of sieges have broken the back of most large cities north of the Seine, and a good handful south: Now, the English and their allies in Burgundy prepare to break entirely the eight-year-old treaty of Troyes. First, they need to pacify the last remaining towns and villages: like Domrémy.

The people, the whispers in the church, know it all already —even those that want to deny her. They know that Burgundy, swilling wine down English guts in his Dijon castle, takes his orders from the English while he fucks the dauphin's mother. They know who gives the orders: a dirty word. Bedford!" spit into the ground. They know that Bedford rests smug in Rouen, ten years after siege roasted its children's bodies.

Most of them are hazy about how far away is *Angleterre,* or who rules it. They've heard rumors about a king no taller than a pony, but most of them don't believe it. The Duke himself wishes he didn't have to. Burgundy, as fat as the rumors but not nearly as calm, is in a hurry now. Rumors about La Pucelle have already begun to stream through the valley and beyond, but he ignores them for now. Instead, he tells the Sire de Vergy, the governor of Champagne: "Strip those dolphin-pins if the skin has to come with them."

A heavy July morning, then: the cows deeply asleep, the sheep already up and howling. "Gerardin's cousin came to warn us," Jacquot tells his children. "He rides with the Burgundians, but he wanted Gerardin to be safe." Jehanne swallows, hard. She is still too deeply fatigued to have heard them coming.

She casts about among her bedclothes for something to wear.

Her angels are terrified too, of what? Do they love their grove so, were they damaged at Vaucouleurs? All she knows is that her mind is empty, silent, the flood of voices snowblinded in summer by Isabelle Romée's vast reservoir of energy.

Isabelle and Jacquot, so at a loss with Jehanne's wildness, are the perfect dictators for something practical like this. Jacquot deputizes Pierre to tell her to go to the barn and begin to wake the cows. "I need you, Jehanne. . . . Where are you?" shouts Pierre, who has avoided his sister since she came back from Vaucouleurs, but now calls to her. "You were right!" half exultant, half terrified.

She is numb, helping sheep escape. Her whip is loud. Pierre takes it from her then: "We need it to keep the cows together— remember?" He tries to remind her of how to do this, how often they've done it together. But she can't bring the memory to her eyes. She hasn't realized how exhausted she was. She stares Pierre down as if he were a stranger, and lets him go forward without her.

The Meuse River is far too narrow for the number of barges being loaded into it, families gathering their most needed possessions and propelling themselves downriver with newly-carved sticks. She wants to dive in beside them and swim, holding

Mengette's hand, but Mengette is right now laden with children, gesturing to her. "Jehanne! You were right!" The ridge is the only reliable way out, on foot or horse.

For Jehanne right now there is only green, grasses and low-lying groundcover softened by the swirling fog. She climbs out of the village, her heavy shoes leaving footprints in the mud: alone for once. She never knew angels could be so scared.

Until the ridge above Domrémy is as clogged as the road to Vaucouleurs: families, sheep, cows, low-lying carts piled with family treasures. She doesn't remember putting her clothing in a box but there it is, atop the heavy silver tray Isabelle has prized since the day Jacquot gave it to her, the week of their wedding.

Until her angels finally emerge: a thick-bodied amputee joins Le Lune in hauling the goods Isabelle has piled on the cart. A tired mother, her dead child's body still strapped to her breast, grows huge, terrifying the cows into compliance.

They all give way easily to Mengette and her family. Yves, the two-year-old Xavier, her newest infant daughter howling at her breast. Jehanne reaches for the terrified-compliant Solange, takes her onto her shoulders, the little girl's muddy shoes leaving their mark on her chest.

"We should have left the day after you talked in the church," Mengette says without preamble. They've never needed one, not since they were eight and giggling in the creek beds. "We've been ready since then. All this haggling over where to go—where else but Neufchateau?"

"Neufchateau!" an old woman takes the word up as if in a chant. Before they know it the town's name is skittering along the ridge, like a demented chorus, *Neufchateau. Neufchateau.* Jehanne grins at the white noise. She can barely hear anyone over the lowing of the cows. Last time they took care of the cows first, before seeking shelter in a neighbor's drafty castle. That much she remembers.

They pass her orchards, her groves, where her angels and

Mariel whisper secrets in the dark. She keeps her throat tight and doesn't speak of it. Behind her, anxious boys have swords drawn, as if Burgundians will jump from under a beech tree. The mingled horde, the white-noise horde, is moving, albeit slowly, all shouting. All headed south, as Mengette said: Jehanne's feet are already dragging, screaming *wrong way!* She bends and hoists Solange off her shoulders, hands her back to her mother.

"Where else," she tells Mengette absently, "is Vaucouleurs." Amo, amas, amat. Credo in Unum Deum. She leans into a cow's side and cries in frustration, in fear. She has to get there before she can save France. Before she can make Englishmen bleed. Her insides cramp, she will herself bleed soon. Vaucouleurs is also where the de Vergy brothers are headed, she knows, but such a fortress will not be easily breached. She could help them, were she there.

Instead she's on these roads, which are truth to tell a relief, not glutted with bodies but fresh, green, calm as a baby's pulse. She loses Mengette in her sea of cows. The humidity sits on her skin like a pressure, a tight cloak. Jesus wept from fear. She can't wait for rain.

Neufchateau is the nearest fortified city, about twice Domrémy's size. Its buttresses not nearly as massive as Vaucouleurs but sturdy, strong, its guardsmen pacified into opening the walls by Jacquot's saved gold. Families beg surcease from Neufchateau's families and innkeepers, offer themselves as tenants in neighboring farms, promise their horses won't eat too much. They try to ignore the glow in the distance, the smoke from their burning crops.

By nightfall things are as settled as they're going to be. Another packet of gold gains the Darcs entrance to an inn, and the voluble company of Madame Rousse, its owner. "For as long as you need," she cries as she takes Isabelle's clothing into her warm arms.

"Domrémy is small," says Isabelle, "and their band larger every day. Why would they stay long, without us there?"

Soon the inn is crammed with families: women, children, boys line the hallways and stairs. The infants seem all cried out, the younger children's curiosity wiped clean by the fifteen-mile walk in the heat. The air is fetid with their sweat and excrement.

Jehanne and her brothers have safely herded the cows into a nearby field and tethered the horses, though they are missing Le Lune, who ran off, wild, angry. "You never did tame her properly," Jacquot tells his daughter.

"You mean she wouldn't leave without me," the girl replies. "You sent me off to direct the cows and left my sister to choke on burned grass."

Jacquot reassures Isabelle that they will be able to return before the sheep have quite forgotten them. But Isabelle is not thinking of the sheep. She is thinking of Jehanne, who has insisted on spending the night with the rest of the horses so they don't run away, her hair mixed with wildflowers. Isabelle's hand clenches: her youngest daughter, her only home. The grief is too huge. She accepts a glass of wine from Madame Rousse.

Still, the first question the doyenne asks is about Jehanne, about their daughter's performance at St.-Rémy. "Your daughter knew they were coming," a timid question phrased like a statement.

"Yes, she learnt it when she went to Vaucouleurs."

"She was she there by herself?" The opportunity to have rumors confirmed is too delicious; Isabelle thinks she sees a smile on the doyenne's face, not quite hidden. What does the woman know, about Jehanne and her voices? Her saints? The spirit that moves her to madness? Isabelle is angered now, provoked into defending her wayward girl, feeling an odd sort of pride.

"She was with my cousin, Durand Laxart—your husband

fought a round or two with him, a year or so back. Now Durand can't be as much in the war; he has twins to farm for. So Jehanne decided to do it for him."

"Twin whelps! I'll drink to that," the doyen declares. He has seen enough today, having had to find room in his village for three hundred people and their animals, children, muddy carts and smelly hair. Why he is endorsing twins is clear to no one, except that it sounds good in firelight. "And to your daughter's news, however misbegotten. It means you're alive today."

Misbegotten, has their daughter just been explicitly called a whore? Jacquot's eyes blaze a moment, before he drops his shoulders. It hardly matters what she's called, out there sleeping with the cows.

He watches the younger women as they lean against each other, stroke their children's hair. Mengette, Jehanne's friend, nurses quietly in a corner, her cheek against the castle's cold stone. She catches Jacquot's eye on her and smiles. At least one of us is eating, she seems to say. At least one village is quiet.

That they hear the thunderclap at all is a miracle in this rabble, even if half of them are very close to sleep. Isabelle thinks of her daughter again, but doesn't rise.

At midnight the rain makes glass of moonlight. It plasters her hair to her face, her dress to her skin, until she wants to strip it all off, run naked back to Domrémy. She feels invisible, as if no one could see her, not Antoine de Vergy or the Duke of Burgundy or the Dauphin himself. Her angels will protect her from harm. She wonders how you burn a village in the rain.

Jehanne is tired beyond arousal, beyond mania, she is tired nearly beyond sense. She hasn't slept or eaten since they left, two days ago. Even her angels are coming to her only in patches, flashes, blending in with meadow soldiers: blond-haired arms, tossed armor, cracked steel. She may fall asleep right here, and fulfill Jacquot's oft-repeated threat. No, Father, *I* will drown her myself, in rain.

She counts the horses again. This can't be possible, but it is: there are only three, and none of them are Le Lune.

With some trepidation she mounts the oldest, most stubborn of the lot, Le Bonne. He never liked her, and likes her less since she dragged his baby sister to hell and back. He also hates the rain, its thunder r-noises on the roof of the barn, the lightning flashes swirling brightness in the night sky. Jehanne starts to laugh. She loves the lightning: its racket matches the one inside her head.

As if to match the old horse, tonight's angel is very old, a Roman tunic on his wizened body. His war stories are in Latin, a language she now nearly understands. He helps her use the same stick she used for cows, to hustle the old horse out into the wet.

When the mud surrounds the horse's hooves she presses on his shoulder, burning him a little, until he kicks it away and moves on. Finally the old horse wins, bucking harder, and throws her; it's only the depth of the mud that saves her bones in the fall. He throws her within five yards of the narrow riverbank, and she knows what to do. She's drenched already; swimming won't make her much wetter, will cleanse her of mud and blood.

She's never tried to swim in this many clothes and she feels them push her, try to send her to the bottom. She doesn't want to go; she knows how many corpses rest there. Concentrate on breathing, on making sure her arms part the water. In the dark she can't see the lichen, the little fish, the bubbles that nourish her in the day. "Just keep breathing," Mengette would say, before they collapsed giggling.

She wonders if this is a really stupid idea. *They'd love to see you here,* warns an angel once thrown in the Nile, as an execution. Witch-tests. She lifts her head above water a minute, coughs, lets water flow from her nose.

She finally crawls out of the water about a quarter of a mile upstream from the ridge, from her groves. She's greeted by more rain, and by Le Bonne. Untethered, without her, he has just headed home.

Her throat fills. She calls to him, "*Mon frére! mon frére!*" He ambles over, sits for her, still angry but as frightened as she. The rain starts up hard again just as they reach the top of the ridge, and they duck back into her groves.

She's never taken a horse back there and Le Bonne is skeptical, hangs back closer to the road, lowers himself for her to dismount. *Not yet*, she needs him, she is not ready to sink her ankles into the charnel.

For not everyone left, it seems: a few boys hung back, anxious for battle or protective of what was left of their crops. Jehanne's throat closes at the single arm brushing Le Bonne's hoof, as if she can feel the dead flesh. The wildflowers are trampled with other horses' hooves, a flat muddy pool where her walking path should be. Someone ran here for safety and was chased, doubtless after they'd already taken the rest. The noise escalates, beginning to ask for blood.

As they get deeper into the grove, Jehanne dismounts. Could they really be gone already? Doesn't it take longer than this to eviscerate a village like a newly-killed sheep? Her drying skin chills a little, as fear settles in her chest. She leans on Michael, putting her legs around his Roman waist and begging him to tell her what she will find at the bottom of the ridge. Instead, he drops her to the ground. She will have to go herself. She may have to ask a dead soldier.

But she's paralyzed, as if her knees were sunk in the mud. The voice of her battered angels, the voices of Domrémy bouncing off castle walls, the lowing of her family's poor cows jam her ears. *Who the hell is this Pucelle? thinking she can save France?* The one who banished the others, then hurt her worst of all. No power here.

The tips of her fingers are numb, her calves weak, her arms

heavy with indecision. She lies in the muddy grasses and lets sleep claim her.

When she wakes, fog kisses her face; in the place of her angels now is another real girl of perhaps fourteen, Hauviette's age, her face plastered with rouge and her wide shoulders bruised. Her name is Carole. She speaks a very rough slurred Burgundy tongue, half French, half English; she touches her forehead to Jehanne's and tells her about traveling with them, all this way. She can barely walk with it.

Jehanne sighs. She could have woven Carole from whole cloth, if asked. She lifts her with one arm and inspects her bruises, then asks about her church, her home. "The Darc house?"

"They are done there, you don't want to see."

"Where are they now?" The girl's eyes widen, words sticking in her throat. Jehanne is patient and waits. She kisses Carole's forehead, her eyelids, closes her eyes against the force of the girl's pain. If she feels the weight of Burgundian bodies, smells their mead on her neck, she may never make it out of this grove.

They stand holding hands, rising to their feet in unison. "Let's go, eh?" Carole shakes her head, but Jehanne's arm encircles her waist. Too dangerous to leave her here now.

Home first, the building with the signature angled roof, where the barriers so carefully erected by Jacquot have long been breached by heavy swords. Her bowls and plates are smashed, all tossed in search of the doyen's gold. The stairs to her room are broken from too many armored feet, the side wall cracked: had she not taken her crucifix they would have smashed that too.

Out back, she kneels to lift half-bodies of chickens, whose guts have been ripped by hungry chevaliers. The rain has kept the blood moist. Carole chokes as if to vomit, but she has been fed by Englishmen this past week: Jehanne has not eaten in all that time and her stomach jumps at the meat-smell. She lifts one and buries her nose in it, traces a bird-heart with her tongue. She takes a deep breath and tries to decide what to do now. She stills herself for the braided voice, *tell me what to do, please*. Instead she hears little Carole cry out, from the other side of the house.

There Le Lune, the young horse, lies motionless, her side mutilated with a circular motion—some enraged soldier's slap at the Dauphin insignia.

Jehanne kneels, lays her fingers into Le Lune's blood, her face wet with fog and tears. Her shoulders freeze. Anger's been a stranger since she crawled home from the sheep meadow: too frightening. Too interested in the flood. Her jaw now so tight she fears her teeth will break.

"It's time to find them," she says aloud. The words lost against wood. "To get their stink gone." She pulls at little Carole's hand. The younger girl straightens, moving toward Jehanne, no longer cowering. She points an arm toward the river.

The public house squats on the Meuse like an unwelcome guest, its excrement flowing into the riverbank. Jehanne leaves Le Bonne a quarter-mile from it, willing herself silent, pressing her hair into a tight plait and easing herself in through a side window. An angel, a pale woman with almond eyes and a set mouth, pushes her all the way in.

Jehanne's feet slide on the damp floor, mud mixing with blood and urine. She holds her breath against vomit. Drunken Englishmen sleep on top of Burgundians and astride other girls like Carole, all mute and some drunk themselves. Jehanne squats in a corner and watches them, wondering if she should set this pub afire or if it will take the village with it.

Then the clouds pull back, letting the sun stream over the river and into the narrow building. The English arms begin to stretch, the first few yawns echo like thunder against the pub's clay walls. She searches their faces but: no. None from four years ago. She doesn't understand what they say to one another. Too fast, some of it English, the rest her language flattened by

Burgundy. Carole whispers explanations, but they're strangled by fear.

The largest among them stirs last, reaches out a massive arm and digs behind the counter until he finds another bottle. The woman under him, her face flushed, sees Jehanne, startled. She places her finger across her lips.

A huge sound then, inside the silence: as if the door opened to a stampeding band, as if horses were stomping on heads. More hands, girl-hands, silenced boys. Maybe it's the blinding sunlight that lets them in. Boys whose voice she knows. Girls she's glimpsed in dreams, with dark arms and darker voices. She strains to see through the glare.

The Burgundians' priest whimpers while the huge captain rolls away from his prize, bellowing. Eyes staring at nothing Jehanne can see. She slides closer, far closer than she'd dare, taking advantage of their distraction to examine them more closely. The captain's mouth in a perfect O, his eyes soften a second, as if dying or fucking or scared. A perfect moment to cut him, if she had a sword and the courage: someone is stunning him somehow, giving her the moment to strike. She wishes for not just a sword but an army beside her.

Lacking either, she retreats back to the door, warming it till the wood of the doorframe glows in embers. Urging the men out of here instead, though other phantom girls have driven off their horses.

Then another thunderclap ends it, as if the rain's bored with it all. The men shake their heads like horses lifting out of a drink in the river, as the threat recedes. The biggest one finds his sword and uses it like a walking stick, to guide his way out. One by one his boys follow, lift themselves out of the pub, make their way up the muddy ridge. Jehanne keeps herself very still by the wall until they're gone. Finally Carole laughs, emboldened. "You showed them."

Jehanne shakes her head, stunned, her angels silent. What just happened? And who did it?

She lurches out of the stinking public house and throws up in the river. For the first time since the de Vergy brothers came, her shoulders are cold with fear. Her lips don't stop moving. Recite the gospel Father was just teaching her, Jesus chasing out the money-changers. Jesus damaged by soldiers too. Blows on her arms from them. The clanking of armor. Her blood heats.

She kneels at the riverbank and immerses her bruised arms in the river-water, rubs it into Carole's scraped hands. She can't pray here, right now. They approach the church then, her hands flat, open, weaponless.

Her church, where just a week ago she stood like a Pope shouting warnings, is silent now: empty? Jehanne goes first to the statue of St. Margaret, that small pregnant smile and billowing cape. Someone has already tried to take off the statue's head: The altar split by lances, the candles a frozen rained-on cesspool. The altar-tableau got the worst hit of all, tiny figures strewn across the floor like dead fish.

She picks up the pieces of Jesus in Gethsemane: his head has been completely knocked off, its halo-circle bent and splintered. She bends again and scoops up more and more, filling her hands with tiny broken peasants, animals, the feet of ten disciples. Then she kneels in a patch of sunlight, makes herself feel it, as much as she fears it. Fears the drops of salt. Fears the braided voice with its impossible demands.

When it finally comes, the voice is not kind. What the hell is she going to do? The hum on her skin, her aching head. The roar. Girls and boys she knows only in the voice. They're what stunned the captain at the public house: how? A bruised unreliable phantom army, promising to join her if she will come in from the border. They'll distract the English, while French destroy them.

The voice is loud and almost incomprehensible, like the

white noise at Neufchateau, at Vaucouleurs. Right now, it tells her, di Baudricort is busy defending his fortress against two thousand of de Vergy's men. *Into France with you, now.*

Her body stays still, until she feels angels untangle her hair: then she opens her eyes and embraces one, a narrow boy from Alexandria with whip-marks. Together they turn to watch Carole as she rushes to the back of the church, to its lone occupant, someone who didn't leave Domrémy with the rest.

It's Alain, Hauviette's younger brother, his small dagger used against him by laughing Englishmen. He is missing half of his fingers. His eyes are dead, and his jerkin is torn at the back.

Jehanne's shoulders hurt looking at him. She wishes he were dead nearly as much as he does. She'll sling him behind her on LeBonne and bring him to Neufchateau, where his parents have been weeping for him. That should also mollify her own parents, who will keep secret that they didn't send her to find him. And Pierre will wish he had come with her.

It takes Domrémy a few months to recover from these raids. At bottom, the town itself is far from devastated; the last crops are gone and the public house may as well burn, but the few remaining farmers shrug and pick up their ploughs. Le Bonne goes back to being a plough horse and Jehanne is steady on him, pleasing her parents as she works to nurture her orchard, her groves. Jacquot starts wearing his dolphin on the outside again, though his Dauphin is far off, on the other side of border: in a palace at Chinon.

In the late afternoons, instead of the church, she rides Le Bonne: she's learning for Vaucouleurs, for Chinon, for the Dauphin. Pierre, impressed now if still confused, agrees to help her: he shows her how to hold to the heavy branch, not quite as heavy as a sword but still good training right now. They go off into the groves, practice in hilly ground—as far as she can get from the empty sheep fields, the blazing sunlight. The noise, the scream of steel, abates temporarily.

Father Guillaime can't begin to repair his drafty stone church. He almost didn't survive the trip back to Domrémy, and his moves are shaky now. Jehanne and Alain instead borrow the hands and skill of Jacquot, of Mengette's husband, of anyone willing to help peel away the muck and blood. The priest watches helplessly as his church becomes a center for gossip and war news, as ploughmen take a break from their lost harvest to re-cement St. Margaret's neck. "Way, di Baudricort, he held them all off!"

"Well, that Vaucouleurs is huge, it's not human sized." The speaker is in his sixties, a former pot belly now concave from hunger. "Easy to get lost there, *non c'e pas truet*, Jehanne?"

"*Ah oui*," Jehanne mumbles. The ploughmen are thick-bodied, angry, she can guess how stupidly they'll die. One of them has the same hair as the commander, the one who lay his sword next to her and didn't leave with the rest. Woolly, graying, to his shoulders. She kneels to the floor by the statue, scrubbing at the scratched fluids that flow through the floorboards. She keeps listening.

"There was hundreds of them there. They had Englishmen, Burgundians, traitors from Larzicourt and Blanzy. Fine horses, finer women, with breasts like—" The man stops and turns, bowing in embarrassment to the priest and the girl and the mute boy. He turns back and takes his position by the stone wall, pushing one of its disrupted sections into place. "They hammered at the place for all of fucking July, but his bombards was huge and blew up more than a dozen of 'em." That last sentence breathless from effort.

"So they finally gave up?" Father Guillaime asks the question, weakly. If he's the one to ask, maybe he can remind them that this is a church, that they should watch their language. Jehanne has stood up from the stone floor and is helping carry a heavy tub of clay, to help cement the repaired wall. Her face is muddy, stolid, with a useless half-smile, as if she were a fishwife cleaning a trout. It doesn't look like the Jehanne he knows.

"Oh, *pére*, I wouldn' say gave up. Di Baudricort, he promised he wouldn't try to attack any Burgundians, right? Not the same as vowing loyalty to their lord but De Vergy decided that meant he'd won, for now. He just ran out of men, *d'accord*?"

"Bet the Queen of Jerusalem was relieved!" The big man laughs, leaning all his weight into the wall till Father Guillaume fears it will crack.

"Who?" Jehanne's voice, faint, still brings an answer. She's remembering one of her angels, the bruised Jewish prostitute, her brothers sliced underfoot. Jerusalem?

"Yolande of Aragon! The bitch from Anjou, the dauphin's mother-in-law, they talk about her at Vaucouleurs. Fucking queen of Jerusalem and Sicily, and every little kingdom she can eat in between. She keeps closer eye on the war than our so-called king."

"She's still a girl," the short one chimes in, his red-furred knuckles now covered in white dust. "She has no armies to help him win. He'll run off to Scotland. I bet he has a girl there."

The big man sighs. "Perhaps your mother-in-law's not as fierce as mine, or his. She'll keep 'im stuck at Chinon, even without Orléans. She won't stop till he's king."

Together, the two men lift the final stone for that portion of the wall. "Proof is in the war, my friend. Nine years since Troyes and we do nothin' but give up. Get my boy home and we'll learn English." One last *push!* and the stone's firmly in, the farmers then slapping their palms against the wall to apply the cement.

Jehanne stops them, takes the big one's hand and directs him to work more slowly, to apply the cement more discreetly, hide the cracks in the church. His eyes widen at her bold touch as his hands redden a little, seared. "Don't start learning English very soon," she says, her voice shaking. The one who said *prih-tee wuhn*. He walks backwards, nodding. He understands now the words he heard skittering around Vaucouleurs, about the Maid from Lorraine with her blistering hands and empty promises.

The ploughmen leave well before nightfall, bowing to the priest and the Maid equally. The priest is exhausted; he tries to remember to look at the girl, to try to ease her out of her battle formation. "They're doing what they can, Jehanne. You made sure they would help. Thank you."

She looks at him with heavy lids, she looks at him with loose shoulders, she lets tears immerse her cheeks when she smiles. "I should have been there, at Vaucouleurs," she whispers. Then, what could have been a non sequitur but isn't. "Teach me, now. Tell me about the Queen of Jerusalem."

His shoulders slump. He thought she was done with that. But the words are clear and bell-like and the tears are melting the fishwife smile, bringing her back to herself. He bows internally.

The church repairs are complete by the first frost, but Jehanne doesn't leave Domrémy until mid-December. By then the village has almost completely recovered, collecting those who fled from all corners of France. By then, she has ridden for miles and miles, pushing Le Bonne hard, sometimes in the middle of the night, her *faux* sword in her no-longer-blistered hand. By then, villagers have received confirmation of what the ploughmen heard. Orléans has fallen, flies the English flag behind siege-barriers. The Dauphin has retreated deeper into France, to Chinon. Rumors have him fleeing to Scotland soon.

Pierre has had enough, now: enough of farming while his baby sister runs off with crazy schemes. He knows they need tall, strong boys like him in the battle for Orléans. With his parents' heavy permission, he takes one of their horses, and says a quick, awkward goodbye to Jehanne. "Don't hurt yourself, *ma petite soeur.* Wait till spring comes. You said Easter, yes?" resigned to her plans, but thinking to put them off indefinitely.

She looks up at him. "Second self," she whispers. He was, she was, the two of them burrowing into earth. And now going without her. Finally, "I'll see you at Orléans," her angels push through her tongue.

His lips purse, swallowing a laugh. *Batard.* How quickly forgotten. She watches his tall shoulders recede as he ascends the ridge.

When he's no longer visible, she looks down: three half-decomposed corpses block her path. Have they been besieged, and she not known it? No, these are angels: from besieged Rouen. The corpses melt into the ground. She walks the narrow walk to the Darc house, wondering what she has just said. Orléans? All the braided voice whispered was Vaucouleurs, Chinon. Who said anything about Orléans?

Jacquot keeps himself busy trying to collect tax, half-heartedly: who is left to give the taxes to? The Burgundians? and preparing the ground for the long winter. Meanwhile Isabelle takes refuge in prayer, sitting in the back of the church while Jehanne studies with the Father. She's been in correspondence with her favorite priest, Friar Jehan Pasquerel of Tours, and is busy planning a pilgrimage to Puy-en-Velay. "This is a damned perilous time to be crossing the Loire," Jacquot grumbles, but he knows Isabelle better than to forbid. Her surname isn't Romée, pilgrim, for no reason. And he knows his wife needs something to sustain her, lest her heart break from their heavy daughter. All that time in church is also time to watch Jehanne, and worry.

Hauviette and her husband return to Domrémy, not from Neufchateau but Larzicourt—a smaller town already pledged to Burgundy years ago. There Hauviette, pregnant now, hid in the cellar until her husband came for her. Now, Burgundy's crest in slim bronze has sprouted on her shoulder, half-hidden by her full red hair.

That first Sunday, Hauviette doesn't speak to her wounded baby brother. She sits in the back of the church and toddles Mengette's baby.

The priest's voice is reedy, frail; Hauviette giggles into baby Xavier's ear with it. Jehanne's eyes fix on the trefoil as she sits behind them, her lips moving to the words of the Mass. She holds tight to Alain's hand.

Father Guillaime sings the Latin into her ears alone. She makes him read to her every day, show her where the words are on his scroll. He no longer protests. She's proven herself, and if God wants her to learn Latin she will.

At night, she traces the words she remembers on the ground below the Lady-Tree. Words of martyrs: *Barnaba, Ignatio, Alexandro, Marcellino, Petro, Felicitate, Perpetua, Agatha, Lucia, Agnete, Caecilia, Anastasia, et omnibus Sanctis tuis: intra quorum nos consortium, quaesumus, largitor admitte . . .* "all the Saints into whose company we beseech you admit us." Jehanne giggles at it, at this Mass that dares not mention her angels, her broken children. She spends many nights this way, the time shortening as it grows colder. She can't kneel easily in the frozen mud.

In the morning, when she comes home, Isabelle greets her at the door with a wide cloth, warmed by the fire. She wraps it around Jehanne's shoulders, and whispers a prayer into her black hair. "Are you going on a journey, *ma petit pucelle?*" she asks. Jehanne wishes she had the energy to ask her to tell the stories again. Instead she whispers, "Did you ever see the Queen of Jerusalem?"

"I have not been there," Isabelle misunderstands her. She helps her daughter up the stairs to her narrow bed. "God blessed me to see Lourdes, but not yet Jerusalem. If this war ever ends . . ." She crosses herself, and covers her daughter with a thin sheet

"It will, *maman,*" Jehanne promises as she closes her eyes.

When Jehanne tells her parents she's leaving, she doesn't get the objections she expected, their resistance punctured by the raid on Domrémy. Instead, they declare to the town that their child, La Pucelle, "leaves now to save France," and invite Father Guillaume to her goodbye dinner. Isabelle makes extra saint cakes, and a soup so green it might be the valley floor.

At the dinner Jacquot looks at his daughter, his *petit fleur* replaced by a jagged dandelion, her face taut against cheekbones, her fingers rough in broken gloves. No armor, then, but a soldier indeed, and un-drowned. "Jehanne—what was it that you were trying to tell me, about your Voice?"

"When?" Jehanne fills his bowl with soup. The fall has aged her father, she notices; his face is a little collapsed, a little wider, with wrinkle-impressions as wide as a cornrow on his cheeks. "You mean in the summer? When we were ploughing?"

"Yes, *ma petite generale.*" Jacquot lifts the soup to his lips, leaving a good one-quarter in his beard. "Ever since the de Vergys came, I've been saying to myself, 'There's something your little Jehannette was saying that you missed.' You tripped your horse, remember?" A quiet chuckle, muffed.

Jehanne looks from her father to Isabelle to Father Guillaume, suddenly reluctant to bring it all to the table just now. She asks her angels, today a wary dark figure with stringy-muscled shoulders and a short man with a topknot, if they think her parents are ready for their truth. Her fingers shake uncontrollably. The voice doesn't want to be exposed here. "Sometimes it makes my head hurt," she says, slowly. "I told you everything else."

Isabelle makes her way around the big table and slips an arm around Jehanne's shoulders. "Do you need anything?" she says. "Should I make you a new surcoat?" She's rarely seen her daughter this openly nervous, with less bravado to get her through.

Jehanne looks up at her, gratefully. "If it might have the

same red color," she says. "That's how they know me, there." She doesn't mean Vaucouleurs, but her first destination, a camp deep in the forest. She wants to get there before the snow hides it too well.

"Do you think di Baudricort will receive you?" Jacquot asks.

"This time he will," she says. "He'll help me. I will meet the Dauphin before Lent is through." She doesn't mention the Queen of Jerusalem, her most unlikely ally, her real goal in reaching Chinon.

"Easter with the Dauphin," Isabelle says dreamily. "My little girl. Not a nun, but a holy warrior." Then she sits bolt upright, her color suddenly high. "Will the Dauphin be going on the pilgrimage to Puy, Good Friday next?" she asks.

Jehanne's eyes widen, startled. Good Friday in 1429 is set to coincide with the Feast of the Ascension, a holy day indeed, and why Isabelle has been organizing a group from Domrémy to go on pilgrimage to a sanctuary at Le Puy-en-Velay, barring a raid that kills their horses. She closes her eyes, asking her angels if they know. A hard thing. *Not as hard as crowning the King.* No real answer but her need.

"I will try to join you," Jehanne says simply. "Not *adieu* but *au revoir*" may be a lie, may not, but it's satisfying enough to them, and to her.

She leaves Carole behind, telling her to help tend the few sheep that have returned, and ascends the ridge on the back of yet another horse, the broodmare Madeleine. Alain rides his family's oldest, least needed colt, his face still frozen cold, his eyes still dead.

Régine has aged in the half-year since Jehanne last saw her, the scar on her throat somehow less healed than before. She is wrapped in blankets, the winter chill threatening frostbite. "*Quel dommage,*" as she takes Alain's hands first of all. Then: "Come under, now." Behind her are some of the others that greeted Jehanne last time: the tall Parisian girl, the Scottish grandmother with the bruised mouth, the Breton boy who embraces Alain like a brother or co-conspirator.

They pick their way among new piles of corpses from the summer raids, under the first ice: long enough ago that now they have no faces.

Then a grave but not a grave, a deep gash in the earth, first left when a tree was pulled up. Régine leads them into it, and they keep walking till darkness becomes their daylight, underground. A few candles are lit on the soft walls of the cave, which grows larger and larger. The long corridor widens until it can hold a score, a fire burning at the end. She recognizes the girls and boys who greet her: she met some in the grove. Most are stunned, exhausted. Not angels but real, she has to remind herself, but part of all of this.

This time, she stays in the camp a fortnight, as she'd promised she would do, would carry their voices to the walls of Vaucouleurs. A quiet angel, a dying Sicilian broken as much for his land as for heresy, listens with her as to his last confessions.

Kasia, the white-blond girl from Prague, comes and sits beside her, mute, her arms tight with rage. Her anger humbles Jehanne, who waits until her blood heats enough to let her see clearly: Bohemian footsoldiers tying Kasia up for days, till she can barely walk. She watches her beg rides across frozen rivers, rob coachmen to get to this place. *Teach me how to be as angry as you,* Jehanne begs. *I will need it, soon.*

After Kasia comes a boy from Tunis, near Jerusalem, who tells her the Duke of Lorraine laughed at the sight of his slim ass. "He told me I looked like his last mistress, only prettier."

She waits most of a day for an old, one-legged knight from Rouen to tell her his story, but he refuses. His rage denies even her offer of food. It doesn't matter: there are others waiting for her.

The only one she can't shake is an odd, long-limbed Lorraine boy, with hair as gold as Pierre's and a stupid smile. He keeps telling her over and over what the Burgundians did when they came through his village. No matter what Régine says, there he is. His voice in choirboy notes as his hands move quickly, as if trying to wash the semen from his hair.

Just as she's about to leave, of course, comes the inevitable: the girls from Orléans. One is fat as Carole, with marks on her fingers where jewels used to be, others are skinny maidservants with silenced mouths. It's the old knight from Rouen who brings them into the cave. She doesn't need to ask.

On her last day, Régine leads her to the deepest cave. Her angels hold her still, loosen her hair from its knot, until the dim Lorraine boy and the Bohemian girl help Régine cut it at the collarbone. Jehanne watches as the strands fall to the floor, threads of blood.

Next comes a thick dress, the wool cool against her skin, faded, sleeves too long. She wraps her face in the cloth, smells the woman who wore this dress before she died. She tells the woman she knows the future. That when France is no longer cut up into Armagnacs and Burgundians, there won't be burning fields. That there will be lives without swords or rape or screaming steel.

She is lying: she doesn't know this for sure. She only wants to believe it. So does the braided voice: starved hope, starving time. The noise escalates. Make it stop.

Jehanne leaves for Durand Laxart's house on New Year's Day. It's snowing so hard that half a mile takes more than a day's travel. Her horse Madeleine glories in it, glad enough to be free of the cave's dark. "In that we are quite opposite," Jehanne tells the patient, middle-aged creature, who doesn't know about summer-sunlight and soldiers in sheep meadows. But the snow provides its own dark, its own silence. She lets her hood fall back, and the white suffuses her tired face.

four

IT WAS NOT Merlin but Marie of Avignon in the twelfth century, whose visions saw France destroyed and rebuilt, who wept at a suit of arms and forecast that the virgin who wore it would save France. Since that time, many women and children and broken boys have littered the country's fields and roads, Jehanne Darc among them. Now she gathers up Marie's promise, if not the armor, and bears it to Vaucouleurs.

By the time she arrives, she's preceded by a reputation that has built and echoed and shouted before her, embellished by the testimony of Domrémy, Neufchateau, and those who have never seen but only heard of her. The siege of Vaucouleurs, as short-lived as it was, has sapped the energy of an already-beleaguered fortress: families who thought themselves made invulnerable by the city's walls have lost sons, seen their storerooms exhausted. Each time the story is repeated, it grows.

Durand Laxart has heard them all, now. "La Pucelle, that's all you hear from all those refugees," he says. "Shopkeepers too. Le Royer the wheelwright, says every day his wife is boring him silly with talk of La Pucelle." He's talking half to himself and half to his wife, who's got a twin on each breast and is only half paying attention. "Even some soldiers: *La Pucelle will save us. Marie of Avignon said so.* Was Marie of Avignon carried off by soldiers too? Is this some sort of bloody conspiracy?"

"What do you mean, carried off by soldiers?" Jehanne Laxart's soft voice sharpens. "Is that what Jacquot told you? or just what he fears?"

Durand swallows hard: "What he fears, I think." What he guessed from Isabelle's shamed face, years ago. "Isabelle also said she would be here by the New Year. I wonder if La Pucelle has already got herself into some trouble, without me."

Durand goes outside to scrape the snow from his front step; as it thickens he hurls it away from the house in great thick blades, until his shoulders are sore. He hopes against himself that she's not coming, after all. He has enough to do to protect those two little ones, his big drowsy wife, without worrying about that little slut.

The next day, the girl arrives at Burey-le-Petit, layers of sweat and mud on her forehead, her black hair and red dress soaked in snow. And it's that drowsy wife, rather than Durand, who greets her, brings her in quickly, wraps the half-frozen girl in thick blankets.

Durand, off cutting firewood, doesn't see his wife peel the girl's clothes from her body, begin to bathe her like another infant. "I know the water's not warm but you smell of your own shit. I'll be slow, and only do this bit by bit."

He doesn't hear her soft comment, when she gets to the space between Jehanne Darc's legs: "Ah what did the soldiers do here? This scarring's old. Does this hurt?" She's gentle with the washrag, but needn't be: Jehanne's eyes are focused elsewhere, her whimper nearly inaudible, as if she's dreaming all this. Durand's wife nods. "Long ago, eh? Don't worry miss; this is so bad, it healed thick enough you could almost pass for virgin."

By the time Durand arrives, the two Jehannes are rocking his twins like a pair of Madonnas: one wide and placid like the one in their church window, the other lean and almost Asiatic. He's reminded of the statue he saw once in Paris before it was besieged, a Madonna cut out of ivory with a merry smile. They look up from the babies and tell him it's time to go to Vaucouleurs.

"Oh, so she's got you believing in her too, then?" Durand demands of his wife, putting bluster in place of fear, *what did she say to you?*

She answers him with a gentle question. "Shall we see if the Le Royer the wheelwright and his wife will take her, then?."

Durand looks at his wife, a hard look. She knows. "That's brilliant. If Madame Le Royer is so enamored of La Pucelle, we'll see how they cope with the real thing, this skinny mad girl."

"Her clothes are drying by the fire," Jehanne Laxart says softly. "They will be dry before the sun is down. Will you take her inside the walls, then?" He nods, just as his little boy starts howling beside her.

Jehanne kneels and lifts the boy, holds him to the sky. "*Hosanna in excelsis,*" she says, pressing her cheek to his warm forehead. "He'll be a Frenchman," she tells Durand. "Not an Armagnac or Burgundian. Just France." The rosary round her wrist glows, until Durand wonders how her wrist goes without burning.

Vaucouleurs has recovered from de Vergy's attack, for the most part, though the common people within still look for salvation from the Maid.

The thick red surcoat looks almost like armor in the gray morning light, but for the small figure within it. And it's the young soldiers, this time, who part the gates for her, swing her in from atop the walls. "La Pucelle!"

The old men guarding the bombards, on the other hand,

can't leave off laughing. "The slut of Lorraine!" they stretch out their arms and proclaim, slapping Durand's back.

Durand keeps his face stolid, watching the girl's back stiffen beside him as they keep walking. With the siege over for now, the fortress is full of relaxed activity, not bombards being loaded but wheelbarrows full of corn or dirt, sheep bleating to protest the shear, children chasing each other round the perimeter. They're stopped two or three more times by old women and young men begging to be blessed by "La Pucelle." Jehanne tries to smile, but her eyes are focused on the perimeter, and she's grateful when they finally make their way to the stone corridor where Le Royer grinds wheels for the war.

"*Mon ami*!" Henri Le Royer, a slender elf about five-foot-two, stands and kisses Durand on both cheeks. "This is she, then?"

"Oh yes," Durand puts his arm around the girl's shoulders. "My cousin's daughter. I'd never have predicted it."

Le Royer nods. "And why are you here, sweet miss? What brings you to Vaucouleurs?" Then, before she can answer, he puts up his hand: "Wait till my wife can hear it too. I have waited a long time for this!" He bangs on the front door of the small living space, and keeps banging over and over: "Now, Catherine, now!"

A well-dressed woman emerges from the LeRoyer house, her head in a long white headwrap, her eyes already laughing from her husband's insistence. When she sees Jehanne she sinks to her knees. "Oh, *mon Dieu!* La Pucelle!" She gestures, insisting her husband join her, till the madness envelops Durand and he is forced to his knees before his own niece. "Have mercy on us, oh holy one!"

Jehanne sighs. She takes Catherine's hands and raises her up. The men rise too, with relief. "Never kneel," she says into Madame Le Royer's big black eyes. "That is only for God. And His angels." The words roll off her tongue with relief now, the words rehearsed so many times, code words that will put a sword in her hand. The sword that skewers infants. No. Jehanne swallows.

"You must have *de jeuner* with us," Catherine urges next; dawn has just broken and her hands still bear the faintest traces of flour. "The bread is quite hot." Jehanne's response to Henri's question is thus delayed as they all move into the wheelwright's house, to breakfast on the new bread.

Henri pours his wine into clay cups for them, and dips his first piece of bread: the wine itself is a viscous light purple, staining the fingers new colors. Jehanne keeps her tongue on the fresh bread, warm and soft as pudding, thick enough to block her teeth.

Durand cuts her another piece, explaining to the others "She has ridden a long way, by herself." He wonders where she was, in between Domrémy and his house: but if he ever had a right to ask, that right is long gone.

"God sent her!" the dame Catherine exclaims, refilling Jehanne's glass and looking at her with a daughter's worship. "Marie of Avignon said it would happen!"

"But why Vaucouleurs? And why now?" Henri finally asks.

Jehanne swallows. "I am come because only Robert de Baudricort can help me speak with the Dauphin. I bring him help from Heaven, I bring him help he can get nowhere else." The words sound stupid, do I need to say the whole thing? *yes.* "I must go before mid-Lent. He will not regain France without me," *without us.* the braided voice thick with glottal sounds, rich with rage. "I have to be at the king's side before Lent is over, even if I have to walk until my feet are worn down at my knees." That last feels like a threat, not to them but to her: her angels are hard as bones. They want English blood. They will make her walk until she has no knees.

She watches Henri and Catherine's faces, and asks about their children.

Catherine turns red and grows silent. Jehanne has asked more than she wants to know, right now. She is already carrying too many stories from the forest. If she grows to contain the Le Royer child she may burst. Was he ripped open like Alain or only killed? Did he kill a girl in his fury? Why is dame le Royer not only sad but angry now? Jehanne tightens into lassitude, the morning wine finally sending her yearning for all the lost sleep. The saddened parents start to blur before her eyes, her skin clammy.

Savior of France my ass, Durand thinks as the girl sinks to the ground. He wonders how many mad episodes it will take for the "La Pucelle" hysteria to finally subside .

But then she starts speaking Latin in her sleep, fast, furious, the words clearer than all her God-explanations. Catherine Le Royer scoops her up easily, like a wayward cat who won't stop yowling. Durand exhales. "She can stay with you, then?"

"We will be honored," le Royer assures him. Durand relaxes. He can go home to his twins, now.

Notre Dame de Vaucouleurs is a small, proud mimic of the one in Paris, with its sloping stone arches of stone and an explosion of stained glass that mocks the tiny rose window. A very simple altar-tableau, with larger figurines, seems to have survived recent battles.

Father Jehan Fournier, the pastor, is even older than Father Guillaime, but livelier, as if war has kept him too busy to age. Too many boys needing to be shriven before battle, too many mothers needing soothing afterwards. Too many confessions with sordid details about what a lance and sword can actually do to a human body, to return to their givers in agonized slow motion. While he's rarely been near a battle, he feels like he's survived, personally, each of the last half-century. Who has time to grow old?

But his eyes are beginning to betray him. He can barely see the scripture he reads at noon mass. He looks at the mothers and sisters who fill the pews, hears them whispering to each other. About that girl, probably. The one they call La Pucelle.

Likely a witch, he told de Baudricort. "She comes from Domrémy, after all, where so-called healers danced by the Lady-Tree. Not till three years ago were they finally stamped out." The commander comes to see him every day "for my daily dose," as he says. Although he confesses, and means it, his reason for visiting is the other—to hear what Fournier knows, the other confessions of Vaucouleurs. "You're my best spy." Fournier knows, after all, who's considering going to Burgundy, who's in love with de Baudricort's new mistress, who's still reliving the last battle in midnight screams and vomit. As rumours of La Pucelle find their way into confessions, he's told de Baudricort of them, already bored.

He's tending the fire after two o'clock mass when the door opens and admits Catherine Le Royer, her face wrapped in woolens, holding the hand of a short swathed figure in a red surcoat. Madame le Royer kisses the girl on her forehead and kneels at the back of the church, while the girl moves toward him, eyes flashing, hands extended. She is tiny, round, fattened by her warmth-layers; she looks tired as she kneels before him.

"*Jeune mademoiselle,*" he asks, "what can I do for you?"

"I have not confessed in days," she says, trembling.

Pious or pious-seeming? . His heart sinks, until her next sentence. "But I know you're too full of confessions today." Confessions of killers, she doesn't say: but what does she mean?

She stands then, and looks him in the eyes. Will he hear her? Can she tell him? He has to know. He has to be given that chance: her angels are firm on this point. She makes sure to pronounce the Latin correctly. "I voci audio, et voci proprio." *I hear their voices, and those from before.* He is now only the second person, after Father Guillaime, that she has told in plain prose what is happening.

Fournier looks closely at her flushed face, the mixed fear and anger in her clenched hands. He looks for the signs of a witch.

Jehanne stares back. He doesn't believe her yet. She has wasted the truth on the little priest. She raises her voice now, as if testing it, her tones near-musical. "Terra autem erat inanis et vacua et tenebrae super faciem abyssi et spiritus Dei ferebatur super aquas." *And the earth was empty and formless, and darkness was above the face of the deepest darkness. And God's spirit moved above the water.* She watches his face closely.

Fournier's jaw drops then, his failing eyes finally meeting hers. After a long minute, he smiles. "Genesis, with implied commentary? God moving against our darkness, through you?"

She nods, her lips pursed as if suppressing a giggle. He laughs more freely and extends his hands, keeping them extended until she moves close enough for him to grasp both of hers. "I voci audio," she repeats.

He gives her a measured look. "We will talk further," he finally says.

Before suppertime, De Baudricort comes. He's heard, and there is only one question for the priest. "Is she mad, or a witch, or a whore?"

But Fournier can't answer it. "I don't know."

"What do you mean, you don't know?" De Baudricort's not-insubstantial form makes his chair tremble.

Fournier puts his head in his hands. *It's simply hard to tell,* will the man endure such an answer? "Give me time to watch her. In the meantime, you may as well see her. Tell me what you think, too."

When de Baudricort finally agrees to receive her, Catherine Le Royer, viciously excited, makes a banner for her, embroidered

JHESUS MARIA. Jhesus wept in Maria's lap. The reception hall is huge, and very cold: even in January-brightness she can barely make out the shadows of men. She pulls her hood tighter.

And for the second time, de Baudricort laughs at her, banner or no.

Though this time, de Baudricort has heard much more about her. Were he to believe all the stories, he would believe she could liberate France with menstrual blood and women's tears.

If only he could, he thinks, staring into his bitter morning beer. If only he could believe her. Holding down one of the only Armagnac towns in a sea of occupation is not easy. He is so tired of losing. If the girl really came with allies it would buck up the troops, at the very least.

Right this moment his own men are craning their necks to look at her, sneaking a peak at this tiny thing with the banner who recites Christian doggerel to him. As if he were a priest and would be impressed. *If God sent you,* he wants to say, *why do you need me for safe passage to Chinon? Find the King without me.* "I have bigger affairs to worry about than you. Men's affairs. Go back to the church and pray for Orléans."

She swallows. To know about Orléans you have to dig under the snow. "I am here to lift the siege from Orléans," she tells him, but the words are sluggish on her tongue. Again. And again he laughs, his hand easy on his scabbard. The clanking of armor. Her blood heats. Make it stop.

She closes her eyes and calls for an angel, gets an aged nun who whispers the next words to him. "I need a sword," she tells de Baudricort. "I'll find my true sword on the way to Chinon. But I need one now, to learn, if I'm to be of use." She lifts the crafted wood by her side . "Better than this, no?" hoping to get a laugh from him.

He doesn't smile. "You *are* a traitor," he growls. "You want me to give you a sword and waste men on you, so you can lay waste to the best part of my France. Go the hell home and leave me alone." He instructs his men to carry her out of the audience hall; the moment they touch her she collapses, unconscious.

"Should we take her to the gate, then?" One of them is still fearful, remembering her burning touch from last summer.

"Oh, take her back to LeRoyer. He's her host, not me." He pretends to be looking into his cup as they lift the girl, but he can't help but notice the young ones genuflecting before her: they believe. That belief could be useful, if she's not the traitor he fears. Or a witch. He wonders if Fournier's got any more from her.

Afterwards, de Baudricort can't sleep for days. Here she is, in his garrison, eating the wheelwright's food and drawing crowds in the little church, where they watch her light candles, look at her glowing rosary. That rosary starts to slip into his dreams, mocking him.

"Maybe she is. A witch, I mean," says Angelie, the square-jawed camp follower who shares his bed. "I saw her light candles all day long in the church, they was selling pennies for a view of her—for the church, of course," she adds, crossing herself hurriedly. Angelie watches his face to make sure he's not angered: she's newly arrived, and could be thrown back outside the gates on an order from him.

Baudricort groans. "If she was a witch wouldn't the Father know it?" He wonders if Fournier has become besotted with Jehanne's blue eyes. If she were a witch, if she were possessed, his own church would certainly be a place to start. He kisses the top of Angelie's head, absently.

Angelie turns her body and snuggles against his back, contentedly. "All I know," she says, "is if that's not a witch, she's for sure a saint."

The big man sits up as she falls asleep, rests his face on the cold stone wall. He has started to write a letter to the Dauphin, telling him about the girl's request to see him. He knows it's badly spelled. He decides to burn it. He'll write to someone else, with a scribe's help, someone far more shrewd than the royal boy in the castle. Someone far more interested in the Dauphin's becoming king than the boy himself—someone whose alertness to threats has, so far, kept all of them alive.

The Dauphin. Charles VII. Who is this fellow anyway, that Jehanne is so anxious to see crowned?

Twenty-six years old, a poet, physically fragile, untrusting: part English, he's cousin to his conqueror Burgundy, who nearly ten years ago sold his soul, threw in with the English, and installed Charles' own mother in his castle.

He spends his days casting horoscopes and reading Homer. He's not at all sure he even wants to be king. He dreams of going to Scotland, where his old allies have said he would be welcome. But even they are afraid of the woman who keeps him here.

The La Pucelle stories that reach him are even more absurd than the ones de Baudricort hears. Charles hates hearing from de Baudricort, when every letter may mean Vaucouleurs is lost. When he receives the letter with the girl's request to meet him, he throws up. He asks to go to bed.

He writes to another cousin, the Duke of Lorraine, who of all people owes him this. *One long war*, that Duke told him once, *my whole life's been one long war*. He wonders if he thinks himself the only one. Or if that justifies the amount of Burgundian toadying he's danced through in his time.

Jehanne has found her new groves: the walls of Vaucouleurs. She climbs up at sunset, her boots unstable against the ice. Her red surcoat glitters in the winter sun. "Look, there she is! La Pucelle!" As always, some of the guards kneel to her, while the older bombardiers just chuckle. They watch her until she moves out of sight, pressing herself behind a half-barricade, her thick black gloves the only remaining sign of her.

When she reaches a turret, Jehanne finally stops, sits and looks across, from outside the lookout tower. The sentry on lookout yawns: from his perspective there's not much to see. Under the snow the towns sleep like statues. From this distance, the frozen rivers could be long, narrow beech leaves.

Jehanne breathes out, watches her breath dance in the air. It's too cold to stay still for long: her face is chapped, her lips freeze to pain.

She likes the silence of nightfall, the smoke from fires in distant towns, people trying to stay warm. When Vaucouleurs has settled into post-midnight drowse and even the bombardiers snore at their stations, she can hear her angels. She breathes in, holds tight to what's next. Get to Chinon, find the Queen of Jerusalem, meet the Dauphin. Take an army to Orléans. Her phantom army will help somehow, when are they going to tell her how? Tell her what they did, that day in the public house, and how? The voice has new tones, it grows in power as Jehanne does, holds more voices from more ages within its roar. She can barely make out what it's saying half the time.

At night, when she lies down on a pallet once occupied by the Le Royer son (the one whose story she resisted hearing), she falls asleep thinking of the public-house —straining to recognize her sister soldiers, the ones who distracted the Englishmen and waited for her to strike. In her dreams she kisses the girls of Orléans, wondering if she misses them after all.

In the morning, she gets up and joins Catherine le Royer in spinning, just as she once did with Isabelle. And as before, the whirling is calming to her, the muscular effort bracing: she can lose herself in this dance, get a rest from the angel-pressure. Spinning exhausts them.

. . .

As the weeks go by, she can't leave the Le Royer house without crowds gathering, following Catherine's lead in genuflecting and pressing flowers into her hands. "La Pucelle, La Pucelle," she's getting used to the phrase, wonders how many know of its double meaning.

Even some boy-soldiers do it. One gives her a shawl sewn by his mother, and a sprig of dried flowers. She looks up and sees de Baudricort: the soldier, seeing his captain, stands up quickly, bowing, and runs off. The captain says nothing.

She retreats to the church, only to have them all follow her there. Finally she decides her days will be confined to spinning and her afternoons to Father Fournier's Masses, as much as the old priest fears her. Only the night is hers. The braided voice approves.

One afternoon, mid-way through her stay at Vaucouleurs, de Baudricort appears in the spinning room with Fournier. The latter bears a cross and his strongest prayer jacket, the former his full armor, as if about to cut off her head. Madame le Royer quickly bows and crosses herself: then the old priest, shaking, hurls a hurried Latin chant over her bent head.

She closes her eyes and tries to make out the words. Fournier drops heavy incense on her head, its oil burns her skin. And she was worried about the screaming of steel, or Domrémy burning. She calls for her angels, but they recoil, shy and angry simultaneously. Next to her Catherine Le Royer is on her knees.

Madame Le Royer and Baudricort are watching her as if watching a birth, wondering what kind of child will emerge. Fournier gets toward the end of his set piece, and repeats himself more clearly. She finally hears the word *diabolus*.

Oh *merde* ! Those are words of exorcism! She looks up, enraged, eyes flashing. Her blood heats, and not just from the oil. The hum under her skin wants her to set the thread she's spinning on fire, to blister all of them. So does she.

She would give her life to burn them all and be done with this stupid mission to Chinon, to this hallucination that she can save France, this guaranteed string of people who think her a witch. But Mariel, her healer from Domrémy, stays Jehanne's hand, brings her down to her knees at Fournier's feet. She stays silent, and waits, until Catherine Le Royer says softly, "Let her up, please." Her voice lighter, calmer.

Jehanne swallows. Yes, even Madame Le Royer needed this persuasion. *"Credo de Unum Deum,"* she says through gritted teeth.

Then, in manic Latin, too fast for de Baudricort to absorb: "Father, you betray me with this foolishness." Fournier doesn't meet her eyes: he can't. He shakes a cross over her head and waves more incense round her shoulders, till Madame Le Royer coughs and waves him out of her tiny workspace.

After that, de Baudricort watches her with more interest, less fear. The troops love her, and so do their mothers. *God knows they need some hope*, he writes to Chinon.

In the dream she wears chain mail, her knees and shoulders sheltered by battered metal, her elbows scratched by the under-garment. The armor is heavy; she's strong, and bears it up like a craft on the water. She tries to remember, when she wakes, the correct way to hold a lance, but too often she's burning a village instead, too often the lance skewers a random child. St.-Remy, Domrémy, Nancy. This duke's subjects hate him, hate her, hate his young mistress until her hair is on fire. Alison Dumay is swathed in the duke's jewels, fine clothing torn to pieces. Alain's short arms waving helplessly. Burgundy's tricolor in flames, Armagnac dolphin bleeding, small animals crawl into her helmet.

The next morning at Notre Dame the dreams have her crying at the altar. *Père* Fournier asks her what she wants.

"This will only end when the English are gone," through gritted teeth. The voice pushes and urges. Get the English out and no more women burn: even the Duke must know. High pitched angel voice, name like consonants pinched together: *trung.* The noise escalates. Make it stop.

Hope a fresh taste in her mouth, like lemons. Like new apples from her father's orchard. She will fight to stop the burning. Her blood to nurture such fruit. She smiles at Fournier, as she did first telling her father. "I must go to Nancy," she tells him. "The duke of Lorraine, he has my armor." Battered metal, a dead soldier's arms. She'll wear them until the king is a king.

She's asleep when the messenger finally comes, bearing a safe conduct from the Duke of Lorraine, so she can travel unmolested from Vaucouleurs to Nancy. When she wakes, a strange man stands at the foot of her bed. She starts, asking Michael first if he's assumed human form, but getting only silence while the young man smiles, bows, waits for her to get dressed.

His movements belie his well-fed belly, with limbs seemingly moving all at once and eyebrows left over from sneakier, more relaxed days. She's seen him before: he's a squire to de Baudricort. "Does your lord ask for me?" she asks.

"That's your department, I hear," he chuckles. "To tell us what our Lord wants." He extends his hand then. "I am called Jehan de Metz." He tells her about the message from the Duke, and that he has been charged with seeing her at least part of the way there.

She sits straight up, then. "My dream!"

He listens to her well-practiced explanation of her mission, watching carefully. Her words are fluid enough to be insincere, but with tears underneath: "if I have to walk the whole way on my knees." Her eyes are clear, her shoulders thrown back, her stance low enough in her hips to be ready for battle: if it weren't for her tiny voice, he might suspect her of not being a woman at all.

She looks a little like his son, he realizes. Far too skinny, but the same grasping hands, the same bravado in the shoulders, the same brow twisted not by age, the mark of the times.

He'd realized long ago that his son was a little too dim for battle, and left the boy to tend horses. The Burgundians—or English, he's never known which—realized it too, and even left Roger alive when they stole all the horses, on the way to Rouen last spring. Young Roger, never voluble, now sleeps with the horses. The priest in Metz, the one in Nouillonpont prayed over him, but couldn't coax sense from him; they cried when he did and whined for more money for their ruined churches.

De Metz watches this boygirl, now, like his son but a girl too, softer lips, eyelashes far darker than her hair. He listens as she rattles off mixed French and Latin like a priest, or a heretic. He has had it with priests, but her heresy is interesting.

It's he who secures for Jehanne her first set of men's clothing. "You are small, like my manservant." he says. She holds the jerkin in her arms like a lost brother: This is not the dead men's armor she dreamt of.

She borrows Durand's horse, and him. He's wearied enough of screaming infants to be glad of the call, and she rides behind him fearlessly. He looks at her ashen cheeks, and says simply, "Who fills your dreams now?"

She smiles despite herself. "Lorraine, his broken armies." French so flat after Latin, her mouth doesn't want to speak it. "Women fighting," she clamps her teeth down against Catherine's giddy predictions. She swallows hard. Not words meant for Durand. She misses Mengette, who she could tell anything, even if half the time she knew the girl was too busy to listen.

· · ·

The road to Nancy shows tentative peace: unbroken ice bespeaking slumbering fields, not battles. Jehanne's teeth chatter under her hood until they get there. In Nancy, Lorraine's servants welcome them quickly, offer hot food and warmed rooms. The duke, old and sick, is asleep, the guards say. They must wait until morning to be received.

Though they bow and retire as instructed, Jehanne knows she won't sleep: she crawls out of bed and into the castle's dark corridors. She's alert, looking for danger, listening for voices. She can't feel her feet. She wonders if this is a trap the Burgundians have laid and she and Durand and de Metz will be found in pieces, perhaps by de Baudricort, perhaps by Alain and his pregnant army.

She begins to climb the castle stairs against dreaming, a quilt tight around her body and her riding hood still clinging to her head. Catherine, right now a quick-witted Irish girl with thick blond hair, climbs with her. Silently: even the melded voice flats out clear.

It's on the second landing that she finds him, in his own ridiculous nightshirt. The old man's shoulders are bony, his blue eyes liquid with fever. She's surprised not to see him in bed, surrounded by fawning attendants. "I thought you were dying," is her first greeting to her nominal ruler.

"I am," his words as he sizes her up, as if he can assess her shape and strength inside the lumpy quilt, the woolen stockings and heavy shoes. Or is he looking to see if he can assess La Pucelle's charms? But he coughs; she wonders if he is instead looking for a source of water. He continues, "You mean to free Orléans?"

"I mean to free France," she corrects him, glowering. If he insists on this conversation in the middle of the night, then he shouldn't insult her.

"The dauphin wants to know, are you a miracle or a traitor," Lorraine coughs. "I'll tell him I know," more coughing.

"God sends me," the more often she lies the more easily it comes, and besides what else to call the braided voice? But the rest of the speech won't come, not now. She looks at him and the wide body of his thirty year old whore is decapitated before her mind's eye. She has to swallow, hard, to avoid throwing up at the sight of him, of her. Finally she says "They will kill your Alison, you know."

The laugh stops, as if someone stepped on his laughing throat. "Now you give me love advice, Madamoiselle?"

The word "love" is what gets her laughing, in turn uncontrollably. As if she were talking about love. "God bids you attend to your wife, your children . . ."

"Alison has borne five for me."

Not every one of those babies was desired, she guesses quickly. "The people hate her, sir. Even more than they hate you." Easier to speak truth than the *Dieu* lie, no matter how true it sounds when she calls it out. Then she says another truth she doubts he expects, a secret kept from even Alison. "The Tunisian boys didn't know her, so they just hate you."

"Oh! Now she brings me news from Tunis!"

"Only from one boy, named Said. He said you gave sweetmeats in exchange for his." He threw up after saying it, but she won't tell Lorraine that. "Tell the Queen of Jerusalem I bring her news from there, too. From her soldiers' bastards."

"*Mon Dieu*, she is a witch." Another laughing fit, this one yielding to a coughing fit that bends the tall old duke like a reed.

Finally Jehanne yields, and offers a shoulder. "Do you want help going back to bed, sir?"

He leans heavily, and is quite slow moving down the stone steps. She's dizzy from his foul breath. He points her to a large, drafty cavern of a room, with a bewildered manservant tending a fire. "My lord!"

His lord urinates on the way into bed.

. . .

After conferring with a shaken Alison Dumay, the duke of Lorraine sends Jehanne off with a black horse, a bag full of *ecu tournois*, and his blessing to transmit to the Dauphin. The journey back to Vaucouleurs, is slower, now. Dressed in men's clothing, her hair hidden, Jehanne is stopped more often, and has to show her safe conduct from the Duke. New jeers: "Mademoiselle Darc? What, is this La Pucelle, then?" De Metz and Durand beside her, alert for traps.

While she was gone there's been a routine assault on the city walls: she can smell burned flesh from ten miles away. The smell grows the closer they get to Vaucouleurs. They can see no visible fighting, beyond the smell. Jehanne's throat clenches. It can't be time yet, not with her still unarmed.

She begs instead to go around the fortifications, to St.-Nicholas-du-Port. There is a shrine at St-Nicolas that her angels have begged her to see. "This will give the flames time to cool," she says.The hum under her skin presses at her, not to return until.

Like all the other Meuse Valley towns including Vaucouleurs, St.-Nicolas hugs the frozen river; its tiny church clings to its only castle. Jehanne begs to find shelter from it, a moment inside to breathe. The men station themselves on the outside of the castle, as if their lances were cannons.

The church is enough like St.-Rémy to prompt a jolt of nostalgia, with slated gray stone and thatched roof, its narrow spaces blocking not just smoke but light. Jehanne kneels by the crucifix, pouring gospel through her lips. *Et lacrimus est Iesus.*

The local priest, like so many of the villagers, has fled for safer ground, it seems: Jehanne's wishes for a confession are wasted. It takes about ten minutes for her eyes to adjust, to see the small enclosed room fully, but even before she does she hears the giggles. More angels? No the laugh is quieter, white plumes in the cold air the first thing she sees.

Finally her eyes adjust and she sees them, crowded into a

corner behind the altar, as if they have spent their lives running from priests. They make their own altar-tableau, this one life size, not a halo to be seen.

She's found another colony like Régine's, but smaller, drawn only from the surrounding area: hidden only because no one expects these people to have lived.

Jehanne beckons them to come forward, like a backward priest-invocation. Most are close to her age. Girls like Carole, camp followers tossed aside; a healer, like Mariel back home, but un-crucified as yet and wielding her bags of herbs like another weapon. Boys not soldiered, sheltering in one another's arms. Some priest has told them all they would be safe here.

He has also told them about her. "La Pucelle, La Pucelle," the word in their mouths a magic incantation, one a few of them spit. She wants to send them all to Régine's cave, as if there would be room there. She feels oddly comforted, after so much time with so many men. These are her people, the ones who know. The braided voice inside her smiles.

She lifts one of the tired camp followers into her arms, lay her on the altar and smooth her sweaty forehead. The camp follower, older than Isabelle, keeps holding her hands still in a prayer-gesture, and Jehanne almost says *Stop that!* The *Dieu* lie feels most dishonest with these people. The woman's dress is stiff with dried sweat, scratches Jehanne's hands. She whispers prayers in more languages than Jehanne knows.

A bratty blond murdered-girl angel, whose sprightly air reminds Jehanne of Hauviette, plants her slender arms round the runaway soldiers and tells them how brave they are. Jehanne crosses the church to join them, her heart racing from the sight. Un-armored, stripped of steel, the boys smile at one another: when they see her approach their eyes widen. She squats and reaches for their hands, pulling up hard: she's got sick already of people dropping to their knees.

The tow-headed boy rises with her, his head still bent: What is he afraid of? That if he meets her eyes she'll strike him down? His mouth is moving, silently mouthing "La Pucelle." She touches his pale hair, an uncertain gesture of blessing, and he looks at her finally, grinning like a child with all his teeth. Then a tall woman with white curly hair takes his hand and Jehanne's: a healer, she calls herself Alberte. Jehanne wants to bow to her, but instead makes a request, coughing. Alberte confers with her friends and produces a mask for her, to help with the necrotic smoke at Vaucouleurs.

By the time she leaves the church to return there, the group has dispersed a little, more naturally strewn throughout the church. It's their home, of course. Their safe house—even for the healers, threatened with death by ugly bishops. The thought makes her giggle uncontrollably.

When they actually get to Vaucouleurs, the smoke seems also to have dispersed, the changing Meuse Valley wind blessing them for once. Jehanne yawns, fatigue suddenly claiming her. As night falls, the same wind turns her skin ice-cold, and she shivers as she approaches the Le Royer house.

And standing in front of the door is someone she hasn't seen since she was twelve. "Monsieur Poulengy?" At least ten years younger than her father, his scarred face says where he's been: as Jehanne swings herself from her new horse, he sweeps her off her feet and twines her shortened hair in his stubby fingers. "Jehannette, what has become of you?"

Jehanne shakes him off gently, letting him follow her as she leads the horse to water. "I have been hearing the voice of God," she says casually, as if telling him it's about to snow again. The voice inside her, whatever it's best called, isn't frightened of Bertrand de Poulengy, who visited Jacquot and Isabelle when Jehanne was just learning to tend the sheep. Who she'd thought dead. Perhaps if Jacquot ever talked to his daughter, besides telling her to marry, and not to—"Monsieur, is my father still threatening to drown me if he finds me in soldier's clothes?"

Bertrand De Poulengy laughs then, a big laugh nearly as big as Jacquot's. "Your father adores you," he says. "More than that, Jehannette, he believes in you." Staring at the snow-covered ground, "So do I, it seems."

It's over dinner and generous amounts of mead that the planning begins. De Baudricort, freed by messages from the two Charleses one atop the other, has agreed to provide her with men and arms for the journey to Chinon. "You see the men right here," de Metz adds drunkenly, "and we'll see about the arms in a moment." He watches Jehanne as she carries plates of bread to the table: in this light, and as tired as she is, she looks more like a girl. Softer, more scared. His blood warms a little, noticing her shoulder, the tilt of her eyes, the curve of her lips when she's thinking.

After supper Le Royer feeds the fire, and the group bends over a map. "Chinon is about a fortnight's journey . . . if we don't run into trouble. We'll cross over into France at Gien. Until then . . . who knows?"

"Don't worry, La Pucelle," de Poulengy reaches out to rub her shoulders. "We'll get you there."

"We go to the church first, yes?" She's uneasy not to have gone there yet. "I haven't been confessed since I left Nancy." And that confessor was bewildered, terrified, more than a little hung over. While now that she's passed exorcism, *père* Fournier lets her tell him her dreams and visions. Only he has heard Jehanne's most persistent nightmare: in it, her killer is a small child with a very big crown.

She wishes le Royer would have the grace to offer her some mead, too. She extends her empty cup, glaring at her host just a little. "Do you have a map of Orléans?"

. . .

Nightmare: her arm becomes a lance. It slices her new boy-clothes. The baby boy with the crown holds a large scroll. She lifts it and sees a huge map, Lorraine and Alsace and Burgundy all combined, England a dark-red bleed across the sea. The baby king orders her to read the words beside the map. What girl reads? she asks him. He giggles, huge little-boy giggles, and tears the pages. She can't stop him.

She crawls out of the dream and the dead boy's pallet to walk the walls. Now that she has boy-clothes she can do it easily, like an undergrown sentry, face hidden in her helmet. No one need know she's just a girl whose sleep was stolen by soldiers.

She finds the North Star and tries to turn her face to Orléans. The stars trace the map in her dream, form the words she couldn't read, clearing now. *Serbia, Bulgaria.* South of there, *Knights of St. John.* Homes of the voices in the flood, her angels by turns. Words in curves and slashes. *Chinon.*

Angels kiss her cheek, praising her recognition of the words. Very good. Their breath is sweet, springlike on Jehanne's frozen face. Now practice Latin. You will need it at Chinon, too. And at Poitiers.

Jehanne brings the words before her eyes: she will be able to read, by Orléans. *Introibo ad altare Dei,* she offers obediently. *Ad Deum qui laetificat juventuten meam. I go to the altar of God, who gives joy to my youth.* An angel slaps her, a worn-out girl with sores on her lips. You'll need more than the Mass, she says. The slap lands hot and bright on her chapped cheek. The soldier who slapped her in July sun, trying to get himself hard. The thirty-ninth lash in her throat.

Jehanne stumbles, leans against a curve in the south tower. *Et lacrimus est Iesus,* she whispers.

The braided voice: the voice that holds the slap and slaps back. Do better or you will lose Orléans before you start. Do better or we may as well go back to Domrémy. Marcus, Mattias, Jehan, Lukas. You choose. Then give it to me again.

Jehanne retreats to the stables, where she finds her horse. The sable-colored filly the Duke of Lorraine gave her is asleep, slumped against the stable wall. Jehanne warms her cold face by burying it in the filly's mane. She can feel the young strong heartbeat, fearful. She wonders if she should name her Le Noir Lune. A black moon like the new moon, the day they have chosen to leave Vaucouleurs.

et lacrimus est Iesus, she whispers. Jesus is a drop of tears. frozen now. she feels the lashes on his back. *Hierusalem, o Hierusalem, quae occides prophetas.* Prophets die, the holy city kills its prophets. And its women. What about the queen of Hierusalem? She feels her tears mingle with the horse's soft coat. Spring softens the air around her ears.

"Between Fournier, the letter from Lorraine, and my credulous troops, I may as well believe in her as another," De Baudricort tells Angelie, as they rise from a late-morning frolic. "You'd better go: I'm having a monk in, to write a letter for me."

The letter, this time, is not to Chinon but to Provence, where the real power lives. He's dictating it because his soldier's rough hand is all right for quick notes, but not for the Duchess. His scribe is an old monk, too blind to be of much help with communion, but whose hand on the quill is florid, artistic, just right.

De Baudricort clears his throat. "From Robert de Baudricort, Captain of Vaucouleurs," he begins, the old monk copying slowly, carefully. "To Duchess Yolande of Anjou and Provence, Queen of Aragon, Sicily and Jerusalem." At that last word he sees the monk's eyes widen. "I know, brother, it's rich but she wants to believe it. Now, again. "Hoping this finds you in excellent health . . ." He wonders if the man will nod off in the middle of writing.

.   .   .

After the dauphin allows Jehanne to come, he sweats in his night-clothes, waiting. He wonders if she hates him yet. He tries to imagine her: short, says the letter from Duc de Lorraine, fierce blue eyes. He tries to see her in body armor and glowing helmet, lancing the Duke of Burgundy with her tongue.

Burgundy, meantime, is still swatting rumours of La Pucelle, like out-of-season mosquitoes. "The people will come up with local gods now and again," he tells Isabeau. "I suspect this is another from Yolande of Aragon," he tells her. Another woman to fear—fostered by the one who has managed to stymie him for almost twenty years.

He doesn't bother to tell the tiny English king, Henry VI. He doesn't trouble him with these affairs, even though the eight-year-old boy has already convened a session of the House of Lords. Young Henry hates thinking about France, he knows, as much as he hates the idea of losing it.

Burgundy likes it that way, likes him safely occupied in England. He gestures for a servant to wipe his brow, and laughs. "He's probably the only one of us not taller than La Pucelle."

Once he decides to support Jehanne, de Baudricort makes good on his promises, and a few more. He provides her, de Metz, and de Poulengy, with servants, horses, and a few young chevaliers to fill out their contingent—including an archer, who he also tasks with spying to make completely sure he was right. He's spurred also by news from Orléans of the dourest sort: an effort by the city's defenders to raise the siege has failed badly and its favorite son, the one they call the Bastard, has been injured. "The English are calling it the Day of the Herrings," he tells Angelique, crossly. "Because we couldn't even stop the convoys with their Lenten food. Even if the girl's mad, she's still probably an improvement."

At the supper feast the night before they leave, he gives her a small sword. She doesn't curtsey but bows, consistent with her clothing. "Many thanks, my lord."

He's impressed: she seems taller than before in this clothing from de Metz, and older somehow, as if the cold weather has roughened her skin. She meets his eyes with a clear gaze. "You're welcome," he says. "Must you really go tomorrow?"

"The dauphin needs me."

A one-note band, he sees. "I know, I know, and you'll be legless soon trying to get there. Last thing we all fucking need, a legless virgin crawling across enemy lines. You may as well take a horse or two." He lets a servant refill his beer. "I wish you luck with my lord."

He then stares at her, hard, until she doesn't even think of topping him with yet another *Seigneur,* of saying "Well, Our Lord tells me to . . ." Instead, she's gracious. "Thank you for your hospitality," she lifts her glass.

Baudricort orders up another flagon of wine. "May you pass the test of the King's priests. And may you give the Batard d'Orléans something to cheer about, while his foot heals!" The hall fills with cheers.

After the feast, de Metz walks Jehanne back to the Le Royer house, and bows as if to say, *At dawn, then?* She bows in return, then has to suppress her yawn when she walks into what she thinks will be a darkened house.

It isn't darkened. Instead it's quiet as eggshells but crowded, mostly with women, people she only sees in the little Notre Dame chapel, usually through the corner of her eye. All this time here and she knows no names; they've spent that time gawking, as if she were a performer in a puppet show. Now all these women, these mothers, are gathered around a pile of clothing that seems to grow as Jehanne watches it. Catherine Le Royer is beaming as she hasn't since the day Jehanne arrived—the day she refused to hear the Le Royer son's story. Jehanne's eyes widen as she realizes why: she'll hear that story, and many more, soon enough.

"We joined together to make you soldier's clothes," Catherine Le Royer explains, her wide floury face pink with excitement. "Making new cloth is hard with all the wars, but so much cloth barely used . . ."

Jehanne's stomach turns. She stops, swallows her revulsion: this has been done in love, in faith. This will help her stop the noise. The braided voice scolds her: *Jhesus, Iesus, Jesu, Allah would all say yes. say merci. say bless you.* She says all those words and kisses Catherine on the cheek, lets her tears season the flour.

Then she kneels to examine the jerkins, blousons, carefully stitched boot cuffs, all hard-scrubbed clean, dyed new colors. All made from lost sons of some less-than-hundredth year, or of daughters' trousseaus saved for and wasted when the girl was lanced, her face in a ditch or safe in some church. She knows it will all fit. She will wear the lost children of Vaucouleurs on her skin.

five

THE GROUP THAT LEAVES VAUCOULEURS, the afternoon of February 15, 1429, shelters the former shepherdess at its center, who now rides a black horse and seems indistinguishable from a small footman, or a bird.

Jehanne Darc, Jehan de Metz and Bertrand de Poulengy are joined by two others, provided at the last minute by the captain of Vaucouleurs: a knight called Richard Larcher, and Colet de Viennes, the royal messenger, who has by now carried countless missives regarding La Pucelle back and forth to Chinon. "He'll know where to find loyal men, along the way."

The group also, at first, includes the huge beery figure of Robert de Baudricort, whose shadow dwarfs the Maid's tiny figure in early-morning sunlight. "Arrives by herself, passes out at the sight of me, and leaves with a delegation of four men! I'd say you've done very well, my dear, and pray you're not making of us fools."

Jehanne's fingers tighten on the lance he gave her. She's practiced on foot, but holding it while riding a horse is still new to her. Her new-moon horse whinnies at the touch of cold metal. She swallows hard at the feel of it. The captain who hurt her, crying when he did it, the crush of echoes pushed at her by the flood.

The flood is gentler now, and she holds her angels' hands as if they were Mengette's, working her way past the unmanageable roar. Her time at Vaucouleurs has both calmed and intensified the pressure inside her.

"You like that lance, do you girl?" de Baudricort asks, reaching out a paw to rest on her shoulder. "The boy who gave it to you was very dear to me: treat it well." She starts: she knows the sword's owner was a traitor who wore a deceptive dolphin when he was killed. But does that mean he's lying? Bone-painful, such treachery.

"It's very well balanced," she gives her only honest answer. It is, in fact, better than the sword he also gave her, but she knows her real sword is yet to come. *St-Catherine-de-Fierbois*, the voice whispers: that's where they'll find it, on the other side of the border. By then, she hopes, they'll be travelling at night: she may be learning how to use a sword, but she's still terrified of direct sunlight.

"Well balanced, there's a diplomatic answer," de Baudricort shouts.

Behind them both is Jehan Daulon, Jehanne's manservant: a tall slender man whose hair is reddish-blond and badly cut, sticking out from under his helmet. Jehanne's own has been growing like a weed, and Catherine le Royer refused to cut it for her; she's piled it in a tight plait under her helmet, like a new secret cap. Daulon is shy of her. He knelt next to her awkwardly, this morning, during communion at Notre Dame.

As the group proceeds toward the Gate of France, they're nearly blocked by the crowds that have thickened around Jehanne since the raid on Domrémy. Only de Baudricort's roar and de Metz's impressive, bronze-tipped lance part the way for them. Jehanne can't decide whether to look at these tearful girls and praying mothers, some of whom sewed the clothing she wears and carries. Catherine Le Royer has opted to stay home, praying in front of her spinning wheel, content with Jehanne's tearful goodbye.

"La Pucelle, La Pucelle!" She feels blinded, unrecognized in these boys' clothes, this homemade banner of hers her only marker. They see some saint or madonna from their *maman*'s stories. They don't see her.

Sometimes she feels her angels don't either, nor the hum in her skin, the flood of girls and boys. She wonders how to tell, now. The roar of the crowd matches the roar inside her, neither piercing the gray fog that threatens to envelop her now that she has what she claims to want. The sun begins to dip in the February twilight.

It's de Metz who leads her out, as de Baudricort orders the gates opened and they're released into that other crowd, refugees trying desperately to achieve the safety of the castle. A kiss on her hand, which she can barely feel through the glove: goodbye from the Vaucouleurs captain.

It's her fantastic luck that word hasn't spread to the masses flailing at the gate, neither the big myth of the God-chosen virgin or the truth, whispered by broken girls in multiple languages and understood by a select many. Neither seems on the mind of these people. They're far too committed to pleading with the children at the walls, the old men at the bombards, for admission to a safe place.

She was one of them once: not on a horse but on foot, with Durand, her only tool her burning hands. How long ago it feels now, how anonymous they are. She peers hard, looking for Francine, the little girl she found last time. If you were here I could get you behind safer walls. But in the dark they all look the same, swathed in cloths with small torches in their hands. They could be soldiers, or saints, or madwomen about to burn the fortress down.

Colet de Viennes, the royal messenger, is the one who

shouts: "Make way! Make way!" He's used to having to shout, and crowds are used to parting for him and his royal colors, about to be hidden as they slide through nearly enemy territory. He doesn't say *for La Pucelle*, which might have been deadly; she skulks behind him in his entourage, an anonymous boy, which is much better. She can't move very quickly, anyway. The fog inside weighs down her limbs.

The crowd parts—"like the Red Sea!" Daulon whispers to her—to allow the row of horses through and beyond the crowd, as the sky darkens to velvet. From here they head toward St.-Urbain, where Isabelle once thought to place Jehanne in the convent: she wonders idly whether the Mother Superior there has connected La Pucelle with the wayward damaged girl Isabelle Romée had thought to place with her.

As the ground unfreezes and re-freezes, the path that passes for a road has been doing the same. No horse can move forward quickly in it, even after they leave the camped families and teen-age riot boys behind.

Jehanne is glad when actual fog, off the river and mountains to the east, starts clinging to her skin, matching the one inside. She's trying to reach for her angels, but even they buck under her unaccountable sadness.

Maid, you have exactly what you came to Vaucouleurs for. You have an escort to Chinon. You have armor and a lance and you know where your next sword is. You have a promise of help at Orléans from Alençon, the knight who knows it best, outside of the Batard d'Orléans himself. This is the beginning of the battle for France, this is why these people are behind you. Why then the tears that still dampen your cheeks, stick inside your mouth like spit?

The answer is everywhere around here, in her escort. Their body armor clangs around her. Her lance clashes against her armored saddle. The whinnied complaints of Le Lune Nouveau, at the heaviness of their baggage. The clash of armor, the scream of steel. The noise escalates and she hasn't yet struck a single blow.

She has spent the past six weeks surrounded by this. Armor, swords, falling rocks. The one who slapped her to get himself hard. The commander's glinting shield. The one who pulled at her hair. Every day she's brought back to that long-ago sheep meadow. Five years since, almost. But yesterday. And then and then and the rest.

"Mademoiselle?" anxious chirp from Daulon, who has finally noticed her tears, nearly a half-day since they left Vaucouleurs. At twenty-eight, his arm still aching from when it was broken in the summer siege, he didn't volunteer for this, and is now mindful of de Baudricort's order: "Keep her warm and safe." He rides closer to the girl staring bleakly before her, lips moving silently. "Mademoiselle, are you all right?"

She can barely hear him over the roar inside her. The girl from Ryukyu, fingers enmeshed in her own. "I'm perfectly well," she lies. "How far have we come?"

She cranes her neck and finds Bertrand de Poulengy, Jehan de Metz, all the others. Ten men all together, and she their commander. She swallows hard and shouts. "Come together!"

Colet de Viennes rides up first, waving his hand furiously. "We must be quieter than that," he says reprovingly, his voice tight. "These aren't friendly villages." Behind him, Jean de Metz makes funny faces, trying to get Jehanne to laugh. But the more their armor clangs, the more cold sweat sours her breath.

De Metz points then, to a stand of young pines, on a cliff-side. "Behind that hill—we stopped here on the way back from Nancy," de Metz says then. "At St.-Nicolas. It's a friendly town. La Pucelle found a shrine," of course, what was she thinking? this approach unfamiliar, the last time they were on that hill it was shrouded by night. Her horse recognizes it, though, whin-nies a little.

Jehanne feels her heart open, as if she were in love: they are going toward that shrine, the church with the healers and pretty boys and tired but rested camp followers. If not the ones she met, others have likely taken their place. She has missed them.

She still dreams about Régine, about the girls from Orléans, about the boy from Tunis who slept with the Duc of Lorraine. From St.-Nicolas she remembers most Alberte, a young healer who made her a mask to shield her from smoke, and the runaway soldier-boys with hands entwined and giggly faces. They need her.

"We'll have our first mass there," she says. "We've all just confessed, after all." She made sure of that, on the verge of a journey.

Her angels are excited too, and bid her speed up: the fog lifts, the clank of armor not forcing them and her into a tailspin. She smiles for the first time. "*Avant!*" She kicks Le Lune Nouveau into a gallop, and soon enough is at the head of the pack. She never raced a horse round the village, like her brothers, and with all this metal weighing her down wouldn't be likely to do so now. But she savors what modicum of speed she can get, right now.

By what dint of persuasion, personal charm and direct orders from de Baudricort has this group come together, now? How long will they stay together?

Jehan de Metz is still haunted by his son, whose trousers Jehanne filled for a few weeks. He's never seen a woman quite like her, and can't decide if he's in love, in lust, or about to kneel to her holiness.

Cote de Viennes, the messenger, is so tired of dodging bombards, so tired of having to get a new shield because the old one's bent beyond repair, that he's honestly relieved at being asked so straightforward a favor. A wiry old man with graying curls, he's served the Dauphin's father, the demented Charles

VI, and finds the young man "only a modest improvement." Like de Baudricort, he's enlisted with Jehanne because the alternative—letting a seventeen-year-old girl go willy-nilly along the roads where he himself has barely escaped death—offends both his religious and aesthetic sensibilities. "Let Sire de Vergy wave her underwear and gloat? *Non, s'il vous plait!*" In any case, his wife lives not far from Chinon; in a sense, this mission is simply on the way home.

Richard Larcher, de Baudricort's foil, has promised to bring any news from Chinon directly back to his sister, the famed Angelie. He has also been tasked by *père* Fournier: should Jehanne, now that she's persuaded half of Vaucouleurs of her sincerity, foam at the mouth or speak in tongues, he will say the appropriate exorcising words and sprinkle her with holy water, so that she'll then dissolve into a muddy dust.

And Bertrand de Poulengy is to Jacquot and Isabelle what Larcher is to the commanders of Vaucouleurs. He's known Jehanne's fierce stare since she was nine, since she screamed at Isabelle that she would die before being shut up in a convent. He was one of her first riding-teachers, not that she would ever remember. Thirty-seven years old, his daughters are all married and his sons preparing for soldiering—except for one, who may replace Father Guillaume at St-Remy very soon. Though Jehanne is the real priest among them; he told Isabelle long ago "She won't be a nun, but she'd make a damn fine priest." He said it again this past winter, as he saw her poring over scrolls in the church, chanting in Latin.

It was Durand Laxart who came to him a few months ago, telling him of her voices and describing her "chanting to me Marie of Avignon's prophecy." When he asked Jacquot about it the doyen told him, reluctantly, about her palm of flame. He decided to come to Vaucouleurs and see for himself, little knowing he would end up on this god-forsaken journey across enemy land to a prince he suspects of lazy treason.

All four of them are agreed on one thing: "See how she behaves in her first church away from Vaucouleurs." They're watchful on the road, they'll be doubly so in church. They're waiting for her to disappoint them, and France.

At Chinon, Charles VII has cast numerous horoscopes, trying to divine the best course of action here. Should he skulk off to Scotland before she gets here? Will his mother-in-law let him? Is he getting a little dotty, like his father, who by the time of his death was known simply as Charles the Mad? Is France coming apart altogether, or is the Maid's cry of "France for the French" a harbinger of something yet to come?

All he knows is that Burgundy and England are together tightening their noose around Orléans. Soon it will be too late, unless the mobs are right, unless she *is* the genuine article.

In the last horoscope he casts, his attention is caught by an unusual conjunction of Mars, the planet of action and war, with Cancer, the sign of compassion. Should he attend? Or stay with the earlier ones, which suggest he should squash her like a buzzy insect?

He sits down to write to Yolande of Aragon and send her the latest horoscopes. He also encloses his own fair copy of the latest poems by Charles, the Duke of Orléans. He knows she'll agree that Charles has become quite the poet, after fifteen years as a prisoner of war. He'll likely die there, she says.

Early spring has swelled the shred of river that feeds St.-Nicolas-du-Port, until it flows beyond its confines. The trees are beginning to bud, too. Jehanne's heart lifts at the sight.

She wants to drink this water, swim in it, though as an anonymous shepherdess—not as some *petit generale*, Jacquot's

and now de Poulengy's name for her. She wants to hold
Mengette's hand and swim back to Domrémy.

Larcher, a six-footer with nearly as pronounced a belly as his
captain, is the first to arrive, declaring himself famished. Despite
the friendly territory he keeps his voice quiet; Jehanne agrees
with him. He follows her into the church, along with de Metz,
while the others stand sentry outside.

Unlike the previous time, there is a priest there—a middle-
aged man with beer-breath. He looks up from tending the fire as
Jehanne and her guard enter, offers them warm cloths against
the bitter wind. "This weather is like an ungrateful child," he
says as they press their faces into the bits of cloth. "Everything
thaws, but the wind freezes your bones."

Jehanne uses the muffled moment to think. She thought this
church still abandoned. Did all her *compagnie* leave? The runaway
soldiers, the healer? Did they recede into the crevices of this
church? Her heart is in her mouth. She lowers the cloth and kneels
before the altar, gesturing to de Metz and Larcher to do the same.
"I am sent by God—" her voice cracking, this is a horrible start.

But the priest kneels in turn, his hands shaking just a little.
"La Pucelle?" he whispers. Is he afraid of her?

Deep breath: time to use this fear, this is what she came to
do, and to demonstrate to these men that she's real. "Can you
please say a mass for us, while we are here? We have a ways to go
today, before we get to St.-Urbain."

The priest sinks his head into his hands then. "My altarboys, they're not diligent," he wails softly. "Mass is hard enough
once a week."

Jehanne reaches out and takes his hand, gently but firmly.
"We'll do it together, then. What is your scriptural reading this
week?"

After some consultation, it's agreed: "not a full Mass, but we
can do something." While they talk, a good half of the village, it

seems, arrives at the church to gawk: mostly mothers and grand-mothers with stunted swathed infants, a few injured farmers not off trying to harrow. Their whispers are muted, a fog of sound.

What follows is "the fastest Mass in Christendom," de Metz says later. He's impressed by Jehanne's Latin and her clear-eyed resolve. Jehanne says the Old Testament reading, which is from Exodus: she assures the priest it's in her memory, and doesn't let him see her eyes linger on the scroll, where after all this study the words finally speak to her a little, helping her memory.

"Apparuitque ei Dominus in flamma ignis de medio rubi et videbat quod rubus arderet et non conbureretur." *An angel of God appeared to him in flames, in a bush that was burning and was not consumed.* She wonders if the bush had a braided voice. If Moses existed, and was urged on by the voices of whoever the Pharoah had killed that week.

In front of her, accommodating, is a Jewish girl dying in Egypt, long jagged scars on her cheek where her master cut her; that baby again, crawling at her feet and crying; that elder warrior twisting around the pew. All searching for the church's little colony, the outpost of Jehanne's phantom army. Jehanne tries to blink them away. She needs to concentrate on the accuracy of her scriptural reading, keep her eyes locked on Jehan de Metz's, on Larcher's, *Dieu* the lie that binds these men to her. And to Moses, she thinks. His people were slaves, after all. Her fingers warm in sympathy.

When her vision clears, what she sees is a damp, half-empty church. A handful of people in the back, behind Larcher and de Metz, sit wordless, dumbfounded. The old priest has joined in on her last words. She bows to him and kneels in the front pew, looking at the rough-hewn altar, the shrine to St. Francis.

The priest reads the Gospel with a reedy voice, hurrying through it needlessly. But behind him, next to the St. Francis statue, Jehanne finally sees Alberte, the healer, peeping shyly from behind the carved robes. She has to restrain herself from standing to embrace the older woman.

The line for communion, when it forms, is longer than she expected: Jehanne stands behind de Metz, waiting patiently for her bit of stale bread. Beside her is a camp follower, now grown thinner and paler; an un-soldiered boy slides into place behind her. The line swells until the priest gestures. He needs her help again. Jehanne realizes that he knows full well who is here.

Even in her boldness, she's never thought she would be doing this, handing pieces of bread to women and small children and burly, aging farmers. Over and over again, then: "*Corpus Christi. Corpus Christi.*" Jesus is a drop of tears. Alberte swallows the bread, smiles into her eyes.

When the Mass is over, the priest retreats to his place in a corner of the adjoining castle. "*Bonne chance* and *merci, mademoiselle.* The Lord be with you."

Larcher and de Metz come closer, awaiting orders to proceed to St.-Urbain. She tells them to start, that she'll be along presently, but is answered by a negative: "We'll wait." She turns to de Metz, "Do you doubt me?"

Larcher is still trying to digest Jehanne Darc, peasant girl even if La Pucelle, distributing communion. "I am under orders," he says quietly.

"You are under *my* orders, good sir." She hears her own voice go sharp, weak, an ugly whine. Still, no backing down now. "I need to pray here awhile."

"We need to get to St.-Urbain in time for the abbey to be open," de Metz reminds her.

She can continue this battle or she can acknowledge that a few months of riding hard, her experience travelling from Domrémy to here to Nancy, hasn't taught her to properly estimate time. She nods. "Then wait outside for just a few minutes. This is between myself and *Dieu.*" And about twenty survivors sleeping in the alcoves here.

Larcher refuses to leave. He has his holy water at the ready. He's waiting for her to speak in tongues. And if he stays, if they stay, he'll hear it, too.

Jehanne holds in a breath. She doesn't want to leave without holding a camp follower in her arms. Without whispering promises to the rest. Without hearing from the healers how to survive the noise, until she can stop it. If these men are going to haunt her every move, her life will be hell, even worse than she was expecting. Larcher's armor clanks as he speaks.

"Are you appointing yourself church elder?" she asks point-blank. "What sort of witchery are you suspecting?" She wonders if Larcher, in particular, saw Alberte.

He's silent, and very still. His cold-red skin betrays no blush. She swallows hard and gestures for him to approach her: in his height and bulk he's easily three times her size.

"It is not your role to doubt me," she says quietly, so quietly he has to strain to hear. "I have been exorcised by a stupid priest, I have met with the Duke of Lorraine, I have had to hear voices so cold they would break your bones. You are here to get me safely to Chinon, where priests far stronger than you are waiting to strip me naked and test me clear. Until then, you give me what I want. To do so honors *le Seigneur*. Yes?" Her angels keep her voice steady, her hands still. They don't let her show how afraid she is. "We'll be on our way soon enough."

Larcher looks down at the burning bush girl and swallows hard. He looks over at de Metz, who is looking at her in a very different way. The younger man says, "We'll be outside the door, *mademoiselle,* with the others."

Larcher nods, wordlessly, and follows de Metz out the door.

As soon as they're gone, Jehanne slumps, frozen against her sleeve. Larcher may as well be the first one, the one who broke her, shouting his glory into the sheep meadow. He has the same smell. *The soldiers in your command will smell worse*, her angels tell her. *Get used to it.*

She wants to scream. She welcomes the flood, easier to borrow someone else's pain for a while. A middle-aged woman in one of Charlemagne's brothels, used for so many years she feels nothing. An educated man, inquisitors' bait, with Levantine eyes and soft voice. The hum under her skin pushing her hard. She was wrong: it's not easier. The noise escalates.

Until Alberte touches her, opens her eyes, offers a shoulder to receive her tears. A silent girl who she's never met holds out a scrap of cloth, and Jehanne blows her nose on it, nodding thanks. The unsoldiered boys make a circle around her. One of them, named Francois, was in her communion line: he winks and holds out some bread for her to eat. *Corpus Christi,* he says. The circle bursts into laughter.

They ask her what she needs. She tells them they have already provided it.

The abbey at St.-Urbain has survived a lot in the past year.

Sire Vergy and his band took potshots at it, enroute to Vaucouleurs: what there was of gold on the altar is gone, the statuary now all clay, the ceremonial ark turned to wood and stone. Then came the refugees from all the surrounding villages, turning cloistered nuns from refined families into scullery maids, cleaning up after babies' bottoms. And finally, the death of its monsignor, who has not yet been replaced.

The abbess, Sister Marie-Therése Carpentier, has therefore had a few more things to think about, to remember, than a stray message once sent by Jehanne Darc's mother. St.-Urbain has been ruled by Burgundians so long she'd nearly forgotten there was a war, until this most recent phase of fighting: she thinks in Latin, and refuses to honor the nation-borders defined by warrior blood. She has left it to her younger nuns to comfort the weeping widows and broken children, and is relieved now that most of them have gone back to their abandoned homes. The last thing she really wants is this band of ten from Vaucouleurs.

The band arrives at the church as the sun sets, the sky a bruised purple as Jehanne and the others dismount their horses. The church is pale brown stone, with a tremendous arch over its entry-column; Daulon, Jehanne's squire, slings their bags over his shoulder as they walk the horses to the front door.

Jehanne wonders if she has ever been more physically tired, ever ached so in her muscles. This is not quite as hard as the walk to Neufchateau from Domrémy, the swim back, but all that was last summer; too much time since spent praying, kneeling, learning, walking the walls. Not enough making sure her body is strong enough to do what she needs to do.

Now, they've gone further than the ride to Nancy, and the armor she'd prayed for then has made more demands on her and her horse. Her angels help prop up her soul, when she might fail, but they're blessed little use in getting up steep ridges, with a quarter-ton of iron on Nouveau's back.

How would they have arrived, she and Isabelle, if she had come here five years ago, her bottom still green with meadow grasses? She swallows hard. This is, after all, where she took her first communion, a great privilege only for the daughter of the doyen. The church looked immense then. She was eleven and even smaller than now, and had never been somewhere *really* huge, like Vaucouleurs. Just before the other: they would have known her, then, if she were brought back so soon to take the veil. Bride of Christ. Jesus is a drop of tears. A different way to learn the code words. She would have received the flood in the privacy of her novitiate cell.

Non, the angels laugh uproariously. Not us, we would have burned it down. Churches may be sanctuary, but they hate us too. Jehanne laughs at herself in turn.

"Mademoiselle?" Daulon, her shadow, again anxious.

"I nearly came here to take the veil," she tells him, with a genuine smile and gesturing to her armor. "Now look at me." She turns and de Metz and de Poulengy are right behind her: de Poulengy takes the laugh up, makes it boom against the church walls, until the entire party is subsumed in delicious giggles just in time for the door to open. They are laughing in the Mother Superior's face.

"*Pardon?*" The abbess looks at the armored group, at its center a rakish boy with a sand-streaked face, and begins to move the door back to a closed position. "There's an inn not far away," she says. "Times are hard here."

"No, madame." Colet de Viennes, the royal courier, comes to the front: the group watches her eyes widen, she knows him from the Dauphin's messages. "I bring you La Pucelle of Lorraine." He helps Jehanne unfurl her homemade banner, JHESUS MARIA, and lifts her helmet to reveal the girlish profile.

Sister Marie-Therese moves closer to Jehanne. "It's true, then what they say?" she murmurs. "Lorraine bore a girl who hears the voice of God? I am forty-three years old, and I've spoken to *Dieu* every day for nearly thirty of them, but as far as I know he has never replied." She looks closely at a girl who claims to hear from Him every day: then the cold starts to frost her face and she remembers where they are. "Come inside!"

Within the castle walls she reads the safe-passages from Robert de Baudricort, from the Dauphin himself. Jehanne looks at the papers from behind her, de Baudricort's signature easy to recognize, the "B" two angled balloons. The one from Chinon in smaller more coded letters, they could almost be Latin. She can't read French. Latin is easier. Her secret safe with Father Guillaume.

Colet de Viennes strides down the abbey's passageways as if it were his home. He has his favorite room here, his favorite serving wench. "You will be sad to know that Sister Marie

Margarethe has taken a vow of silence," Mother Superior tells him now. "She no longer serves in the dining hall."

"*Impossible!* Those lips, silent?" de Viennes whispers to de Metz.

They've arrived long after the evening meal, but the abbess organizes a repast for the famished group. Jehanne is stunned at how hungry she is. She may not have been this hungry since Domrémy after the raid, when she plucked a chicken's heart out with her tongue. Now, as they suck goat's milk out of cups and sate their teeth with the remains of tonight's veal, she eats enough bread to fill her belly for six weeks. The nuns are shy with her, in her men's clothing. The abbess hasn't told them.

Jehan de Metz sits beside her, looking at her slim shoulders under the thick overshirt. Now that she's eaten, her color's high and she laughs, telling stories of similar rides in her childhood and urging him, de Viennes, de Poulengy, to tell family stories. "How are your children, your wives, getting on, with you on this pilgrimage?"

De Metz lets the others take a turn. He doesn't want to talk about his wife, or think of her or his son. He's too drawn to this rough girlboy, too embarrassed at how his skin burns when he looks at her.

How will they sleep, all of them? Not tonight, tonight the abbess has given her a separate room, but when they are skulking through enemy territory and sleeping by day? More precisely, how will *he* sleep?

"So I don't know if I will really be a grandfather," de Poulengy finishes, "until and unless the Dauphin gets himself crowned. My daughter swears she won't bear sons to get killed in another war."

"That's why I'm here," Jehanne says quietly. "You'll be a grandfather. The King will be crowned at Easter."

"Whether he deserves it or not!" de Viennes chimes in, to

another peal of laughter. Jehanne lets them do it, relaxes into the back of her chair.

De Metz sees her decide not to protest. Smart move, he thinks. Keep them hopeful. He tries to keep his thoughts on military strategy: she's his commander, after all. He can't be feeling her this acutely.

Her eyes meet his, then: "Monsieur de Metz, why so silent? What of your children, and this journey?"

"My son . . ." He swallows. His son is. His son is ruined. "They came through, the English, and . . ." The silence after his words is thick. Jehanne nearly gasps with his tears. The noise escalates inside his silence.

She goes over to him, sits beside him and takes both of his hands. "He is with me," she says, thinking de Metz's son one of the boys and girls flooding her mind. But he shakes his head, no, his son isn't dead. Her voice firm, then: "We'll make it stop. Together."

Her gloveless fingers are warm inside his. No woman like this exists, anywhere else. He has to make himself sit still. Finally, he shakes off his desire and returns to his plate. "And my wife tells me if I bring back a token of you, La Pucelle, she will honor my absence."

Jehanne looks at him, worried: something odd here, with him. His fingers shook a little when she held them.

She leaves it alone, as they all look at the map together and plot their next stop at Clairveaux, as the meal ends and they drag their weary bodies toward bed.

As the weariness descends the other kicks in, characteristic for her: just as in Nancy, in Vaucouleurs, in Domrémy, she's alert and looking for danger. Besides, there are stands of trees in the courtyard that resemble her groves well enough.

The corridors at dark; with matins at four each morning, monks and nuns alike slide into silence as soon as they lay down.

She starts to look in the corners of things. It's just cold enough that she wonders who can sleep out there and live.

But she's warm enough in two cloaks and two hoods, her helmet too heavy but her sword near: the abbey is fortified for a reason. Warm and sheltered from discovery, she could be any boy soldier sneaking off for a tussle with a girl. She smiles. She thinks of Mengette, of the girl from Prague. She should have been born a boy, and not a priest. She would have been better prepared for this.

She calls to her angels, restless: they're underway now, where are they? She stares, trying to shake off the soldiers' rage. The clanking of armor. She cuts her hand on her sword.

Finally she sees a girl in a long yellow gown, covering all but her rageful eyes. Another Jerusalemite, this one Arab, sunburned skin not masking bruises. A man swimming in the mud in a green uniform and a flattish helmet, a string of steel in his teeth. They make a baleful circle and lure out the shy people among them, faces wrapped in scraps of wool and cracked hands holding mud cups full of rain-water.

She can't figure out who is who, now: are they all angels? Is this a colony like at St.-Nicolas, like Régine's camp? Do they serve her or she them? Her head starts to hurt. The noise escalates, the braided voice wide, shallow, indistinct. Unlike at St.-Nicolas these people are angry, and her angels with them. *Why aren't you there yet? Orléans will die.*

Jehanne's own anger: she sought them out for sustenance, not for them to echo Larcher's impatience. She kneels in the mud and lifts her crawling soldier, and with him a lazy prostitute with about five teeth. She ignores the prostitute's battered face. "I could stop now," she says angrily. "I could tell them all my vision was a lie and beg their forgiveness. I could walk into that abbess' room and plead for the veil. I could leave all of you behind."

Not true, the whore's arm tightening around Jehanne's belly.

And you know it. The damp grove suddenly quiet as a grave, the crack of a branch as loud-seeming as the bombards at Vaucouleurs.

She bows her head: they're right, of course. She lets the soldier bring her down, and lies beside him in the frozen mud. She can almost see corpses under the river-ice. She dreams of the people she met at Régine's camp, as if the mud were a mirror taking her fifty miles west.

She sees the girl from Prague, who misses her. And she sees him, tall and exceedingly slender, twelve years old with a sweet slack-jawed expression. His name is Roger. He helped cut her hair. He couldn't stop trying to clean himself.

And she's scrambling up, out of the mud, shaking off her angels and letting the slow prostitute go back to where she's secreted. Not all of this new army is with her, it seems, unconditionally.

Back in her room, she washes off the mud as best she can, from the clear water that's by her door. It's late enough that she may as well stay up for matins, and let this church's priest confess her. She will tell him, before she tells de Metz, that she knows what happened to the latter's son. That she saw him, in the forest camp. That his father is quite right, in not wanting to know what happened.

The next evening, as the band of ten leaves St.-Urbain, the court at Chinon is in a near-frenzy. Word has arrived from Vaucouleurs that La Pucelle is definitively on her way—with the dauphin's own messenger, Colet de Viennes, in the contingent. And they will be preceded by an arrival both dreaded and expected: Yolande of Aragon, of course, arriving from her quarters in Provence.

An entire set of apartments in Charles' castle at Chinon already awaits Yolande, the Duchess of Anjou and Queen of

Jerusalem. She will arrive with four ladies-in-waiting, three squires, and her own priest. The dauphin orders the cook to prepare a feast for his mother-in-law's arrival. He is more afraid of her than of La Pucelle.

To calm himself, he picks up the newest sheaf of those poems from Charles, like the one he copied for her: he received them from the Duke of Orléans himself, from an English prison. Charles has been there since he was left for dead on the battle-field in Azincort, fourteen years ago: he left his city's defense to his half-brother, the bastard Jehan-Paul, instead writing passionate poems of courtly love. If he can distract himself thus, so can the Dauphin, by reading him; he's admired previous lyrics, like the sonnet that began "The world puts off its raiment old/The year lays down his mantle cold."

In some ways, Charles d'Orléans is his role model. From prison he writes muscular, tasty poems, while sending succor to his illegitimate brother who mans the barricades. The siege of Orléans thus changes his status only a little.

The Dauphin's still in bed as he reads, a manservant arriving with extra pillows, a glass of wine at his nightstand. In his lap, besides the scroll from the Duke is the notebook where he scrawls his own spurious efforts at Dante's art.

One poem, entitled "Rondel," is presented as a love poem, but the shadow of the siege lays on it, and not lightly.

"Too weak to make his cruel force depart,
   Strengthen at least the castle of my heart,
   And with some store of pleasure give me aid."

The Dauphin swallows. It could have been written by the Bastard, from inside the besieged fortress: a cry for help, not very effectively buried. His own poems curl on the page, wilting.

. . .

"The Bastard—that's the fellow to watch." Colet de Viennes' words are soft, and a little slurred from exhaustion and cold.

They've reached Clairveaux, or at least close enough to it that the smoke from distant fireplaces can be seen against the darkening sky. They've waited now for nine hours, squatting in the fields, trading stories. There are no safehoused at Clairveaux, and even though it's a Valois town they don't want to risk it.

De Viennes is the only one among them who has actually seen Orléans, before it was besieged. He's described its fortifications, its trees, its barricades. Now he's onto the people.

"They still call him *Batard?*" Poulengy asks. "It's not like his brother's ever coming home."

"He calls *himself* the Bastard—it's how he signs his name."

"I hear he goes to mass every day, even when there's fighting. They say God smiles on him, and makes him brave." This from Larcher, *père* Fournier's friend and spy.

Catherine laughs and whispers in Jehanne's ear: *find out who he feeds, in the dank castle's church*. Jehanne asks de Viennes, instead: "What does he look like?"

"Like the King, *actuallement*. He's the same age, the same size, but where Charles Ponthieu has only flab and poetry, he has pure muscle and practically unlimited fire. Big moustache. His hair is so blond it's white."

Jehanne nods, and shifts her weight. She hasn't been shifting her weight enough. Half a week in heavy armor and her hip hurts, as if half-pulled out; her knee burns, too. When this happened farming, Isabelle made her rest for a week. But lying down has only made it worse, albeit in half-frozen grass. She bends her head, to look at the map. Her hair falls in her face.

Beside her, de Metz watches her bare neck, the glimpse of her bare shoulder, and curses his erection. He can't believe lust is able to pierce the fatigue. He wishes she would sit up and start speaking Gospel again. That always brings him back to his senses. "How many has he lost, trying to defend?" he asks de Viennes.

The messenger demurs, flattered at being asked. "I only carry the messages: I am not allowed to read them. But in Orléans, this horse—" he gestures down to his angry wiry mare—"stepped on a good number of bones." The clank of armor. The screaming of steel. The noise escalates in the quiet evening.

Jehanne swallows, to avoid throwing up in front of them. She looks up and her eyes meet de Metz's. She's not wrong about him. Her body numbs from it. The one who cried and cried. She stares into the starry field.

Finally she stands up, as the sky finally deepens from indigo to darkest night. "Come together!" she shouts, until Poulengy is beside her, until Jehan Daulon and the other squires have assembled. They are all streaked with mud. "We can get to Poitiers tonight, if we ride fast and hard," she says. "Let's start our journey, then, with a prayer to the Blessed Virgin." She raises her rosary, which is worn from the pressure of her hands. The stones glow like new planets in the night sky." *Credo de Unum Deum* . ..."Jehan Daulon's voice next to hers is musical, like an emasculated choirboy.

Jehanne's voice, rougher from shouting all week, wobbles, until she can meet de Metz's eyes. He prays the loudest.

The woman kneeling by the fireplace is not praying.

Her shoulder aches. She should be in bed. She's forty-nine years old, ancient by these people's lights, though her body is strong enough to have scaled the stairs to this tower without requiring assistance. She should be asleep, too: lights have long since been snuffed, and out the castle window the bombardiers slumber against the wall. But the rain is loud and the air too chill and her hair still snarled from the journey. The ungrateful girl who attends her hurried, combing it, and is now off bedding some cook or footman.

She hasn't started a fire in years, and when the flames burst she's startled. She wants to watch them awhile; flames calm her. They make her feel less alone. God knows her daughter doesn't, working on another baby, sleeping through the days: neither does Lucie, the king's mistress, off suckling that big baby. Though Lucie tells her everything. She doesn't have to rely on Le Brat to decide to write her.

Yolande knows them all, these mistresses. They are her secret weapon, spread out over six kingdoms like nameless sentries: literate women, most of them not mothers, with time to spare and sharp ears. She knows, for example, how Alison Dumay was threatened by Jehanne Darc. From de Baudricort's letters, she know the girl passed her exorcism, but from his mistress Angelie she knows the girl liked to walk along the castle walls, making nice with the bombardiers. She's intrigued how this small girl can already play her game. Or else she needs to know what game is being played.

Even at forty-nine, Yolanda d'Aragon's face yields gasps: the poet who called her "the most beautiful woman in Christendom" needed no hyperbole to flatter her. Her Spanish mother's deep eyes and high forehead mix with her French father's chestnut hair and height: she's close enough to six feet tall to intimidate most of the kings who came to bargain with her. She stares into the flames, somehow doubting her height will be enough with this girl, who doesn't come to bargain.

This girl who already has soldiers kneeling to her.

This girl who could get her Orléans.

Twenty years of caring more about the crown than the Brat. And now so does the girl spouting God.

Yolande gave up God long ago. *Mia nina, papa is never coming home* from Jerusalem or Sicily or one other of his wars. Not even a body. Her newlywed court emptied when no one returned from Azincort alive. Bodies dragged home, in coffins. Three of her five castles battered by illiterate armies. Torn apart. Footmen's bodies, nearly her own. Her husband, duke of Anjou, off in Naples defending one of their kingdoms, and leaving her to this. When home he wakes up screaming for blood. No God. Just war. Her palms are punctured with fingernail marks.

The flames finally make her sleepy, as she knew they would. She puts out the fire and heaves her large-bellied body over to the bed. The sound of the rain helps her sleep.

When Jehanne and her band finally arrive at the Poitiers safehouse, they are soaked as she was swimming from Neufchateau to Domrémy. Their horses have nearly drowned in it.

The rain has slowed their progress by at least a third: whether taking shelter in stands of trees or ploughed through, it's felt the same. The rain like the night the de Vergy brothers mutilated her home, her church, her crops. In full night-vigilance, she almost doesn't want to hide from the Burgundians. She wants to cut them now. A battered German general in a white dress uniform holds her back from giving any such order: not time yet, Not till Chinon. Not till she has an army.

Larcher and Poulengy are the ones with the salient point: that the Burgundians, crafty but lazy, are likely saving their strength for another day. "We can move forward with a little less fear." Jehanne forced into agreement: they had better brave it, get drenched, rather than wait until closer to dawn.

It's de Metz who does the honors of banging on the door of the village doyen's house: finally a sleepy-headed sentry yanks them in one by one, through the kitchen door. "We'll take care of your horses."

In the kitchen, the bakers are already busy making a fire. Jehanne nearly faints at the smell of fresh bread. She also realizes how she smells. She's soiled herself at least once. This closed-doublet closed-hose life has definite drawbacks.

But she has to wait until they get up the narrow stairway, slowly, not to clank so much. The noise escalates, but in a way that only makes her laugh. The braided voice has retreated for the moment.

The doyen doesn't know there's a girl in the group, only that Colet de Viennes is among them: the room he assigned is large, without walls, some storeroom emptied by the current troubles and thus perfect for them. The clank! is now armor being shed, slowly, nervous eyes on The Maid. She nods, no reason for them to continue being weighed down; she turns to avert her gaze. The doyen's wife has filled a washtub for them, which sits full, cold, in the back of the room. It glimmers in the torchlight, like an altar they're all supposed to pray to.

Poulengy bows, and then so do the rest of the men. Then in a group, they turn their backs. She will wash first. "Do I smell that bad?" she jokes. She knows, in fact, that she does. They stand still looking at one another, like an altar-tableau: they're muddy enough to almost look made of wood.

Her skin far colder than the water. She tries not to look at de Metz. She reminds herself: he is a good man, who loves her, who believes in her. Remember Roger, the idiot son, who cut her hair. But the fear, still. The one who begged the others to stop, until he was ridiculed and joined in.

Mariel, with a bag full of poultices, helps her wash herself below, where feeling and sensation are muted, damaged. The one who pulled at her hair. She drops to her knees, fully submerged.

She stays below a moment. The noise is dimmed that way. The braided voice approves.

When she rises out of the water, she sees de Metz's face: he looked. Tears linger on his eyelashes, his shoulders shaking. His eyes are closed and his lips move in prayer. No need to fear, now. Her heart calms in her chest.

When she's finished dressing, the tableau comes to life. Suddenly all is noise, confusion, as one after the other washes and puts on new clothes. "*Alors*, Bernard, your doublet stinks!" "Only because you were close by."

Their armor is piled neatly along one wall, their weapons on the opposite: "If the Burgundians come through right now, we'll have some comic loss of life," de Metz warns.

But for all of them, fatigue has crossed to that point where no prayer, no contemplation, no rational argument can compare to the lure of the horizontal sleep surface. They sleep in a row, like knives in a large scabbard. Jehanne falls asleep in between Daulon and de Metz.

six

JEHANNE PUSHES OUT OF A NIGHTMARE, and wakes with her face against an unfamiliar stone wall.

In the dream the baby king is back, and this time laughs at her. You think to free France? he ask, and locks a gate in her face.

She stands up, one hand against the rough wall, the other on her lance. *Ah weh,* she tells him now, oh yes. She has no idea where she is. She blinks until she recognizes the shapes along the opposite wall, clustered together like puppies —with De Viennes, the courier, on top, as if to fit his aristocratic bearing. And the building is an abandoned gatekeeper's cottage, owned by some knight lost at Azincort, whose sons have fled to the south or just given up.

Jehanne laughs: Not Vaucouleurs, then. And not Domrémy either, despite the presence of her childhood ghost de Poulengy. She even knows that, for the first time she can remember, perhaps the first time in her life, she has awakened in territory not held by England or Burgundy. Here they call themselves French, and most wear the dolphin. She just wishes she could remember its name. Anywhere is better than where she'd dreamed herself, the baby king's laughter.

Jehanne stands unsteadily, wraps her surcoat around her, and pushes open the building's heavy door. She uses her lance to propel her across the snowy field. It's midnight, her favorite time to call on her angels.

Over time she's learned to do this, not to wait for armor-noise or her own rage, but to receive the braided voice like a necklace. It looks a lot like prayer from the outside, bolsters *le Dé mentir,* the lie she needs and hates.

Around her are unfamiliar, coastal trees, though de Metz's map has told her the sea is far away: low eucalypti, moss-covered fruit trees wrapped with fungi. She half-kneels on the cold ground and asks, *Where am I?,* still not knowing if the answer truly comes from the voice or her own buried knowledge. She opens her mouth and lets the snow tease her tongue.

Almost there, the reply like a slap, the voice so loud she's a little off-balance. St.-Aignan. Ride faster.

St.-Aignan. Of course. She remembers now getting here, even finding this castle. And she knows what they mean, too. Fierbois is close, and with it her sword. An angel drifts in like a snowbank. My church, she says, you'll find it there.

Is this the youngest angel she's had? Round, reddish face, narrow eyes, perhaps seven or eight: she's safe in the arms of a battered dead soldier, who puts her down and lifts Jehanne's lance. *Belle!* he croons at its smoothness, its lightness. They hold it together and point at the sky.

She promises to get the others up and go: she's not the only one, it seems, impatient to meet the Dauphin and the Queen of Jerusalem. One angel kisses her on the top of the head, cradles Jehanne's face with burned, bruised hands. The snow has abated now, though not yet melted: good riding weather.

Back in the shelter her escorts are stirring, beginning to pull on their clothes for this next night's journey. "Good eve, made-moiselle Jehanne." Daulon stands anxiously, her armor in his hands, as if he's been standing here all evening waiting for her to put it on. Jehanne bows to him and shrugs off her surcoat, wincing at her own smell. Perhaps there's an inn at Fierbois. "Before we go, I want to practice," she tells him.

Daulon's eyebrows rise, disappearing into his carrot-red hair. "With the lance?"

"*Ah weh.*" Her body-armor snug, she grips the lance with both hands: it still feels a little heavy, though not nearly as much as when she first held it. De Poulengy comes up and grips the other end.

"Are you ready, Jehannette?"

She glares at him: her child-name not fit for La Pucelle. De Metz comes on her other side and kneels to her, to another glare: not that either. She didn't realize she was this cross.

"On your horse and let's have a go!" Larcher, of all people, strikes exactly the right tone.

De Metz helps her get settled, the lance snugly on her shoulder, while de Viennes feints next to the widest tree available. Both make a wide berth as she hurls her body forward, and with it the lance. An odd adrenalin rush when she feels it hit. Splintered wood. not flesh. She grimaces as she tries to pull her lance out of the tree, until de Poulengy, laughing, does it for her. "Human skin won't fight you nearly that hard." The screaming of steel.

Jehanne flushes, her stomach turning. Her blood heats. This time, she slices at the tree's edge, leaving green nodules exposed. Colet de Viennes claps, wanly: "You almost got *me* that time!"

Yolande d'Aragon does not enter a room so much as annihilate it. Flanked by serving-women on either side, her body is swathed in embroidered wool and her face framed by multiple scarves, the lack of a crown more an affectation than wearing one would be. Her son-in-law, Charles Ponthieu, offers her bread like a servant, or else a priest offering communion. He doesn't look much like a king.

"I trust your sleep was fine enough?" he asks, well-bred.

Yolande forces a smile. "As well as can be, with all this furor. Have you seen the missive from the Batard?"

The Dauphin pales. His breakfast not yet fully swallowed, and already behind on important news. "How is he recovering?"

"Oh, his foot will heal, though I don't imagine he'll be glad to battle soon. But there's better news still—about your protege, Alençon."

Charles sits up straight, his eyes lit at the mention of Jehan d'Alençon: a comrade-in-arms only four years younger than he, captured defending Verneuil five years earlier. "His wife managed to pawn all that gold?" Alençon's duchess the daughter of Charles d'Orléans, the prison-poet.

Yolande laughs. "As an initial payment, anyway. He also promised two of his titles away—for now, he says. In any event, he's free—and when he pays the remainder, he can fight for us, if necessary."

Charles grins suddenly "He's had five years of rest, now." By all accounts. the Duke of Clarence treated his cousin more like a guest than a prisoner, though besieged Orléans is torment enough. "What new do you hear from our wounded warrior?"

Yolande's smile looks more like a grimace. "He reiterates that his people are starving. And he asks what we know about the Maid."

The sound of Charles' goblet hitting the stone floor is less dramatic than possibly intended: the ceramic doesn't break and the liquid within is viscous, noiseless. He backs up his chair to allow the servant to clean up the mess. "And who did *he* hear from, pray?"

Yolande sighs. He *is* an idiot. "How many families turned away from Vaucouleurs?" She reaches for her own cup and stares into it, as if fearing poison. "The trees are talking about her, what do you think? Her name is everywhere."

"I think she's a witch," says Charles.

"As if that's a bad thing," says Yolande. "Young people so grossly underestimate the value of a good poultice." She finishes her bread, shrugging a little. "But this one is something queerer than an old witch, I think."

"I think we send her to Poitiers and let the clerics have at her," says Charles, shuddering a little. Priests scare him, always have. His slim frame and fey speech cast no favor with them, either. "A fine fate for a local goddess."

Yolande's eyes widen: no idiot after all. "Brilliant." Her voice softens, then, for the first time. She looks over at the boy she's known since before his voice broke. "So, do you have any new poems to show me?"

Sainte-Catherine-de-Fierbois, as hoped, bears several small inns happy to accept Jehanne and the others. Small crowds threaten to block her way with their kneeling feet, though de Viennes and Larcher are fine interference, their glares alone matching their lances. The clanking armor grown comic.

The band disperses a little, a relief after so much time locked in step. Daulon, his red hair newly washed, disappears with one of the serving-girls at the inn. This far from home he can play at being a knight.

Jehanne is glad for the room alone. Her arms, her shoulders hurt after all that lance practice. Larcher and de Metz were worthy opponents, feinting and dodging her, pointing to ever-more trees to be the enemy she skewered. As trees cried she got used to it. Her chest freezes, as if she were back in the sheep meadow. The adrenalin that has stolen most of her sleep is now high anxiety, for they're less than a day away now: she'll soon meet the Dauphin. And the Queen of Jerusalem.

While the others sleep, she asks the innkeeper where she can find a scribe. They send her to the church, of course: who else needs to read? She trembles a little, wonders if they will let her hold a scroll, the way Father Guillaume did, the way the priest in St.-Nicolas did. Jesus is a drop of tears. The innkeeper's son escorts her to the church, shooing away the gawkers like so many mosquitoes or beggars.

The church of Saint Catherine is larger than Domrémy's, smaller than Vaucouleurs. Still it's narrow, dark. The priest receives her warily—doesn't he know she passed exorcism?—and waves over a young monk with heavy eyebrows and two days' growth of beard.

"To His Excellency Charles VII, Dauphin of France," she begins her voice wavering even with the salutation. The monk stares, his quill still aloft. "Mademoiselle?"

She sighs and stares at him, her blood heating a little. "I am Jehanne La Pucelle," she continues, and waits until she sees the pen-tip fall again. "I am writing to inform you of my intended arrival on the morrow. I know you have been alerted by Captain Robert di Baudricort," she adds. The monk settles himself, sitting back in his chair, his quill casting droplets that curve to words. "I respectfully request an audience with Your Highness, as soon after my arrival as possible. I have come 150 leagues to come to your aid. I hope you think I have done well." She watches each line, each set of shapes, and recognizes the 'a,' the 'c', and the sloping D, the word for God. The monk, who could easily be her brother Jacquemin with his wide neck and quizzical eyes, keeps his mouth in an expressionless line as his quill glides on the parchment. When he pauses again, their eyes meet: and his are warmed with tears. She suspects he believes her, and clears her throat.

"When I arrive at Chinon, I will know you among all others," she continues. "And I know many good things, that you will rejoice to hear." She bids him add the correct salutations at the end, the proper *Dieu* phrases that she has never bothered to learn: then she takes the pen and, very carefully, starts to draw a long J beneath it, its loop an angle against the rest, leading a careful string of letters. Watch the word become her name. J-eh-hanne. One syllable, long roll of letters. She looks down at the letter, and scraps of other words whisper in her ear. Then she takes a deep breath, looking at the man who resembles her brother. "And one more?" she asks. "To not so exalted a personage?"

He nods, puzzled, and sits back down.

"To Jacquot Darc and Isabelle Romée, village of Domrémy." The words sting her a little. She never wrote them from Vaucouleurs: she wonders if they know of this journey from de Poulengy, or not at all. She then tells them herself, in words she would never use in person. *Maman* you don't know how it's been. Splintered wood and exorcisms. Jesus wept. Stronger now. I could pick up your harrow with one arm and throw it. Larcher teaching me the crossbow soon. A long way from the girl crawling home from the sheep meadow. The flood still constant, but.

She says none of this, only that she's well, and that "I still hope to see you in Patay. And tell Pierre I will see him in Orléans." The monk nearly drops his quill then: after her measured, domestic soothing he'd forgotten he was writing for the Maid. They both laugh.

"If you have the money," the monk says, "royal messengers can deliver to Chinon. It will take longer for the letter to get to Domrémy." She bows, grateful. She hopes he survives this war. "Now," she says, "I need to confess. I have not confessed in almost four days." The last time, Auxerre about forty miles off, was also her last mass: blazing candles in the shadow of Burgundian soldiers' quarters. The priest there stolid, uncomprehending.

The dark of the confessional always liberates her. She

confesses here to a priest younger than the one who admitted her: nervous, with huge eyes that stay with her after he recedes behind the confessional's curtain.

Jehanne's angels slide in easily; a black-skinned ten year old nestles in her lap as she leans against the stone wall. She tries to describe the last few days. The feelings when her lance hit the tree-flesh. Her need for a sword. Some of it comes out her lips in many languages. Stop that, she tells her angels, hoping against hope that the priest is asleep.

If so, he wakens in time to give her blessing, and ask for her prayers. Then, his voice shaking a little, "Look under the altar after mass is done. And tell the Dauphin to become King, please."

She pulls at the curtain then, to see those eyes, but he's already slipped from the other side of the curtain and taken his spot across the sanctuary, assisting with communion. "*Corpus Christi.*" He might have asked for her help, she thinks.

Newly sinless in the eyes of the Church, she slides into the front row to receive the pieces of bread. The priest who gives it to her, to them, is the one who barely let her into the church. Her submitting to confession has softened him.

For the rest of the mass Jehanne keeps her eyes focused on the statue of St.-Catherine. The one who sought the nunnery and when denied, begged for death. Isabelle's dream for her, she thought sourly as a child. Until.

The statue is taller than the St. Margaret she wept for in Domrémy. She feels the braided voice before she hears it, feels the thrum under her skin before she sees any more. She bids them calm, *we're almost there,* begs them not to stop her now. St.-Catherine looking so sad. Jehanne holds her rosary for protection, sheltering the battered crucifix in her palm. Jesus is a drop of tears. Are you ready for war? the braided voice asks. As if she has known anything but. Are you ready to kill? The tree's exposed flesh. The smile on her face makes her jaw hurt.

At a tap! on her shoulder she jumps: it's Daulon, who's crawled out of the girl's bed to find her. Beside him, in the row behind her, are de Metz, de Viennes, de Poulengy, their newly-washed faces shining like a trio of young monks. They all look so much younger without armor. Even Poulengy, whose gray hair whistles vigorously in dark curls.

She places a finger across her lips and points to the altar. They sing along with the hymns, uncomprehending. An angel with a heart-shaped smile finds Daulon's flushed face amusing. She perches on his shoulders, making faces at Jehanne.

When the mass is over, the handful of elderly people attending drain from the church. Jehanne stays in the front row, kneeling to St.-Catherine with her eyes closed; the men behind her start to prowl, restless. Jehanne shudders: what do the priests think of her ungainly soldiers?

Finally the priests have retreated, the sun finally set on the evening mass; Jehanne rises and goes to the altar, kneeling under it like a workman planning to remove a table leg. De Metz and the others follow her, looking on the other side. Her confessor definitely said the altar, yes?

Finally de Viennes points. '*Voici!*" Set into the marble, deep in the recesses, is a long, elegant sword, encrusted with rust and debris. Simple neither to remove or, frankly, to use. She can see five crosses engraved at the base. A baby angel reaches out her hand and caresses it, and starts crying. Mine, she whimpers.

Jehanne's hands tingle a little, but she's not inclined to up-end the church to get to it. It will be yours when you need it, whispers a man with a smashed face, lifting the baby angel in his massive arms.

Jehanne asks her men to leave, to meet her back at the inn. Only Daulon demurs, having pledged to di Baudricort her safety. She starts to look in the corners of the church, wondering if it's true, that there are fewer damaged girls and boys this deep into

France. The ones from Orléans have made their way instead to Regine's cave, it seems.

But she finally finds them in the confessional, hiding from her. why? Has she done too good a job of expressed piety? Do they not recognize her anymore? Now, when she needs them most, when she's about to throw herself at the mercy of the House of Valois? Fear chills her skin beyond all reason.

They surround her, hungry, begging for food. Here the priests know about them—and have tried to chase them out. There are fewer of them, certainly: two exhausted whores, a fifteen year old who was raped at eight, and a pair of runaway soldiers still healing from the battle they fled. They tell her about a disastrous battle, at Rouvray. "The Batard is so hurt I don't know if he'll fight again."

Jehanne's hands fist. How can the priests deny these children food? Are they so afraid that more will come? She will send food from the inn, she tells the runaway soldiers. In exchange, "you will guard that sword, till I send for it."

They nod. Then the small group surrounds her, touches her shoulder, her hands, not for holiness but recognition. The noise escalates. Make it stop. The runaway soldiers whisper they might return to the fight. "But only with you as my general." *When France is one there will be no more of this,* the voice croons seductively. Jehanne nods, and says the same. They kneel at her feet.

The young doctor feels insulted by the new snow. "It's nearly March, damn it," he mutters as he ploughs through the narrow, pitted street of his city, a bag full of bandages, tonics in brass bottles. His hair is stringy inside his hood. The only blessing is how the snow helps clean his hands. He raises them to the sky.

When he arrives at his destination, he doesn't have to ask the servants the location of his patient: he's guided well enough by the loud curses, blaspheming every religion on God's own earth and a few not invented yet. 'I can't stand!" followed by yet another stream, until "Oh, *docteur! Bonne matin.* I see the snow has gotten worse," he forces out a sentence.

The doctor throws off his hood. "Softer, with less ice." His patient is about the same age, twenty-seven, as he, but also tall, with white-blonde hair and eyes the color of the winter sky. His face is prematurely aged, with small burns and sword-scratches substituting for wrinkles, and his wrist-bones peek out from his winter clothes, accentuating his thinness. His foot is wrapped in bandages encrusted with week-old blood. The doctor sits down next to him. "Are you going to keep screaming like that, if I remove them?"

"Probably." The tall knight grins a little. "They don't call me *Batard* for no good reason."

The doctor lifts the foot, whose flesh puffs out around the bandages. "I'll say this—judging by the damage here, you're damned lucky that fellow's crossbow missed your heart."

"Miraculously bad aim, if that's what he was wanting," says the Bastard, with a grin that turns to a grimace. "I think he was aiming at my balls." He sits up, looking at the doctor's face to avoid looking at his own foot. "How are my men at the south gate, *docteur* Masson?"

"Healing well," says the doctor, using a small knife to cut the bandages into small pieces. Those that aren't dead, he thinks. "They await your return." He pulls one of the fragments away from the skin: the other man groans, but keeps his peace. "Have you heard back from the Dauphin?"

"Not yet, damn it," this time a growl in the Bastard's throat. "You'd think he'd move faster, we were practically suckled together. Sometimes I wonder if he *wants* Orléans to starve, so he has an excuse to run off to—oh *mon Dieu.* More gentle. Please."

Masson shakes his head, works more slowly, peeling off the bandages as slowly as he can. The snowstorm gains in force, and he can hear the wind slam against the fortified wall, whistling through the window-slits like an unslaked lover.

After the doctor leaves, Jehan-Paul, the Bastard, watches the snowflakes that sneak in, whirling a little over his head. It was snowing like this when Rouen was besieged, they say. They ate snow and coughed blood from hunger. The women and children and old men expelled, starving, piles of peaceful corpses between the battle lines. Rouen an English city now, its spirit broken, its towers shadowed.

Jehan-Paul has had nightmares about it for weeks. *He* will not do what Rouen's failed defenders did, and expel what they called "useless mouths." His own hands still scarred from two years in English prison, after he failed to defend Paris from Burgundy; a warrior since he was fifteen. His own father dead, stabbed by Burgundy's bodyguard when Jehan was five years old. Tall knight, fuzzy kisses, blond beard.

Sometimes he wonders if he's any good at it, either. Paris fell, after all. Like Rouen. Will he have to open Orléans' arms to the invader, before their snow glows red? He closes his eyes. He'll wait for word from Chinon, about the other. The girl. Perhaps La Pucelle can inspire his childhood playmate to commit some of his precious gold, to keep France's most strategic city from falling. As he falls asleep, he wonders if she's beautiful.

The same snow swaths Chinon's castle like an expensive fur shawl, drapes over streets common and noble, quieting the streets. The streets are narrow, houses in the Norman style with wooden crosshatches and thatched roofs; one must look up, above the low horizon, to see the delicate spire of the clock tower.

Jehanne is nervous to tread here, despite having crunched snow from here to Vaucouleurs. The silence feels sacred, perhaps because it's Friday. Jesus is a drop of tears. The castle dwarfs her.

She's never felt more a shepherdess, despite her boy's clothes, despite her armor. She finds a place to sit by the river Loire, slushy now: impossible to swim in, it still brings nostalgia, though a different Jehanne Darc swam in the Meuse with Mengette. She would wager she's more changed, now, than Mengette is after having borne two children.

A different Jehanne Darc left Vaucouleurs, too. Her arms are sore with the difference, her legs scratched with it, her ankles shadowed by the mud that seems never to leave them. The braided voice still splits her head sometimes, but she fights it as often as she receives it: don't they want her to be strong enough to actually fight?

"Are you all right?" de Metz calls, from the door of the inn. "They're serving supper, mademoiselle Jehanne!"

Ahhh, de Metz. She almost wishes she could give him what he tries so hard not to want. Or could at least want it. She wonders if she is a block of wood, now. Surrounded by handsome men, and not even a spark. Their furred chests, glimpsed briefly, could belong to Le Lune. She really *is* La Pucelle. Jehanne Laxart called it right.

When the king's men come the next morning, she finds herself unsurprised. De Viennes did, after all, call Charles VII a coward. He's at the castle now, but she calls the others, quickly, to stand with her. They're soon outnumbered by the king's counsellors, who keep coming, like an altar-tableau gone horribly wrong; seven men, in thick robes of heavy, fabric, some with jewels encrusted in the sleeves. All speak French in a dialect unfamiliar to her. She's glad for de Poulengy, de Metz, even simple Larcher and brash Daulon, whose hair is tousled from yet another chamber-maid.

When they ask her why she came to Chinon, all she can do is laugh. "My letter to the Dauphin, was it not clear enough?"

"You didn't write it," one of them says. "A scribe did. We need to hear it from you."

The phrases cross her mouth like stale bread. "I am sent by God to liberate Orléans. And to bring our lord to Reims, where he will be crowned. I know this from *Dieu* alone. If you do not believe me," gesturing, "ask these men what I have already done. Ask de Viennes, your messenger, who has already been to the Dauphin."

Now it's their turn to laugh and they do, hearty laughs that easily recall di Baudricort. "Liberate Orléans? And how do you propose to do that?"

Jehanne's blood heats. She wants to reach for her lance. More than that, she wants her angels to tell *her* how they're going to do this. It's all very well to urge her to fight, but how to prevent more people from rotting between city walls? She buys time by saying to her questioners: "I will reveal everything only to the Dauphin. He will have no help if not through me."

She raises herself to her best height, and manages through the force of her stare to get the taller one to stop fidgeting. "Do you hear me? God has said this. With me, he will have divine help. Without me, Orléans is lost. Your people will wither between the battle lines." And again, slowly this time: "He will have no help if not through me." She's as unsatisfied by the answer as they seem to be, and one of her hands fists. She wonders if she will set the room on fire.

The braided voice loud now: screams within screams. Then: a waking dream blinds her, she can barely see the priests and lawyers in their nice robes. Instead: A lance crossing a chest, teasing under armor, then leaned into. until blood spurts. Dead eyes. A crossbow splits a liver. Families weeping. A fast succession of such images, till she can barely breathe with it. The screaming of steel. *How we will liberate Orléans?*

Her mouth starts shouting, guttural words. Her throat hurts from their languages. Villages burning. The commander agape in the public house. Too fast, she doesn't know what any of it means. The one who first opened her, grinning. The noise escalates and she's dizzy. Her skin clammy, she sinks to her knees and presses her hands together, tightly. Stay with the tips of your fingers. the drops of salt. Don't on pain of death faint now. *Iesus lacrimus est.* Hot blood on her skin, someone else's. Make it stop.

Finally the flood recedes: un-informative but to its power: her power. She looks up, her face sweaty, and breathes to recover her composure. They're looking at each other, confused, silenced. What does a vision look like? sound like? You wanted to know.

Jehanne stands up and tosses her hair, which has grown too long to be useful and glints in the morning sun. "Tell your Dauphin I am sent from Heaven." She exhales, pushing that useless hair back. "When I see him, I will say to him such things that he will have no choice but to believe me," what? those words are new, since this flood. She wonders what those words to the Dauphin will be, as she offers her battered rosary from Domrémy. "With me he will be crowned. No other way."

The bejeweled men bow to her on their way out, refusing the rosary. When the door closes behind them,. she starts shaking again. She wonders if they knew how terrified she was. De Metz comes to her then, tentatively, and stands closer, jerking her back to her senses. She has worked too hard to lose the faith of her men. She turns to the group, thanking them for witnessing. "Shall we go forth and see what breakfast we find?"

The royal counselors are, as always it seems, divided.

One group is casual, clear: "She's mad." The oldest one then continues, "She may have managed to deceive a handful of your subjects—but then again, her delusions are truly impressive. Speaking in tongues, praying in Latin, it's quite a performance."

"Send her away," agrees another in his group. "The poor girl should be with her family. Or a nunnery. Not bearing arms so close to Orléans."

Charles sighs, adjusting his seat in the hard chair of the Great Hall. He looks over at his mother-in-law to see how she's receiving this: those extraordinary eyes are unreadable. Her mouth is pursed as if from a bitter taste. "But you think differently, Monsieur?" he asks the diffident man to his left.

The man starts a moment, then speaks softly. "She says she has not told us all. That she will do so only with you. And that she will tell you something that will give you no choice but to believe her."

"So says my cousin the Duke of Lorraine," says Charles. That was the strangest letter he ever received from Lorraine, the fearful script after the man met this mad girl. She told him something he never expected, about the Duke's time in Tunis. Then he told Charles to burn that letter, and not on pain of death to let Yolande know.

"There's no harm in seeing her, is there?" asks yet another counselor. "It's not as if she comes with an army already—just a handful of your men."

Charles thanks them all and dismisses them, sighing. Yolande rises as well, startling him. "Don't go yet!" he cries.

Yolande's eyes flash. "My lord?" she asks.

"What do you think? Should I receive her?"

"I thought your horoscope agreed with Cauchon, there. That you should turn her out." Yolanda lets her pursed lips curl into a tiny smile, like a cat's, barely visible.

"I'll cast another, now. But I want to hear from you."

"The crowds that follow her—we consider ourselves fortunate if as many people turn up for a royal wedding," Yolanda says.

"They turn up when a thief has his hand cut off, too," says Charles, shuddering. "I don't want to meet her if she's a ghoul."

"But I do," says Yolande. "I don't know what I will want to

do, then. But it's not often you meet a woman that scares the likes of those old men." She finally lets out the laugh she's been suppressing ever since the counsellors came in, their faces drawn if not quartered. "Easter is coming soon," she adds. "Perhaps we'll have a resurrection."

The castle in Chinon is a small city, fortifications within fortifications. Begun by Roman conquerors a thousand years ago, it has still those curves in its towers, its arches not the Gothic angles of Notre Dame but the proud circles of Gallia. The road into the walled complex is broad enough for chariots, too: as soft rain starts to wash away snow, her horse takes the ascent as a challenge and she has to tap her hard. "No, this is no race. You're just going to a stable," knowing that will make Le Lune Nouveau surly, less anxious to pull ahead.

She pulls her hood closer, to protect her newly-shorn hair from the rain. She cut it herself this time, following the line set by Regine and the younger de Metz. It still looks choppy, home-made, but she doesn't have to worry about hair in her eyes, or about looking more like a shepherdess than she has to. A starved angel rides behind her now, whispering in her hair, *courage, ma petit soeur.* Licking her ear. She laughs.

As they get closer the castle looks less Roman, the clock-tower entrance in that Gallic shape, a country with one eyebrow raised. *When France is whole the noise will stop,* the voice repeats, just in time for them to dismount, for the rain-darkness to be replaced by the darkness of the entrance-hall. The servant that greets them is surly, dismissive, and waves her in the direction of the Great Hall.

A soldier-angel takes her hand then. covering it with his scarred palm, and says sternly, *Not the one with the crown.* He looks like he's been lanced in the shoulder, but not lanced, something whose impact comes in tinier fragments. She inhales sharply, *please don't take me back to that flood.*

The Great Hall is a cavern within a cavern, a ceiling high enough to hold stars and tapestries older than her home. More light than she's ever seen indoors, ablaze with high tapers and chandeliers in high contrast to the entrance hall. It's also crowded with all manner of supplicants and sycophants, the counsellors who disbelieved her chattering with monks and serving-women. Jehanne feels tinier than before. Tinier than the sheep meadow. Knights whose armor glows new. Noblemen with hats sewn with jewels. Women with waists pulled tiny and exaggerated bosoms. She could be in a nightmare.

One of the counsellors sees her then, and greets her: a quieter, older man than most who questioned her. He leads her to a large man with pale-blond hair, whose crown looks too heavy to be borne. "This is your Dauphin," he says.

Jehanne has to stop herself from laughing. They do think her a fool: anyone knows the Dauphin is younger than this man. This one has also drunk a little too much to maintain the pretense. She turns away and keeps looking, wandering the room, looking behind chairs and in corners. The tables in the hall all look alike and she's confused; she's lost her men in the chaos and even her angels have deserted her. Except for the hum, urging her, pushing her forward in not-well-suppressed rage. This is the moment the grove spoke to her about. Her blood heats. The noise escalates inside her.

Finally, next to one of the serving tables, she sees not him, but her. Sitting far lower than usual, her full skirt half-filling the floor; the deep black eyes, that high forehead. An angel from Jerusalem, a battered slave, recognizes her. A wizened servant is filling the woman's cup; she looks off into the distance, scanning the crowd, a tiny smile playing on her lips.

Jehanne kneels in front of her, says nothing at first. "A long way," she finally whispers.

Yolande starts. Why didn't anyone tell her the girl was here? And wasn't she supposed to either make a fool of herself with their pretend king or descend on Le Brat with prayers and lamentations? Not this, not quiet steel. "Aren't you also looking for . . ."

"Yes," says Jehanne. "But more for you."

The way she says "you" makes Yolande start. No one knows me, arrogant child with the Bastard's blue eyes. She doesn't say it. It's true, then: the girl compels. She wants to know what Lorraine taught and how. She tilts her head, just slightly. "Now is a good time," Yolande says. "He has his advisers 'round him."

Jehanne looks in the direction Yolande indicated. Sharp intake of breath: the dauphin is lean, willowy, a little sickly, with hair cut as badly as hers and not slicked down properly. Loose courtier-shirt and a floppy peaked cap, like a court jester's. He's putting back a cupful of mead and laughing.

Swiftly, dodging behind, she finds a spot in front of him and drops to her knees once more. It feels more false than with her impulse to the Queen: more like the chevalier at the Lady-Tree. "My lord," like a rehearsal.

He looks down at her and freezes. She almost laughs: she's rarely seen that much panic outside the walls of Vaucouleurs, when she had to blister soldiers' hands to get their attention. She then tells him in quick succession what she has already told his counsellors, told her parents, told di Baudricort and Larcher. When she says "Reims" she feels his exhale of near-pride, close to her forehead. Then she leans even closer and whispers again. She shows him what she sees.

The ground shifting under his feet, in court. Little Charles and little Jehan-Paul playing boy games before Jehan-Paul became a warrior. His tears in Lucie's bed. His prayers to go to Scotland. Jehanne whispers them in mottled French, she rests her hand within his like a lover. She also whispers about the noise, about the clanking of armor and screaming of steel. Echoes, for him, of Jehan-Paul's letters.

The next time she sees Yolande, she's been brought to meet her on the arm of the Dauphin, who asks a little querulously, "Where shall we put her?"

"Couldray," says Yolande. "The tower. There's room there for her there. Talk to Madame Bellier, she's a godsend." She rises to her full height and looks down at the little shepherdess, in her wet hood and boy-clothes. "I am honored to meet you, Mademoiselle La Pucelle."

"And I you, your Highness," Jehanne answers the Queen of Jerusalem.

After Madame Bellier takes Jehanne to her new quarters, Yolande turns to the Dauphin. "What did she say to you?"

Charles can't answer her. He looks a little green. His knees knock together with even more force than usual. "Enough to convince me that we need send her to Poitiers, indeed. Shall I write them?"

"I already have," says Yolande. "Now, I am wondering if a little jaunt to Poitiers might do me good. My own personal Good Friday pilgrimage." Her rings pinch her cracked fingers, and she wants to go back to her rooms.

When the letter arrives announcing Isabelle Romée's imminent arrival, Father Jehan Pasquerel indulges himself enough to read it right away. Plans and pilgrimages and La Pucelle are far more satisfying than any of his duties running a convent in a war zone.

The young Augustinian is more good-looking than wise for a priest, they say. All in the great city of Tours whisper that that's how the convent stays filled: maidens gasping for love of that delicate jawline, those unusual long-lashed eyes. Certainly he is having none of the attention of the wives who fill the church, stolid and adoring, or even the ones who follow him on every daft pilgrimage, like Isabelle. Perhaps, they whisper, it's those pilgrimages that help satisfy the priest's desires.

Not that he's been on many pilgrimages of late. Tours, a fortified city re-conquered by French forces only just before Azincort, is a stone's throw from besieged Orléans, and receives more than its share of those seeking refuge. Like his peer Fournier in Vaucouleurs, Pasquerel is kept busy hearing confessions from all sides.

Burly men confessing to squashing some random fishwife on the Burgundy side. Terrified girls from Orléans, confessing because they felt soiled, forced into sin by the invader. Nervous young men confessing because they take seriously, *Thou shalt not kill.* Battered children begging him for refuge more than absolution. The confessions haunt his dreams.

So does Isabelle Romée's daughter, who people five hundred leagues across France have whisper-named "La Pucelle." In his dreams La Pucelle is tall, big-boned, like his dead *maman*. An edge of shame, dreaming her so: not lust but a need for comfort. God and his mother combined, God and Marie le Virginie, just as the masses have already christened her. He hears also that she's now living in a corner of the Dauphin's castle, preparing for battle.

Pasquerel sits down then, sinks his head into his hands. His dreams are also nightmares: La Pucelle a figure swathed in dark. Unlike her mother, a woman as practical as she is devout, kept busy with herbs and grandchildren and that huge, blustery doyen of a husband. Isabelle told him something else long ago, something meant to be buried deep in the confessional, and he wonders if Jehanne Darc is just looking for someone to confess to, over and over. He has already heard about how much she prays.

In any event, the letter confirms it: Isabelle is coming soon herself, with a band of intrepid pilgrims from Lorraine. Damaged daughter or no, Isabelle Romée is that rare creature who can laugh and hoist an extra beer while remaining dry-eyed and deeply in love with God. "I would join your convent, Father," she tells him each time she sees him. "But then what would my husband eat for himself?"

Ascension Day at Puy will be glorious, he thinks, even with these troubled times. And after all, when have they *not* been troubled? Pasquerel smiles, finally, and puts the letter away. Time to clean the guest rooms, and prepare for this particular onslaught. "At least we know they're coming," he'll tell the washerwomen.

Meanwhile, there's a convent to tend, with two dozen nuns at last count. Girls with a secret like Jehanne's, less well hidden. Fat widows whose sons were greedy for their inheritance. And a few truly holy souls, who know the scriptures nearly as well as he and don't stint at cleaning privies when it's necessary.

Jehanne is cowed by her quarters at Couldray, high above the Loire.

Madame Bellier, a nice, florid woman with a bubble-laugh, led her up three flights of stairs until Jehanne feared for her hostess' heart, so badly did she pant. "*Ici*!" From the window-slit the river looks small, like a half-frozen ribbon. She wonders where are de Metz and Daulon; she feels vulnerable, unprotected. Her angels seem to be taking a rest from her and she from them: anyway their presence feels less like protection and more like demand. *when will you act?* She shivers in the draft, her surcoat and hood drying over the fire. As her adrenalin subsides, her stomach also begins to gnaw at her. She reaches for the ceramic cup provided by one of the servants.

"Are you comfortable, *ma petit soeur?*"

Jehanne drops her rosary, nearly sending the small stones across the room. That voice is unmistakable, and the servant hurrying right behind knows it too. "Your Highness!"

Yolande, divested of the jewels she wore in the Great Hall, only laughs. "I am tired and nearly ready for my nap. Don't fuss so. I just wanted to ensure that our guest was comfortable." She looks around until she sees the heavy, low chair near the window. "Now go away. I want to talk to her. Alone. Why do you think I didn't bring my women?" She lowers herself into the seat and exhales. "Sometimes," she says to Jehanne, "you just want to be able to hear yourself think."

Jehanne purses her lips to keep from laughing. Does the Queen of Jerusalem have a hum under her skin too? Jehanne's is beginning to wake from its slumber, whispering in tongues. Pushing from under hers, like some hidden treat or festering sore. *Non,* she says to them.

Yolande doesn't hear them, turns to the window as if absorbed by something outside. "They've put you up in the corner," she says. "If the Burgundians ride right to us, you had better be ready with your crossbow, *non?*"

Jehanne swallows, and says honestly, "I am only just learning the crossbow, your highness." Then she finds herself smiling, and swallows hard, surprised as she adds: "I will leave that to the experts, like my man Richard Larcher."

"*Tres bon,*" says Yolande absently. She gestures for the girl to come closer. "My eyes, after forty-nine years, they're not as sharp as once they were."

Jehanne approaches her, pulled by the gray-green eyes. She sees why so many say the woman is beautiful, if not why ploughmen spit at her name. She fights the urge to speak, to tell the Queen all. This is not her mother.

Yolande reaches out and touches Jehanne's hair. "We shall have to get a royal hairdresser to see to this."

Jehanne starts. "*Non, merci.* I must dress and look this way. I am told —"

"By God. Yes, I've heard." Yolande smiles, and keeps the tendril of hair in her fingers. So soft: it glows in her hands. She forgets the bloom of youth, un-powdered. The girl's eyes as if lit from within. No coquetry, yet plenty of calculation; she fancies she can see the girl's mind whir before each sentence spoken. Her hands slide over to frame the girl's cheeks, like a prayer-gesture opened, fingertips just below those blue eyes. "I see now why they joke that you're the Dauphin's bastard sister."

"The *what?*" She starts: she hasn't heard.

Yolande glides over it "Just another baseless story. You look more like the real Bastard, the one in Orléans."

"So have I been told," Jehanne recovers and offers. Not quite true, of course: de Viennes said, *You're as quick as him.* Half-truths what she has to offer, to shield from the real story un-believed. Except: could she hear it? The hum demands to know. The woman's hands warm on her cheeks, a half-caress on the way to control. *This is not my mother: she rules armies.* The clanking of armor and screaming of steel.

"*Belle fille,*" Yolande continues, "you have terrified my son-in-law. He practically prayed for you to be removed magically from this castle."

Jehanne's blood heats. "He needs me," she insists again.

Yolande laughs. "Does he?" She doesn't let go of Jehanne's face. The skin has grown hot underneath: she's angered. Good. A woman's anger is too often suppressed, let alone, turned inward or toward some jealous rival. This heat is different, though. "Have you a fever?"

Jehanne shakes her head, smiling slightly. She reaches down and touches the other woman's cheek, barely singeing it. Yolande drops her hands and rears back.

"Those men at the gates of Vaucouleurs—they weren't exag-gerating, were they?" What is this, she wonders, this fever that blisters others. "I wonder you survived your exorcism, *jeune belle.* Now don't go telling me it's all from God. I'm not ready to believe you."

"Nor should you," Jehanne says without thinking. Someone

who can hear about the lies and why they're necessary. yes? no? A sharp headache then, the flood denying emphatically and forcing a backtrack. "You are having your own priests examine me, yes? They will tell you."

"Ohhhhh, two sets, *belle*," Yolande finds herself saying in a very low voice. "Next week, we all leave for Poitiers. You, me, my yellow son-in-law, his wife, and his patient, over-educated mistress. But first you will meet here with his confessor, and with three other bishops. You try explaining that touch to them." She shifts in her chair and groans, working slowly to pull herself to a standing position. "In the meantime I'll send you a page; if you like him you may keep him, for the duration. And each night, here and in Poitiers, I'll make sure you have women with you. If you're such a *pucelle*, after all, we must keep you so. And we'll learn about *that,* yea or nay, soon enough."

Jehanne half kneels, places herself under one of Yolande's shoulders. Her temperature cools, and she lets herself take the older woman's hand. "Don't be afraid," she says softly.

Yolande throws her head back and laughs: loud, like a seal barking. The servant she banished is back, alarmed face in the doorway. "Never say that, child," she says. "First. *I* am not afraid of you. But if you want us to give you an army—you want them to be." She rises to her full height, shrugging off the girl's arm like a scarf. "If you can give me back Orléans, perhaps I'll teach you enough so that they are always afraid of you."

Jehanne shakes her head, sadly. One truth her voices told her long ago, and these bloodied lands give her no reason to doubt them. "I will not last long enough," she tells Yolande. "Only a year. No more."

After the Queen leaves, Jehanne wonders for the first time what the voices mean. Will she die in battle? Are her dreams true, and she will die at the hands of a tiny king? Or will she simply drown in her voices, and be found at the bottom of a muddy river?

In the meantime, how is Yolande planning to learn her answer to the virgin question, and how can Jehanne stop her?

She watches the sun set, through the archer's window. A corpse from Rouen reaches out his good arm and tousles her shorn hair. *Bon,* he says in a choked Norman accent, gangrene at the tip of his nose. Women, children join him, each blackened by it. They all tell her she has done well. She remains on her knees and cries at their teeth, their stinking bodies.

Not Orléans, they hiss, to Jehanne's annoyance. She knows why she's here. She keeps her hands clasped and her head bowed, so any passerby will think she's praying. She begs them to tell her how she'll win so she believes it. Not to flood her with pain like last time.

Amid their silence she starts real prayers, softly. "*Pater Noster . . .*" Her rosary is beginning to lose beads, its crucifix long without Christ's head.

seven

THE CURVES and whorls haunt her dreams. The curve that means the sound that begins her name. J. Long straight line, loop back. J. The mark of God: one straight line, one pointed circle. *Deum, Dieu.* In her dream she stands with a scroll, reading pages of scripture. Jesus is a drop of tears. The baby king knocks the scroll from her hands.

When Jehanne wakes her cheeks are wet. Her hand on the hard floor traces it: long line, simple loop. The line and circle of God. She holds her hands together to stop trying. Opening her eyes to banish the words, she lets the moonlight stream onto her hands through the archer's window. She wants only to walk the castle, find her angels, and watch for enemy soldiers, village fires, girls burning.

But if she dresses she will wake the women in her bed, the ones Yolande sent, who every night frame her like birds in an altar-tableau. Kneeling by the window, she sees above the covers only their night-caps, bits of hair emerging between.

The moonlight stuns her eyes: too much like sunlight. Her blood heats. *How do you know they're safe?* They who? Not the girls of Orléans, that's for damn sure. The best she can do for those girls is to do well here. Does that mean staying up all night to study scripture? Or carving out a moment of dream-time?

She shakes her head and begins to call on her angels. Today she must talk to priests, convince them of *le Dé mentir.* The same next week, in Poitiers. Her lessons with Father Guillaume, with Isabelle preparing her for the nunnery, all must come out her mouth in full feeling and seeming faith. Though right now, she's far from sure what she means.

The nuns at the Tours convent, skinny from prayer, rush around the tables of the dining hall with uncharacteristic smiles; this despite the gloomy gray day, a huge storm-cloud threatening their peace. The nuns are revived by the new arrivals, hardy pilgrims who nearly battered down the door getting here. Jehan Pasquerel's astonished at how much they all eat.

The tables, already full to groaning of stolen meats, are now supplemented by loaves of Lorraine bread, carried into France in a tremendous sack and dusty from the trip. "Supplies for our pilgrimage," Isabelle Romée explains to Pasquerel, as she kisses him hello. "Special bread for *ma petite fille.* I'm so glad we got here before it started to rain."

Pasquerel swallows. Isabelle still thinks her daughter is going to meet them in Puy. He wonders if she's right. "La Pucelle is very busy just now," he ventures.

"Conquering the king!" Isabelle grins, accepting a bowl of soup from one of the nuns. She thanks her profusely, her fingers thrumming like a schoolgirl's.

"You don't seem near tired," Pasquerel says. He can't help smiling. The color is high in Isabelle's cheeks, and the circles under her eyes have faded since Jehanne left. "Have your grandchildren not kept you up, much?"

"Mon Dieu, c'est Isabelle!" The roar cuts across the room, now: Isabelle looks up and whoops, letting herself be lifted by a

middle-aged squire with a sprawling beard. "Has Darc given me permission to woo you, yet?" asks her old friend Bertrand de Poulengy.

Isabelle looks down at the priest from her friend's grip, laughing helplessly. As Poulengy puts her down she begins to introduce the two men, but Pasquerel waves her sentence short.

"Monsieur and I have met," he says gently. "He will be joining us to Puy-en-Velay."

Isabelle nods, serious now. "I know." She looks at the crowded room, the skinny nuns and quiet parishioners crammed onto long tables, and sinks into her chair. She pats the chair to one side, for de Poulengy to sit, but he shakes his head, already squared away across the room. "Do you always feed this many?"

"It's been more and more,." says the priest, biting down on the next phrase, *the longer Orléans starves.* He looks over involuntarily at the family at the other end of the table, the father long gone, the mother and daughters still ashen, quiet. Other daughters won't come to table. Stories that will soon be imprisoned in Pasquerel's dreams. His mother superior sits with them in cells, promises absolution she can't give.

The noise in the room escalates: between de Poulengy and his men, there is more armor here right now than in months. Pasquerel turns to Isabelle and asks after her family.

"Oh, they're fine," dismissively. "Making babies, ploughing fields, tending the orchards. The de Vergy brothers have completed their worst and moved on, it seems, and now we can get back to our crops. Such as they are." She stands up, scanning the room, her foot tapping in concert with her restless hands. "Even my *petit generale* managed to find a scribe and write me, from St.-Catherine-de-Fierbois. Where is Bertrand?" She finds him and waves, furiously. "Come back!"

"Sit," Pasquerel almost pleads. "We're not leaving till morning."

"But—isn't my daughter joining us here, first? Or will we meet her at the sanctuary, next week?"

The priest bends his head, suddenly deeply occupied by Isabelle's hardening bread. He dips it in the wine, absently, and doesn't speak. Then he waves over de Poulengy himself, almost desperate. "Ask him," he tells Isabelle.

The stout Lorraine pilgrim pales for the first time, looking up at the tired squire. "When is my daughter joining us?" she asks him now. Her foot and hand are still, her merry eyes now wide and soft, like a child's. Bertrand sinks to one knee, like a knight in a court painting.

"La Pucelle goes instead to Poitiers," he says softly. "She needs prove herself to her dauphin, still. When the bishops there have blessed her, then he will give her an army, not before. She cannot come on our long journey." Puy-en-Velay, deep in Auvergne, is nearly as far from here as Chinon from Vaucouleurs, he tells her. And there is an army to raise.

Isabelle swallows, another child-gesture before she gathers herself. She shouldn't have let herself hope for this. Jehanne's letter itself made no mention of it, only to Orléans. "La Pucelle, you are calling her that now too," she says, her voice low, no trace of her brassy entrance.

"She stayed chaste through eleven days of crossing hazardous lands with us," says Bertrand. "And she is learning the lance and the sword." He tries to ignore the tears that escape against Isabelle's will, sliding down her round cheeks. "She prays every night.." He continues, slowly, "I have seen her converse with her voice, silently. Sometimes it gives her great distress. I honor La Pucelle."

Jehanne's mother straightens then, trying to shake off her need to see her lost daughter, to see her instead in the older man's words. "She is not frightened, then?"

De Poulengy sighs. Jehanne is often frightened, he thinks, though she has never shown it to him. "She is in the care of the

Dauphin now," he says instead. "And the Duchess." He knows he doesn't believe either, and neither does she: Jehanne does, after all, mean next to go to Orléans amid men and arms and blood and steel. He would never have let his daughter do such a thing. Jacquot Darc, he knows, still rails in his sleep against it. The short, stolid woman in front of him has usually been the holy one, the one whose faith in *Dié*, in Jehanne's voice from Him, surpasses most of theirs. But right now her shoulders are low, and she fingers the pilgrimage-cross around her neck.

She turns back to Pasquerel. Then she speaks, quietly, firmly: somewhere between a request and an order. "Go with her to Orléans, Father," she says.

Pasquerel shakes his head. He's a convent to tend. "I'm sure the Dauphin will assign a fine priest—"

Isabelle takes his hands and looks at him. Not one who knows, she doesn't say. "Go with her, Father. Persuade our wild Charles to assign *you*. After Ascension Day."

A sharp cry from the far end of the table: one of the daughters from Orléans has caught sight of de Poulengy's lance. A nun peels her from the table and they rush off, leaving her meal uneaten and her mother shrugging. "This is why I usually don't allow those here," Pasquerel says, deep in his throat. "And you want me to follow an army, now?"

Isabelle doesn't say anything, just looks from Pasquerel to de Poulengy, her eyes steely now: she won't take no for an answer. De Poulengy knows that look well, in her daughter's gaze. It also reminds him of something. "Isabelle," he asks, "when Jehanne left Domrémy, did she know how to read?"

His question is matched by a thunderclap, quite as if God had ordered an end to this conversation. Now.

The storm over Tours has skirted Chinon, chasing the newly-freed duke of Alençon halfway across the Loire Valley to get here. Twenty-two years old, pale from five years in captivity, Jehan Valois is nonetheless well-fed, anxious, hesitant on a new horse as he approaches the gates of the Dauphin's castle.

The sun, rising to mid-afternoon, sets the river alight; its beauty still stuns him. All of it. France's innumerable shades of green, poking from under the melting snow; the low houses with Germanic front doors and Gallic roofs; the high Gothic arch of the old castle. Even the high French noses of the people. He breathes it all in with the softening nearly-spring air.

The horse under him still feels uneasy: a young one, a filly but colt-surly, his own horse long run off when he died at Verneuil. Riding now jostling his stomach, five years since his last gallop.

He's happy enough to dismount, let his men take the horses away; watching his banner, his battle standard, recede. Staring at it, as if for the first time: *his* banner? Three fleur-di-lys and a half-human griffin, the banner belongs to his father, dead at Azincort. To his brother, Pierre, now four years dead. And Orléans nearly lost. How weak he is. Pulled by the English from under stacked corpses. Their smell still competes with the rain, his new horse, these riotous plants.

Better to walk in the garden, while he waits to be announced: look at the trees, Valois. Soft smell in palest green. Look at the boy running up and down with a lance: sure, practiced, sliding the lance along slim beech bark, without breaking skin.

He watches the boy awhile, the slow approach, the whirl and duck, the ferocity of the lance slicing again and again. His heart rises to meet the blows. Too long away from battle: too much lost. Fear and lust for it. Would the boy run so hard, spear so freely, if he'd seen what the duke's seen? Has he ever smelled death?

Then at the third approach he looks again, as the lancer's

hood falls back and he sees her. No boy, this. He wants to call to her, but mostly he wants to keep looking.

Strong legs, shoulders, muscled as a boy's. Her jaw tight with rage. Her mouth moving slightly at each impact. He wasn't as agile as this, when he began. Could this really be the shepherdess they speak of? Do these fast blows mean she really could free Orléans?

"Alençon!" the cry behind him now, and he turns: he knows the voice. Thick with winter, ringed with laughter; a voice he's known since he was five, since she entered his cousin's and all of their lives.

"You only grow more beautiful," he tells Yolande now, with some truth. Her olive skin softens her age and those black eyes, as always, seem to contain the memories of everyone he has ever known inside them. "And your letters—they helped keep a poor prisoner like me sane."

Yolande laughs and kisses him. "Poor prisoner indeed, entitled before you were free. And what's this I hear about a pledge not to fight?"

Alençon winces. "You hear correctly. Ransom still to pay. But I can help you prepare your army. Along with . . ." He jerks his head in the young girl's direction. "What is this? Is she real?"

Yolande looks past him to the girl dueling nothing. "I'm not sure yet," she says quietly. "She's managed to convince one group of priests: now we go to Poitiers for another. I'm glad you came before we left. Perhaps you can help us see if she's mad or a miracle."

"Or both," Alençon says. "To fight the English at all right now—many would call it mad. Do you like her?" He doesn't know why he asks the question: for Yolande d'Aragon, all his life, such a question has rarely mattered. She's ordered cut the throats of knights she loved, who threatened her Charles.

But Yolande looks past him again, at the now-sweating child beginning to wilt under her lance. "I can tell you," she says softly, "that it may after all take a woman to break the back of this mealy-mouthed truce."

Alençon turns and watches her, along with Yolande. The shepherdess is as young as he was when he was captured. He wonders if she'll win. Against all those priests and everyone else. And if she'll end with the same smell in her mouth.

Who is that? Bright eyes, plump belly. She sees Yolande kiss his face. Her shoulders hurt, as she runs hard at the next tree.

She's jousting this hard because she's angry, and a little lost. She hates it here. Hates Yolande's spies in her cold bed. Hates the priests grilling her every day, as if suddenly she'll erupt any moment with a different set of answers. Hates the dauphin, the skinny poet, most of all. He's far too afraid of her for anyone's good.

Her lance starts to weigh more than her. She misses de Viennes, the others, standing by her tree-target. Without them she feels aimless, and swings the lance like a battle-axe, a if she could cut this tree down.

The fat young man could have been in the sheep meadow. His armor glitters in the nearly-spring sun. She decides to hate him too. The hum under her skin is anxious, alert. Maybe it *is* the voice of God after all: petulant and vengeful. Where are her angels? She needs to find somewhere private and call on them.

Except there isn't anywhere private, in this place. The night-women are spies for Yolande, her page the same. All report back to the Queen of Jerusalem—the one who could believe Jehanne, but is biding her time. Both of them are. Jehanne still can't decide how much to tell her. Her head hurts. She sees them go off, the Queen and the fat man, and breathes easier.

The other reason she's jousting this hard is a simple matter of the calendar. Ascension Day this Friday. Pilgrims crossing France, toward Puy-en-Velay. Jehanne almost starts crying, thinking of her promise to Isabelle. Instead she whacks another tree.

"Mademoiselle!" She knows the voice, another one she hates. Louis de Coutes, the chief spy: the young man who bothers her from the moment she wakes to the arrival of Yolande's female informers. "You told me when to tell you it was time for the King's mass."

Not king yet, she almost snarls. I'm to crown him, remember? Though without clearer words from her angels right now, she's forgotten the point of putting a crown on that idiot's head. She sighs, and hands him her lance. "Thank you."

Time to take communion from the same priests who've been harassing her all week. This masque has hardened, and she can no longer afford the wildness that scared his counsellors. Utter quiet, utter piety, at least until Poitiers. When do they leave?

"Does mademoiselle need anything before you go?" The page is close to her age and reminds her of Daulon, with curly red hair and freckles that threaten to overshadow the otherwise impressive blue eyes. Not cocksure like Daulon, she guesses he's not finding himself each night in a different girl's bed.

She would like him, if he weren't working for Yolande. "Just —please take my lance up to the tower." He nods and races off, his limbs wavering in numerous directions at once. He's not yet grown into his body.

Jehanne begins to walk the long way to the chapel. The sweat on her neck starts to dry, chilling her skin.

It takes more time than anyone anticipated to arrange the trial at Poitiers. The more skeptical members of the court remain Yolande's nemeses, Poton de Xaintrailles and La Tremoille, who've over the years danced back and forth between here and

Burgundy. The night before they're to leave, La Tremoille invites all of them to his rooms.

La Tremoille is huger than di Baudricort, richer than Alençon, and far smarter than any of them save Yolande. She still suspects him of the murder of his predecessor, two years ago; that he is now in charge of negotiations with the enemy, both Burgundy and Bedford, makes her ill.

But Charles looks at the large man like he's found a saner father than the mad king, and begs him tremulously for counsel on Jehanne. As usual, the dauphin has caught whatever cold has been wafting its way round the castle, and pauses every other sentence to blow his nose. "How can I actually put her in charge of men at arms?"

La Tremoille sits back in his seat, his own throat clenching in sympathy with his kinglet. He avoids the Sicilian bitch's glare. "If she passes these trials, the priests will believe her, and our troops all believe their priests. They may finally believe that God is with us." They haven't since Azincort, he doesn't say. He doesn't need to. His eyes meet de Xaintrailles': both were there, saw ten thousand knights and footmen sink into the mud like crushed vines. Both were captured, and heard it like a brother's taunt: "God was on our side, frog," incomprehensible Welsh and high Oxford tones alike.

"If this girl can bring God back," La Tremoille continues, "I'll turn over all the soldiers in Christendom!" His bass voice is unsuited to the crescendo, and the sentence comes out insincere. His eyes meet Yolande's, finally. She hates to think of them being on the same side in anything, though she can't really move without him.

The girl's been more interesting than she thought: athletic and stubborn and pious by turns. Just as her audience and, perhaps, her inner voice demanded. Yolande wants to know what's in that voice, how fraught it is with a childhood in the midst of the invader, three years old when Azincort dissolved any myth of France. And how much of it is lies. Not that she's about to tell any of this to La Tremoille.

Instead, she blows her nose, having finally caught Le Brat's cold. "We'll see, after she submits to a proper ecclesiastical trial," she says slowly. "Now if you'll excuse me, this old woman must rest her bones before the ride to Poitiers. And so should you, my lord," she tells Charles.

La Tremoille bows. "I wish you both a good journey," he says, swallowing a smile. "And we will see what all your priests and confessors make of this girl in boy's clothing. That must violate some Old Testament prescription or another."

Jehanne kneels before her window, in the moonless dark, begging her angels to make an appearance. Yolande's women are asleep, finally, and Louis de Coutes has finally retreated to whatever room holds his spying eyes. Her arms, her legs hurt: all that jousting, all these stairs. She's never been in a building with so many stairs. She's hungry, now, and more than little cross.

Are you as terrified as I am? she asks. Or simply impatient? Their silence appalls her. Why is she here? Why is she doing this? Why isn't she with Isabelle on her pilgrimage, in Domrémy baking bread for her father?

The answer in slicing memory. Blazing sunlight in the sheep meadow. The one who opened her first, his low gurgle of victory. The boy from Tunis, the white-blond girl from Prague. Where are their sisters and brothers here? Is this castle so impregnable?

Finally an angel emerges, a skinny girl with golden skin and slanted eyes, like the oldest images of the Madonna. She leads Jehanne back to her bed, bids her crawl in between the two women, whose bodies make the mattress sag under their weight.

One of the women stirs, turns over, fixes Jehanne in her open-eyed gaze. Not the same prying gaze Jehanne has recoiled from all week: her eyes are shy suddenly, her gaze drops and recurs. The woman is short, like Isabelle, with buttery hips and a ready smile that dismays when it evaporates, as now. Her name is Jehanne Christiane le Preuilly, called Christiane. She looks fearful now, as if she thinks Jehanne and the angel will hurt her: as if she sees the angel: as if she has her own voices chasing her down. Hair sweaty against her neck.

Jehanne suddenly the calmer one. "Don't be afraid," she says for the first time. "I won't harm you." Christiane's eyes return to the floor, her pudgy hands held still by force. One reaches for her own curly hair and pulls at a strand, hard. Words sticking in her throat fall noiselessly to the floor.

Of course, Jehanne doesn't touch her but lies down again, settling into a crevice next to her. No more: when France is whole. She doesn't say it. The words are meaningless. She falls asleep.

When she wakes, Christiane is gone, but the smell of her tears moistens the bed beside Jehanne. In her place in the room is the annoying Louis, who is gathering her possessions and sweeping under them. "*Bonjour, mademoiselle.*" He looks nearly as worried as Christiane. Has she really terrorized them all?

Jehanne struggles out of bed, lets him help her brush her hair and get into new doublet. She looks up with a start at the sight of an aged warrior angel, appearing on the arm of the Queen of Jerusalem.

Yolande's face, her voice cheerful, tired, her message not unlike that of the dirty girl. "What a big day! Are you looking forward to visiting the holy city?"

Jehanne rises, wiping the dust from her doublet and bowing. "I am, your majesty." She stares a little, for Yolande is accompanied by half-a-dozen servants and is dressed in her court-finest, her jewel-encrusted bodice set to challenge any horse. "Though I am dressed a little more plainly. Will I have the horse I came with, do you know?"

Yolande then grins, a full-fledged, triumphant smile. "You have a secret admirer, La Pucelle. My fair duke d'Alençon noticed your jousting, and wants to give you a horse. If you pass this next trial, he may even be fighting beside you."

That far knight. Her good luck. The braided voice approves: his memories of corpses. Still she grimaces inwardly.

Poitiers, full of spires and churches, has seen war for millennia. In 722 A.D., the barbaric warriors called Franks here overwhelmed the Moslem prince Abderrahman, whose armies had already sliced their way through Narbonne, Toulouse, and Bordeaux until they were so sated by rapine, so laden with jewels and furs, that they could barely move.

And in 1356, nearly a century ago, Poitiers was first lost to the English in this forever war: the Duc d'Orléans, whose son now sits in an English prison, lost a decisive battle to that pitiless English longbow, the bow that slices chain mail like a knife in freshly-baked bread. The Dauphin's grandfather, Jehan the Good, was captured and held without ransom for months. Like Alençon.

Yolande wonders why French archers didn't start to build longbows right then, instead of letting themselves suffer the same at Azincort. No one ever learns simple lessons offered.

Still the spires and golden domes are beautiful, rising above the river Garonne like upturned chalices. The river's surface is creamy with just-melting snow.

Jehanne rides behind Yolande's company, riding beside Alençon. He's lighter than he looks, and seems tolerable company. "You ride well," he complimented her twenty leagues back, and then shut up.

The braided voice reminds her why he's so quiet. She's heard about him from the court, about his being left for dead at Verneuil. He's likely as frightened as she of this war, and as desperate to fight it. Stacks of rotting bodies pressing against. What would she do? Will she die like that?

Out in the open, her angels are closer to her skin, the hum near-gentle. *Remember, no theatrics,* they warn her. She swallows her laugh; not unless you blind me! She knows her mission here; the script is well-worn, burnished by repetition. She knows she can't answer them in Latin, or tell them something they don't think she's supposed to know. *Give them an intensified form of what they expect, what they hope for. Be their newest Marie le Virginie, and try to contain that Lorraine accent. No Dé, no Dié— only Dieu.* She doesn't know if that's her thoughts, saying it, or the toothless murmur of an angel, eighth-century victim of Moslem rage.

In Poitiers Yolande sends her to the home of Jehan Rabateau, chased here from Paris by the English only two years ago. A change in surveillance, then; instead of the women who swathed her at Couldray, she has only Rabateau and his shy wife, who bow to her desire to pray every day after supper. They look worshipful when they glimpse her on her knees, all night long. Unfettered access to her angels.

By day she sits in a large room, in a building only partly a church, with a group of holy knights; prelates as distinguished in their clerical armor as the others on the battlefield. Twenty of them, some still freshly tonsured, some at the height of their power, a few skinny and white-haired with age. They test her on every scrap of Scripture from Genesis to Revelations: they watch her eyes, her face for the answers. They whisper among themselves as she sings her well-worn song. *I hear a voice, the voice of God. It told me to come to Vaucouleurs and then to the dauphin.* When she's asked "Why do you not call him king?" she replies hotly that Charles is not king yet, and won't be until she brings him to Reims. Right now, in this cold place with all these priests, she wonders if they will ever get there.

Questions echo her own, to her angels. "If God wanted to drive out the English," says Guillaume Aymeri, a lay theologian, "there's no need for soldiers, is there?'

She stares at him, relentless. Let me try, sir, I will tear them to bits with my hate. In twisted blood and memory streams, in ways you cannot conceive of, good father. She does not say it, but instead: "The soldiers will give battle and God will give the victory."

He nods and sits down, a very small smile on his lips. Jehanne has to force herself not to look to her side, to where the Queen of Jerusalem watches the show. Why did she come? The Dauphin stayed behind, blowing his nose, in the embrace of those horrible men. Why did Yolande decide to follow her and sit through the hours of tedious repetition, like an endless rehearsal?

She finds out in the middle of the second week, when Yolande comes to the Rabateau house for supper, on a horse. "If you can ride with Alençon you can ride with me." The queen heaves a little as her horse kneels, grunting with approval when Jehanne takes her place easily behind.

Her angels, who have just become used again to her nightly visit, are delighted to be taken along: a pregnant Norman girl with her womb sliced open rides unseen on the Queen's bejeweled shoulders, her belly now flaccid against Yolande's hair. Another, elder angel is by contrast silent, one wrinkled finger across her lips.

"Where are we going?" The March wind is real, and not unfierce; Jehanne wishes for another cloak. But then they're there, at the rooms Yolande has been fearfully given by the Poitiers council. A sleepy maidservant stands wobbly at the entrance, alert for the Duchess's whims. Yolande points to the fire and

Jehanne helps the poor girl get it started, while Yolande starts to unfurl pieces of paper on her dressing table.

"Do you know what this is?" she asks, once the fire has caught and the servant retreated. She holds up the parchment like a precious jewel.

"A map," Jehanne confirms, though it's not one she's seen or understands.

"This is Orléans," says Yolande. "Since you want to go there, I thought you might want to have a look."

Sharp intake of breath. "Have they said?"

Yolande shrugs. "So far as I can tell, you are surviving passably. Here is the cathedral," she points to a rose blot on the parchment. "Notre Dame des Miracles. This is the first gate, closest to the Loire: the Bridge Gate. The other gates are Burgundy, here, Bannier, here, and Renard close by."

"By which I will enter?" Jehanne murmurs, asking more her angels than the Queen. Until this moment Orléans a word, an image, a broken girl's face. Now a map. Now somewhere she will really go, with men at arms beside her. The clanking of armor and screaming of steel. Her hands fist. "Now, where are the English—which of these gates?"

Yolande looks at Jehanne, hard. "All of them. And they don't die, but multiply, like maggots." She reaches out and touches the girl's soft cheek. "Why do you want to be the one who crushes these bugs?"

Jehanne pales. The urge so strong. Because the noise escalates, my duchess, and I want to make it stop. We want to make it stop. Can she say that much? Or if she does, will she find herself wanting to blurt it all, to blurt the twelve-year-old in the sheep meadow pulling her own hair? Instead she points at the map, now. "This letter—this is the *buh* sound? Like Bannier?"

Yolande starts. The last conversation she expected to be having with a peasant girl, dressed in boy's clothes. Does she think herself a knight or cleric, then? "Why do you want to crown my son?" When Jehanne doesn't answer, she repeats the question. "Why do you want to be the one who goes to war?"

Jehanne looks at the ground. When her eyes meet Yolande's they're bright. "There are girls deep in the forest," she says softly. "Boys with fingers missing. When France is whole so will they be."

Yolande's hand strays to Jehanne's hair, loosens it from its loose braid. "Where does your voice come from?"

"*Diéu,*" Jehanne says reflexively, though she knows that wasn't the question and won't be believed. "With all their voices behind him." At Yolande's raised eyebrow, she adds, "You ask why I fight. They're everywhere. Some of them alive."

"Like Christiane," Yolande murmurs, now running her fingers lightly across the girl's shoulder. "Like you." She'd wondered at first, whether La Pucelle might have been through it—the kind of battle reserved for women, their bodies scarred by men's weapons. Disgraced. As shamed in their defeat as ,Alençon in his. But this girl? Christiane and the others have seen her bathe, they have told Yolande: yes, a maid. She had dropped the idea weeks ago. Until. Who is she fighting for? "What you want is revenge?" She understands revenge.

Jehanne breathes tight to keep from shaking. Can she let this stand? She reaches out and picks up the parchment, the map of Orléans. "I know about the siege of Rouen," she says softly. "I don't want rotting bodies round Orléans. The voice is clear: get the English out. Make it stop, whatever it takes." The words sound soft in her mouth, like mulled wine, though all of it true enough. The no-longer-pregnant Norman angel starts sobbing uncontrollably until a boy with bag full of rocks lifts her, carries her away. They fade into the air around Yolande, whose eyes have never left Jehanne's face.

Finally Yolande sighs and turns back to her dressing-table, retrieves another sheaf of paper. "Can you read this signature?" she asks.

Jehanne shakes her head. "I only know some . .." She bends to the paper, until the scrawls come more clearly into view. "That *buh* again . . . and that word there, like on the map." Then she looks at Yolande, a grin crossing her face unmediated. "The Batard d'Orléans."

Yolande claps, a schoolmistress. "He has heard about you, too. But mostly he is railing against the English who cut off his food."

"Tell me who," Jehanne says quietly. The tears that threatened, when Yolande asked her why, are hardening on her cheeks in the late-night cold. She stands then, a general with her troops. "Tell me their names."

Yolande sighs. "The first, and most important," she says, "is William de la Pole, the Earl of Suffolk. He was the one who murdered Rouen, and then Ivry. He knows better than anyone how to starve a city. Now he stands at the barricade, hoping to do the same to Orléans." Yolande points to the name, even though the girl's illiterate. It's always helpful, to remember who you hate.

Jehanne nods, staring at the curve that begins the last name, like an inverted J, with the loop on top. Suddenly, she wishes she'd brought her lance; something, beyond the tiny sword that never leaves her side.

The barricades around Orléans are still alight with Lenten candles.

Some soldiers, homesick, bear talismans sent by their sisters and weepy mothers; others, still healing from the last battle, are whispering prayers that they survive through Easter.

William remembers numbly when he did that sort of thing. When the victory at Agincourt seemed impossible and that bratty king Henry, now a long-dead emperor, a sheer idiot. Now he sees the tiny lights under the besiegers' barracks, and tries hard not to laugh. They call themselves soldiers, and still they need to light the night.

After all, most of what they are doing, right now: nothing. "What kind of soldiering *is* this waiting?" one young pup cried to him, just before he died.

Patience. The spider's victory. "Another few months before they get hungry enough," he told the boy. Hungry enough to listen to him, to open their gates to his lords. To Bedford and Burgundy, who are right now both asleep in their own beds, not pissing on themselves in some fucking barracks, like these boys. He's as tired as that boy was, of these penny battles. Part of him does want to ask, when do they roll into Bourges, go to Chinon, and burn the Dauphin out? Not the way it's done. We'll make Charles *want* to kiss my fine wide ass, says Bedford.

At fifty-three, William Poole, Earl of Suffolk, is still wiry, as if years of nervy battled had burned off any spare flesh, and he's as comfortable on horseback as in his whore's bed. He spends the night on a circle round his city, his city of wood, ringing the delicate tracery of stone churches with his quickly constructed wooden towers, mini cities with bombards and platforms for archers, temporary housing for a hundred men apiece. He and Salisbury named them in a burst of irony and nostalgia: *Paris, London, Rouen.* As if anyone who made Rouen bow wants to remember that. He half-wishes his lord, Bedford, had agreed to let Burgundy have this city, whose inhabitants had shamefacedly made their cousin an offer. Bedford *is* willing to have another Rouen.

William rides between his cities now, still proud of how they've held up, how relatively few English corpses lie under them. The sentries still awake wonder at the old man's wide-awake calm. If he sleeps he dreams, he tells them, "and dreams are a drug from Hell."

By dawn he is at "Paris," a barricade newly re-constructed, after the pathetic French attempt to cut off their Lenten food.

God knows they need it, though now that Lent is nearly over his stomach gasps after some flesh. He's greeted by sleepy sentries and by Thomas of Scales, his fellow commander, who rubs his eyes and bids his girl go back into hiding. "Good morning, then!" Thomas is taller than William, with still some flecks of black in his gray hair: he offers Suffolk a piece of bread, as he shrugs into chain mail. "I hear a frog messenger is coming our way, with some word from the king of Bourges."

When Colet de Viennes arrives, he's damp with sweat and holds his lips quite still, as if such news might really be in his quiver. *"Bon journee, Monsieur de la Pole, de Scales."*

"Good morning, tired herald." Suffolk grins at the circles under the excited herald's eyes. "What news has you trying so hard not to smile?"

"My news," says de Viennes, "comes from someone of whom you have only heard rumor. I bring a letter from Jehanne La Pucelle." He does smile, now. He saw this letter dictated, heard the unexpected choirlike voice declaim its words. As he unrolls the parchment, he wonders if he can echo its power.

"King of England, and you, duke of Bedford, who call your-self regent of the kingdom of France." It's Suffolk's turn to suppress a grin, to swallow his belly laugh in respect for the messenger's long ride. "And you, William de la Poule, and you, Sir Thomas d Scales, who call yourself lieutenant of the aforesaid Duke of Bedford . . ."

"And he begat Adam who began Cain who begat Jesus Christ. Get to the point!" De Scales mutters, loud enough for de Viennes to hear.

"Render your account to the King of Heaven." De Scales does laugh then, and hard; de Viennes ignores him and keeps reading. "Surrender to the Maid, who is sent here from God, the King of Heaven, the keys to all of the good cities you have taken and violated in France. She has come here from God to proclaim the blood royal. She is entirely ready to make peace, if you are willing to settle accounts with her, provided you give up France and pay for having occupied her." De Viennes carefully raises his voice with each word or so, and gets the result he anticipated; groundlings of all sorts, soldiers and camp followers, have filled the space between Suffolk and the bombards, just as Jehanne had hoped. "And those among you, archers, companions-at-arms, gentlemen, and others who are before the city of Orléans, go back to your own countries, for God's sake. And if you do not do so, wait for the word of the Maid who will come visit you briefly, to your great damage."

Suffolk turns, noticing the same as de Viennes, and shouts, "Go back to your breakfast! This foolishness means nothing to you. This is just the brat prince's latest *amusement.*"

No one moves: as still as a church service, even the morning doves and rabbits seem to be listening now. "If you do not, I am commander of the armies," says de Viennes, "and in whatever place I meet your French allies, I shall make them leave it, whether they wish to or not. If they do not, I shall have them all killed. I am sent from God, the King of Heaven, to chase you all out of France, body for body."

"Enough!" De Scales finally stands now, and marches over to the herald, shouting to his troops, "Desist! How many of you are armed for today? How many of you are ready to destroy another garrison? Why are you listening to a girl's tantrum?" He holds out his hands until de Viennes, cowed, extends the parchment.

"More of the same, the same, more God, she will make the biggest uproar in a thousand years. If we give in, than this becomes a holy city." He looks like he might destroy the note, but instead hands it to Suffolk, ignoring protocol. Ignoring de Viennes entirely, in fact: the hard-working messenger might not exist. They don't even notice him turning his horse around, his fleur-de-lis banner a mere ripple in the dawn light.

Suffolk scans the parchment, slowly: while he learned to read as a schoolboy, this French is knotty and strange to him still.

Latin, yes, the old French-English, yes, but this? He recognizes easily *Roy du ciel,* and the threat, *tout occire,* all will be killed. What bloodthirsty girl talks like this? Has she grown the dauphin's lost testicles? *corps pour corps.* Body for body. Till the last.

Finally he gets to it, *at aux horions verra on qui ara meilleur droit de Dieu du ciel.* "Bring her on!" he roars to de Viennes. "She says, 'we will see who has the better right from God.' Does she forget Agincourt, where God slayed ten thousand of your knights? The sieges of Verneuil and Rouen? Let the cunt come, with her crosses and her prayers and your drunken soldiers. We'll flay them like the herrings they are."

De Scales laughs, agreeing. "Come in and we'll have an honest breakfast."

Suffolk nods, waving off the remaining groundlings who are still craning their necks, wondering about this latest theatre. *Corps pour corps.* The promise haunts him. How does she mean to do this? Does the Dauphin have something hidden under the Lorraine girl's skirts?

He looks across the Loire, at the calm-seeming hills beyond the barricades. He tries to imagine the girl's army. And perhaps it's his sleepless night but he imagines an army full of bloody stumps and tired camp followers, holding as weapons the embers of their burned homes.

eight

THE OLD MAN pushes against gravity and wins, one more time. Waking up is an enterprise not unlike church, when you're an old man of sixty years.

He pulls himself off his pallet and stretches, grimacing. Stepping into the small alley, he picks up the firewood piled nearest the north corner. Time to chase off the late-spring chill in this, the little building that's his tiniest of domains. The public house he's run since he was twenty shows the same signs of age, and has to be coaxed every day from the verge of total decline. Just like his city, under siege for what feels like years, now.

Auguste Blanchard's weapon has been strapped to his back so long that there is a dark stripe on his right shoulder, from sleeping on it; it nearly replaces the arm he lost ten years ago. Sixty or no, he's tussled with the English enough to salve his pride, lately. "I showed those damned chevaliers a thing or two," he likes to tell his patrons, his troops, the militia of his town and his heart.

Most of them are nearly as broken down as him; they've spent years with the name of Orléans carved into their tongues. Some of them, like him, have lost limbs in her service.

Auguste pours wine into one of his spare cups, lets it warm his insides. He's three times the age of that interloper the Batard, and remembers Azincort like an untreated toothache, like a greasy hangover, like a stubborn dream that he can't shake. A dream of swimming in mud, not unlike the mud at his feet now. And unlike: in the dream it fills the air, his mouth, mixes with blood.

His reverie is interrupted by hoofbeats in the alley: this early? It can only be, and is, the child-man who's just joined his militia, a welcome infusion from some lost vein. And he's right: the young man approaching is far younger than he was then, and has that strappy energy that says he's never yet killed a man but isn't afraid to.

"It's morning again, *mon vieux*!" the boy half-sings, a loaf of fresh bread under his arm like another sword. "Can you believe it?"

"Believe what?" Auguste takes the loaf from him, as expected, and trades it for another cup of wine. "That the English have left?"

"No!" The boy's eyes widen. "You *have* been sleeping long. She's here! With her knights, her pages, and a confessor —the one my mother sent!" The words tumble out now like a water-fall, or the breaking of an old crusted dam, lingering for a millisecond on the words *ma mére*. His mother. His sister. This is a family event to him.

"How long now," Auguste asks, "since you saw her?"

Pierre Darc dismounts, finally, and follows Auguste back into the pub. "Who? My mother —when I last visited Domrémy , not six months ago. My sister?" He looks at the low ceiling of the dark public house. "I would say a year and a half, and God's calendar would confirm me. I would say eter-nity, and my own memory would support it. But *mon vieux,* I have just seen her and I can tell you the truth: she has never left me."

Auguste groans: a man in love. "Don't speak so about your own sister. Can you help me start a fire?"

Orléans opens to her like a spring flower in a drought: limp, begging for rain. Even the prayerful mobs seem enervated, distrusting hope.

Jehanne rides beside Pierre, who rides Le Lune's sire, a sturdy old warhorse.. The crowd grows, chaotic, groping for salvation. Inside she's slow, uncertain how to move.

The braided voice chides her. *Smile, wave, this is the new theatre,* this La Pucelle celebration, not unlike the Poitiers masque. The same: just as dependent on *le dé mentir.* Except what lie? God as code. No words to them for the girls and boys. Let the *dé* suffice. The same to the soldiers.

The further in from Burgundy Gate, the narrower the streets seem: all filled with bony bodies. On her other side, on her best horse, rides the tall priest, the one Isabelle loves, given to her like a bauble. He looks like someone just broke his heart, or else bled him till his Provencal skin turned blue. Useless, she thinks. It's not that cold.

Of course, she's not cold because of her new false skin: her favorite gift from Yolande, her white-iron suit. The smooth armor encloses: bakes her skin. Hot when they molded it to her body. Hot as the sheep meadow, or one of Isabelle's new cakes. White not for color, not for purity of soul but purity of form and function: no decorative shapes, no tiny cathedrals on the shoulder, just power.

What's unexpected: she loves it. It's her shell, protective, Jehanne as beetle. It weighs more than she does. It also hides her body from the merciless sunlight.

Nearby is the Tourelles, the nearby tower where the English lurk high above, as if suspended in some demented heaven. From it words flow toward her, English word-sounds: sick music. Even the words she knows. *Prih-tee. biche. Ho-er, Wiche.* The curses of their groundlings are kisses, soft murmurs, puppies in her burning hands.

Groundlings curse, knights brood by stealth. She's seen them rarely, the leaders: Classidas, de Scales, de la Pole. Their slap across her herald's face.

De la Pole she knows best, fears most. She made the Batard point him out, a huge statue in his rusty box, like a demon from an altar-tableau. Quiet as a cathedral: or a sleeping-draught. He makes her want to scream into his silence. But she doesn't hate him yet.

Who she hates: the Batard: this weak priest. The Batard knelt when he saw her the first time, and soon enough spat on the ground. Only Alençon can talk to him. She can trust Alençon because he is so close to her age, and because he has already died once. he could almost be one of her angels. Not the other: big blond baby, the Dauphin's mirror with a fouler mouth, who knows nothing but how to kill. *Don't lie to me.* The braided voice insistent, blocking up her ears, reminding her: she has to contend with him.

The Batard's off to Blois now, with Dolon. With Pierre's new friend, Gilles, the maréchal who taught Pierre the lance. He'll come back with double the army, claims the blond bastard.

She looks beyond the crowds and the delicate church towers, fixes her eyes on the siege barricades, dead cities around the dying city. She can't sleep here. English puppies in their wooden towers, like lesions on the skin of Orléans. The people kissing her feet can smell them. She wonders if they are all real, or if angels have slipped in among them.

"La Pucelle! Over here, over here!" She turns: a young man with his trousers down waves his penis, his tongue out, drunken or suicidal. Part of her wants to kill him, another to laugh: at least he doesn't think Merlin sent her. She asks her horse to lower so she can touch him, planning to burn him a little, like the soldiers at the gates of Vaucouleurs. Instead her standard, not Catherine Royer's homegrown but a silk banner made for her at Blois, alights at the edges, and the crowds recede. She reaches back then and cups the burning silk in her hand.

Murmurs around her: "*Quelle miracle.*" She closes the gorget over her face, to hide her laughter.

After the procession is over and her armor shed, secured safely in the home of her host, Jacques Boucher, duke's treasurer, Jehanne declines dinner with Alençon, pleading a need to pray. To be alone, to think, without knights and priests. Even that rebellious statement is a lie. The side she can't leave is her brother's.

Pierre leads her down side alleys of the city, where bakers and archers drink. As far as conceivable from the scholars who plagued her at Poitiers. Pierre has lived here long enough to smuggle her in, "it's just as well you look such a boy."

He doesn't mean it. Rarely has he been as aware of his sister's breasts, her woman-voice. The Jehanne in his mind all this time, as he found his way here, was the lean ten year old, or even the flattened twelve year old crying against soldiers: not this soldier herself, leaning on her lance and laughing, deep in conspiracy with a knight just out of prison.

Still: brother and sister jump on one another's sentences:
"You saved the banner—"
"—they made it for me in Blois. I had to, I need it for—"
"—for the battle so they know who you are. Especially—"
"Talbot. And La Pole or whatever he's called—is he as . . ."
"As ugly as he sounds? Worse!"

As they make their way down a narrow street, he shouting behind her, their words overlap, as if they were arguing a tight point in a game.

Cities still alien to her: close, suffocating. Jehanne feels so much younger here. Teach me what you know, Pierre. Where are the slugs? What are your dreams? In this moment she wonders if their years of estrangement ever happened. His body learning war, her voices exacting it.

Now he takes her to a tavern, the last place anyone would expect La Pucelle. But here no one is following, calling "Pucelle!" either in taunt or worship. Instead she nods silently, as instructed, when the one-armed old man hands her a brew, listens as he slaps Pierre on the back: "We'll have a victory now, eh?" When Pierre points to his boylike companion, Auguste's eyes widen, but he neither prays nor bows. "Praise, mamselle," he mumbles as he shuffles off.

Jehanne relaxes then, wrapped in the night, grateful to escape the crowds. She's pleased to have escaped that priest, too, she tells Pierre.

"He's handsome all right," Pierre says, lifting a glass to his heedless lips. He knows he's grown far too fond of the rough brew this tavern puts under his nose. "You see why *maman* has been in love with him all these years."

"Pasquerel? Like a girl," Jehanne freezes at her own disparaging word. Did she just say that like a curse? She carries boys and girls under her skin. She doesn't need one dressed like a priest.

Which reminds her. "Did you marry?" while she was off in Vaucouleurs, in Chinon learning to split trees with a lance? She knows he's been back in Domrémy at least once. And his jaw lined with near-beard tells her how long it's been since those searches for slugs.

Pierre nods, a touch shamefaced. "Sylvie Bert," he whispers, like a secret.

Jehanne nods in turn, knowing why. "You couldn't wait, so now she does. And weeps." She closes her eyes, prays Pierre's death won't slam against them, or worse. "You'll have *bonne enfants,*" she says softly.

In the six months since Domrémy Pierre has thinned down, hardened, with muscled arms and skin toughened by cold. His flaxen hair (which stayed blond long after Jehanne's darkened) now runs past his shoulders. He looks healthy enough to sire a brood, and just might, he thinks. Including a few bastards along the way, but he doesn't want to talk to his sister about that.

He nods when Auguste puts down bowls of pottage: the dense stew of peas and shredded vegetables a feast to his empty gut. Jehanne, who ought to be starving, stirs hers absently and goes silent.

He's lost her after all, he sees now. As the sun goes all the way down her eyes look past him, over the tavern walls and beyond. It's as if night has claimed her, as surely as she walked Jacquot's groves.

"Dolon will be looking for me," she says softly. "And Alençon." And the angels, who've settled in right now on either side of Pierre, one large and throat-scarred, one tiny and staring, like little Francine from St.-Remy.

Now it's Pierre she hasn't found a way to tell about them. Pierre, if you hadn't left me behind you might know them. They're growing in number now. Sometimes she can barely hear Alençon for all their buzzing. How do they plan to help her deliver their victory? *God will deliver,* she said at Poitiers. meaning them, meaning her. who? And where are the girls of Orléans, the ones who didn't escape to Régine's camp? She misses Régine most of all.

Pierre is looking anxious now: she feels sorry for him, suddenly. How can she tell him what she's thinking? Maybe he can help her anyway. She reaches across the table, taps Pierre's shoulder: "*Mon frère*—I need your help."

Pierre grins. "At your service, *mademoiselle.* How many troops should I gather by sunrise?"

Jehanne starts to grin back. "The *ribaudes.* When can I meet with them?"

Pierre's eyes widen: Sent by God damaged by soldiers and she wants to meet the army's whores? "I thought you said to gather the soldiers." The last thing he expected, this.

Jehanne's smile impenetrable now. It *has* been a long time. "All of them, *bien homme*, all of them." She raises her untouched glass to his and grins. "*Tout cela.* God's works are our mysteries." God as code: to Pierre too. She starts to chuckle, then to laugh, a murmur deep in her throat that opens up to a deep alto bark: open, infectious, trembling.. Echoes skitter across the tavern, boom in the owner's basso, lurk in the moans of the pigeons on top of the tavern's low roof. The old men at the other tables try not to stare. Her angels laugh too, some of them.

A few hours later, she waits for him at the doorway of the Boucher house, watching the sun rise shyly on the siege walls. They're taller than anything else, besides the cathedral. She hasn't slept.

All night she knelt in her bedroom as always, waiting for word from her *petites generales.* They prefer to appear these days in a gauzy film over her eyes, rather than in substance. Too many others. Not a tall ravaged man but a cold wind that is him and the twelve boys behind him. Not a little girl behind a raped barn but a cheek, a giggle, a damp hand in hers: blood? They are all pleased: she's here, time to move. She howled at the Batard that they can't wait, but he doesn't understand her code. How could he have led her past, around, avoiding the English she came to fight? It was when she asked that he spat at the ground.

For he has carefully not let her near where it counts. Jehanne's presence, like Pierre's, has come in spite of the siege, not initially as a challenge to it. Her entry, from Tours via Blois, doesn't mean the people of the city are eating, or that the wounded are healing any faster.

She bites her tongue, thinking of it. This way, she's already set to fail the test so carefully set out for her by the judges at Poitiers—who told Charles VII, finally, not that she was definitely sent by God but that she might be, that victory at Orléans would be the test, that God *might* want her to have an army. Mealy words from rich mouths spitting out dead Muslim bones. Entrusting her to this man who doesn't trust her.

Nonetheless they've bet much on this initial gamble: the white iron gifted by Yolande, her seven horses and two heralds, the bishops and knights and tousled foot soldiers. Even the lodging in such a relatively grand home as Boucher's: no ten to an inn now. Yet she misses those odd nights.

She misses Poulengy, de Viennes, even Larcher. She's grateful for Dolon and de Metz's remaining, and pleased that Pierre gets on with her men as well as she had guessed. This morning, he and de Metz help corral her troops so she can speak to them.

Melted snow means mud, slowing them and her down. They sit in clumps, small groups on the dried mud, eating crusts of stale bread. She feels the way she did when she first arrived at Régine's camp, faced with the same task: listening, convincing these bored scared soldiers. Rough boys like the ones who scared her once. White haired fathers who could be Jacquot. Their accents mystify her, as does the excitement that leavens their mistrust. Daring her.

What do they see when they look at her? A sister, a mother, a soldier? She needs them to become a blanket, woven with her, into her back: spread over France and suffocating the noise. The thought, she thrills to realize, not a directive from the braided voice. She, Jehanne, is dreaming this war.

At first, she moves from small group to small group, asking questions. "Born in Poitiers? *Tres belle* . . . How many children?" She tries to block the angels lingering in their laps, evade their memories: but how, especially with the Orleannais? The screaming of steel. Her blood warms. When France is whole: We will. Code words as powerful as *le dé mentir*, and maybe as hollow. The braided voice under her skin calms. The soldiers are stripped of ghosts, *l'armée sans fantômes*.

Still she's exhausted before she's talked to twenty, and there are five hundred of them. Besides, the sun will soon finish rising, exposing them all. She gestures to de Metz and he helps her re-mount her horse.

Once seated she lifts her sword, the one she found at Fier-bois, sent for the same week they molded her iron. On it, as she remembered, five crosses, now free of the rust that had molded the sword to the altar. There is, next to it, carved JHESUS MARIA, just like on her standard. She should have it dyed into her skin, the ultimate *dé mentir*, the god lies indeed.

She hopes all the talking hasn't closed her throat. She murmurs to herself like a chorister preparing for Mass, and raises the sword as high as her farmgirl arms can stretch. "*Bon journee!*" she calls, her voice not choir but high priest. "Prepare to liberate this place!" She tries to ignore the laughter bubbling up in corners, not least from her angels.

Jean Pasquerel is on the scene late, in both body and soul—and not just this morning.

Some kind of river pestilence has seized his stomach ever since he and Jehanne's mother returned from Puy-en-Velay. And Isabelle's daughter is far harder than he expected: swathed in her voices and stressed by weeks of interrogation, she's told him bluntly she's "had enough of priests." Why is he here? instead of tending to his convent, his wounded flock?

Because he keeps promises: because the word from Domrémy's priest, via Isabelle, is that her voices really are from God; because he can't leave this girl un-confessed before battle. What kind of test does *he* have to pass, with her? and why does he feel he's already failed it?

He looks over at Alençon, also here late—he'd uncharacteristically let himself sleep. The golden knight a touch like Jehanne himself, not in his looks but his nightmares. His confession poured into Pasquerel like a well-worn tale, no longer mindful of how it scorches. He's dead already, he says. "At Vernueil. It's why they say I'm fearless." Still he's far more tractable, interested in confession than the woman Pasquerel is supposedly here for.

Tonight, at vespers, he'll ask his patron saint Francis for clarity. Should he go back? Right now his task is to follow, not get caught too much in the mud Alençon's steed is kicking up before him.

When they finally arrive at the soldiers' camp, sunken a mile or so east of the Burgundy Gate, what they see is both mesmerizing and a little frightening: rough-hewn soldiers with half-destroyed weapons beating those same weapons on the ground, and chanting in union like a group of demented monks from the days of Pope Gregorius. "*La-poo-cell! La-poo-cell! La Pu-celle!*" The woman astride her horse, swathed in armor, looks simultaneously older and much younger, like a young girl newly in love. Pasquerel can see she's suppressing a grin.

When she sees them, she waves to quiet the mob of soldiers, as if embarrassed, and rides over to the duke and the priest. "Good morning, my fair duke. Good morning, Father."

Alençon sees it in her face: her first command. The best drink and food there is. Mobs shout your name. The feeling indescribable. The girl's back is erect, her shoulders thrown back, her eyes clearer than he's seen before. That sugar in her veins. His first at thirteen, when a grown man first knelt to him and said "my lord." At sixteen when he first went to war in the Battle of Broussiniére. before he knew. War as sport. He sees it in her happy fist, is she really a girl to have such glee?

Pasquerel is looking for the fear he knows must be there

somewhere. Unless Isabel lied. But he saw it before: it's why she's been so stiff with him, he thinks. Seeing him, knowing he knows Isabelle, flicks open scabs long-healed. He doesn't blame her. He wonders if he should just retreat to Tours, and she find another confessor.

Alençon waves to the troops then, calls out: "To your positions!" but they just keep chanting, until Jehanne reaches for the duke's hand and raises it next to her own. She shouts, her voice hoarse: "My fair duke speaks aright! We'll fight together soon enough!"

It's to her voice, not his, they finally disperse. A few make comic turns of it, chanting nonsense syllables as they go: "*Tout cela, tout cela, ha ha ha ha. Hi ho hi ho ha ha ha.*" Like those helping her father in the orchards. Except they turn on her voice.

She lets the glee hit her blood, finally. The braided voice thrills, is affirming for once: *well done, ma petite Pucelle.* not a *pucelle* not some anonymous virgin but a Pucelle, La Pucelle, the icon the soldier. Poo-cell. She breathes it in: seventeen years old, numb from the waist down and now armed with a thousand swords, their swords. the clanking of *her* armor. The screaming of *her* steel. The noise will abate, and fall before her noise. When France is whole.

She tells Alençon she wants to get closer to the English forts. He protests: "Dunois comes back tomorrow!"

Exactly her point: the Batard would block her. Will block her. Already has. The braided voice insistent: *now.* a stab in the gut, to remind her what they mean. What they can do. That flash in Chinon: *how we will win.* The elation fades just a touch.

Alençon looks at her again: hopeless. She's high with it, all right. And who knows: she could be right. "First, let's go back and get a few reinforcements and some sustenance," he says. "Have you eaten yet today?"

She stares at his irrelevance. The English are taking her

measure, her angels are pressing at her, and he wants to eat? But the words fill her mouth with saliva, and she shakes her head.

"We should at least get you some beer," Alençon says quietly, "after all that shouting to your troops.."

Her troops. She smiles again.

Dreams are a drug from Hell.

William Poole knows why he said that, now, his body having finally seized sleep despite him. With all these troops massing at the word of the Dauphin's whore, he's never wanted this exhaustion less. God gives even the bad dreams, his confessor says: listen to them. He can't do it. In any event his confessor is dead, delivered after sixty years of pronouncing last rites. His dreams were probably of corpses telling him to come home.

Suffolk's are far more coded. Especially since she came. She's in them all, now. Her armor, her white iron like a statue, seems to him some woman-fantasy, generous breasts narrow waist. Designed to raise his temperature and drive him into some handy camp follower. But in his dreams her mouth is full of blood. He can't wait to see her face.

He wants most of all to be free of this drag on his limbs, the slow drain dreams leave long after he's dressed and making his rounds. His men notice it too, offering him their bread and water, though Scales has grown sick of it and just waves him over.

"They're coming, my friend," Scales says without preamble.

Suffolk starts. For a moment he thinks Scales means the troops the Bastard is rumored to be bringing, and wonders why everyone is as slow as he. Is Scales waiting for him to give the order?

But "they" are a small group, perhaps a dozen, clad only in *jaseran*, armor made from tiny plates that give soft music as they move. No white iron today for La Pucelle, her head uncovered except for a hood.

"It's her!" "The witch!" "The Bastard's girl!" The shouts of his men drown out the song of the *jaseran*, answered by similar shouts from her squire and other horseman. The show gives time for his eyes to seek out the important figures: first a squat knight in raw iron and then the girl, quite literally, of his dreams.

The color is high in her cheeks and her eyes are clear: he doesn't think he's ever seen a woman whose eyes didn't automatically drop at the sight of him. Or recoil, but not this steady glare. Is there blood in her mouth? No, but instead a shout, like a well-trained priest in a drafty cathedral: "You haven't yet answered me!"

Answered her? Oh, her letter, full of French invective. Like answering a gravestone. The document until now just as in need of an actual reply. *Corps pour corps.* Since she sent it scores of hers dead here. Does she know that? His arms sluggish again, he still shouts something back, hoarse and weak to his own ears. Scales, beside him, does better, his voice huge enough to fill Notre Dame Cathedral. "Go home and make your prince's babies!"

Her hands fist, small silver weapons. Her eyes do drop now. then look off, quite as if she's looking for instruction. This is the God moment, Suffolk supposes. She says something to the baby knight, drowned out by the noise, and they move away, toward his London, his Rouen. Suffolk doesn't bother to follow them. The girl just wants to play. Let his lieutenants do their jobs and his clerics pronounce curses. As soon as she's out of sight, Suffolk is going back to sleep.

Beside him, Scales stirs suddenly. "That knight he's not supposed to be here!"

"What do you mean?"

"That griffin. Just now released by Clarence. Only half-ransomed—he agreed not to fight us."

Suffolk starts laughing then, quietly at first, then as if some illness had struck him. "He's not supposed to be here? And where on earth do you imagine *you're* supposed to be?"

Office des lumieres. Hora incensii. Vespers: torches: they inaugurate the night. Even when she was little its magic held her, even in Domrémy's little wooden hovel of a church, where too many fires might inflame the altar-tableau. Then when night became the only safe moment, vespers was hers. Father Guillaume taught her the Magnificat first of all, and it was she at twelve that lit those candles, before night cast its comfort and she was freer to walk the groves.

Vespers in Orléans is too staged to inflame her much, at first. The choking incense reminds her most of the exorcism attempt at Vaucouleurs.

Notre Dame de Recouvrance is a slender church, delicate, as if it's been fasting. Its iron-stone facade sits quietly inside the besieged city. It scares Jehanne a little. From the smell, she suspects dead bodies in its wine-cellar.

It's obvious that vespers was once a far grander affair here: the heavy incense, the heavier robes worn by its weary priests, one even loaned to Isabelle's pet priest. Jehanne didn't go to him before mass. Instead she sought a cursory shriving from one of the elderly Orleannais, murmuring Lorraine patois she knew he wouldn't understand into his terrified ears. Without her armor she knows her femaleness is even more blatant, doublet or no, blade strapped to her leg or no, sword in her belt or no. She wonders if her routine confession will hasten the old man's death.

Still Pasquerel does seem comfortable up there, reading the first set of Psalms. *"Defecit in salutare tuum anima mea in verbum tuum supersperavi . . . Defecerunt oculi mei in eloquium tuum dicentes quando consolaberis me?"* His voice thick with exhaustion. "My soul fainteth for thy salvation: but I hope in thy word. Mine eyes fail for they word, saying, When wilt thou comfort me?" Just like him to ask for comfort right when people are bleeding.

She's asking the same, of course, though not of the cathedral's grand ceiling or the grand paternal *Dieu*. Just ask them, crowding her now. Late angels, now whispers. Ask them for what she needs.

Which is not comfort but assistance: she knows she needs more time with those men. To make them her shield, her weapon. She hopes the braided voice will stay with her while she does.

The pew she's sitting in feels packed with them, though empty of others. The noble men and women of Orléans, the university men in thick robes and their bejewelled wives, are looking at her as the dirty Lorraine shepherdess, not as La Pucelle. Their noses as if they can smell the sheep meadow, they've left wide spaces on either side of her.

The pew thus has room for the girls, the boys, for Mariel and the Moslem girl and the ones whose pressure she can only feel. They sit next to Dolon and across de Metz and Pierre's laps. Angels' eyes meeting hers, excited, approving. Tasting hope's brandy.

She lets herself smile. They have rarely been this close to actually happy.

If only the nobles would stop looking at her. If only the jewel priest would offer her proper words of war.

Pasquerel watches her watching him. He still feels a schoolboy. His head hurts and he wishes his prayers had given him some clarity about what to do, here. But St. Francis said nothing about war, and Augustine always eludes him.

He tries not to look at the people in the front rows, whose reluctant confessions he heard this afternoon: the old priest, probably bored with them all, was grateful for Pasquerel's willing help. Now he knows too many secrets about the stout university man who wrote the letter to Burgundy, his tall wife in the gold gown who beats her servants and hates her children. Their numbed daughters silent, refusing. Perhaps they would talk to Jehanne. Perhaps, in fact, they already have.

The girl in the back row looks exultant, younger than when he met her. Less womanly, too: her hair tied behind her, blouson lying loosely on her breast, she's less a feminine symbol than the woman in white iron. Oddly she also seems less haunted. *I thought you knew what war is, Jehanne.* The last person he'd expect to be caught up in the fever. Or is it because she knows? Is he about to become captive to a teenage girl's revenge-dreams? Are they all?

Isabelle, what do you expect me to do here? "Keep her safe," the buttery woman wept into her mead, onto his shoulder. "Keep her chaste." All Pasquerel can do now is keep reciting psalm*s:* "Praeveni in maturitate et clamavi in verba tua supersperavi." *I prevented the dawning of the day, and cried: because I hoped in thy words.* He meets Jehanne's eyes then, and sees hers widen.

Isabelle told him how her daughter hates the sunlight, glories in the night. He's seen it himself, Jehanne staring out the window at moonlight, hiding from sunlight in cloaks and tears.

He continues, "Praevenerunt oculi mei ad diluculum ut meditarer eloquia tua." *My eyes to thee have prevented the morning: that I might meditate on thy words.* Jehanne's eyes brilliant now. He sees Alençon move to comfort her, and the girl shake the duke off like a stray insect.

Finally the bishop nods to him and walks to the altar, picking up the Psalterie and nodding curtly: the old man, archbishop of Reims and one of Jehanne's Poitiers interrogators, is not recovering well from the journey here. Though gentle with Pasquerel, he doesn't waste words even in thanks. He turns pages on the stiff-backed volume and launches, his voice faint in the hot-breathed cathedral.

"Benedictus Dominus Deus meus qui docet manus meas ad proelium digitos meos ad bellum," he begins. Pasquerel nearly faints. He looks over at his *petite generale,* late Isabelle's *petite prétresse.* As much as anything else, his choice a public challenge to the Maid.

Blessed be the Lord my God, who teacheth my hands to fight, and my fingers to war.

Now Jehanne's holding Alençon's hand again, her face intent, as if she were again speaking to the troops. The tears that threatened her at Pasquerel's reading spill happily down her cheeks.

Pasquerel is confused. Jehanne's rape opened the sky for God to speak to her. He has to believe that. But do those happy tears mean that God is bloodthirsty? His bishop's face is unreadable. Equally so when they say the *Magnificat,* or when he leads the nobles in the humble "*pater noster, qui es in caelis . . .* " The words every child sucks with mother's milk, dribbled out by anxious women and knights sagging in their seats. Even Jehanne is leaning against her brother, back to conspiracy. "*Fiat voluntas tua, sicut in caelo et in terra . . .*"

Jehanne swallows hard. ". . . *in caelo et in terra.*" On earth, in heaven, codes for what? In which do the angels swaddling her chest live? The questions have hopskipped her mind at every Mass since the sheep meadow: now, with that bishop staring her in the face, they splinter her head. He asked her at Poitiers: *how do you know the voice is from God?* striking at the heart of her *dé mentir.* She'd said simply, *I would like for you to hear it, and tell me anyone else it could be.* He'd likely faint instead, she didn't say. Right now she feels sorry for him. but then reminds herself: *Yolande hates him.*

Pierre squeezes her hand. He's unimpressed by the old man's bluster, even now. Pierre's limpid tenor leads the cathedral in the final "*Kyrie eleison, Christe eleison.*" Christ be with you. Jesus is a drop of tears. Jehanne almost wonders why Jesus didn't burn the Romans instead. As the last of the light dies, the torches make all the faces into ghosts: *office des lumieres.* "They're meeting us after," Pierre whispers.

At first she thinks he means her angels, and refrains from pointing out that one has been nuzzled in his lap for the entire vespers mass, her three-year-old face blotted by time. She just nods and kneels as the bishop exits the cathedral, ignoring the Orléans nobles and lightweight knights as they follow him, opening the door to a moonless night.

When the first *ribaude* sits next to her, her skinny waist pulled tighter to emphasize her large rump, she thinks it's just the church's secret colony, like at St-Nicholas or Fierbois. But then the pew fills with them: some barely older than she was at the sheep meadow, others hearty veterans older than Isabelle. Pierre has done what she asked and brought them together, for her. Her other phantom army. Why did she ask for them? Where is Pierre?

Now that she has them here, of course, she has no longer much idea why she asked. Does she want to be sure they please to the troops she just met with, as they prepare for battle, or to tell them to stay away? is she most worried they're already hurt, like the ones she met at Régine's? How exactly will *they* help her? has she, really, any idea?

Finally she simply treats them like the others, like the boys with the lances. From one to the next to the next, holding their hands, trying to memorize their faces. Katerin has a cleft palate and worries about her boy's heat rash. Marget no longer bothers to learn their names. Michéle started whoring after her own sheep meadow afternoon, when her father spat in her face. Jehanne wishes she could remove her before she dies.

Just as with the boys she's soon exhausted, and this time not so exhilarated. They remind her of what the screaming of steel can mean. Still she keeps moving from one small group to the next. Not all of them are friendly: a tiny Annabelle openly asks, "what kind of a general this is?" How can they trust a girl like her to keep their boys safe, "and with them our food?"

Then the cathedral door is opened again, by Alençon. Behind him the thunder of hundreds of horses: the sound sends the *ribaudes* flooding out the doors, excited and scared simultaneously, practically knocking the chubby knight off his horse in the process. Alençon leads a riderless Le Lune Trois by the bridle, gesturing.

Jehanne knows whose hoofbeats those are. The armies the Batard promised to bring. From Gien, from Chateaudun, from Montargis. They will want to see - not her, not Jehanne, but La Pucelle.

Pierre watches her ascend the horse, looking simpler without her white armor. Still she is less his sister than before. And he wonders about the taste of blood in her mouth and her speech. For a holy girl, she enjoys talking about killing.

The Bastard's assault on St.-Loup is already way underway when she gets there, her dreams having dragged her along the ocean floor to this place.

She never sleeps in the night let alone the afternoon but this time she did: the dream that hard, the phantom army crying for an answer she can't give. She dreams a queer exotic city raped by crusaders; now near-empty, fertilized with corpses. Not grass below, or even mud, but a fine-grained sand, like glass. Like ash. The word whispered in her ears one of abandonment: *désert*. A fireball makes day of night, something out of the Book of Revelations: children screaming with burnt skin. Ash indeed. Deep dark eyes. Make it stop. No armor no steel. Tall soldiers in queer helmets shouting flat words like the sheep meadow. Headache-producing noises, images pulsating and retreating. The ground shuddering, dissolving into tears. Make it stop.

Then finally a loud noise not from the fireballs and burned mothers: "La Pucelle!" A reedy voice, high-pitched in panic, volume taut with rage, "It's begun, mademoiselle, shouldn't we be there?"

Jehanne opens her eyes and reaches for the door. The face she expects is Alençon's, but instead it's Auguste, the tavern owner, from Pierre's militia. "The Batard is back—he's started something to protect the food he brings." The color is high in the old man's face, his jaw tight trying not to smile. "Do you think we should join him?"

Jehanne tries to shake loose the desert in her brain, let the rage at the Batard seep back in. He could have gotten a message to me. I would have slept on the ground near the English, let De La Poule insult my ass while I slept. "Where?" she finally manages. French is a foreign language in her mouth: the dream's that heavy on her sluggish limbs, her tongue.

"St.-Loup!" the old man shouts, drawing the sword from his side-holster and raising it to the low roof. His shout brings a maidservant, Louis de Coutes, and Madame Boucher herself, surrounding the veteran soldier. She turns and asks the mayor's wife where St-Loup is. "East of here." Jehanne drags her well-creased map from the folds of her doublet. The well-dressed town lady cringes at its smell, before she presses at a corner. "An hour's ride."

"Half an hour!" Auguste says. "And we're all ready to follow you! Pierre has them all at Burgundy Gate."

Pierre's name brings her chin up, rouses her tongue from its babel-haze, finally sets her adrenalin in action. Her brother knows where he is without ghosts. She trusts him more than she trusts Auguste, whose eyes are veiled by Azincort as surely as hers by the sheep meadow. She beckons Louis inside and begins the too-long process of sliding on her armor.

As she raises her arms for the breastplate, she closes her eyes to search for angels. She can feel their waiting on her skin, like a hot wind out of her dream. Desert angels. She takes a deep breath and listens to her gut, her stomach. No words except a name: an odd instruction, which she then passes on.

"We need Dolon," she says to Louis de Coutes. "And we need the priest. The tall one from Tours." She has no idea why the braided voice likes that small child in a long body. Perhaps he reminds them of Isabelle. Maybe it's her who wants him, so she can bring Isabelle to battle with her.

The English are happy occupiers, even of the smallest fortified town on record, in which category St. Loup certainly applies. Their bastide here is rickety, a child's contraption battered in battle, then turned adult-size by the catapults and reinforce-ments within the past year. It holds more soldiers than first appeared: more and more English bodies keep swarming out its sides, hurling fireballs from its top, sending floods of arrows toward the wall of French bodies pressing against them.

This attack is diversionary, meant to soak them up while desperately needed food supplies reach Orléans. No-one has died quite yet. The Bastard of Orléans has got himself a new set of armor at Blois: it makes him a moving sculpture, un-scratched, the long pieces of plate dancing across his chest as he circles his horse around. He hasn't slept in days.

Will it work? will they get through without losing anyone he needs? Have the mayor's men started to receive the bolts of thread and bags of wheat coming his way by water?

Everything's a diversion, he thinks. This skirmish a diversion so food can get to Orléans. Feeding the Orleannais a diversion so the Dauphin can negotiate their freedom from Bedford, find some subtle exchange of oranges with Burgundy to get Suffolk and Poole to return to their caves. Or else give over, surrender, so he can be free also. War as theatre, to let the bargainers do the real pushing.

But then the bitch came. The one approaching now. The smell of blood is filling his nostrils and still he imagines he can smell her. Still astonished by those iron breasts he guesses a hundred soldiers hold close in their dreams as they abuse themselves. She's not the beautiful Pucelle he'd himself imagined: too thick-waisted. Too thick-headed, too. She thinks this is real, not a puppet scene. She's going to be the ruin of them all. Behind her, and that brother of hers, is that sorry excuse for a town militia, enervated by hunger and age and rage. They adore her, of course.

Still he half-bows at her approach, moves off with her some distance from the fighting, Her face is agitated, distracted. "Good afternoon, mademoiselle."

She keeps her mouth shut, tight with rage. Her eyes search the ramparts as if she'd know the English there.

She's already a little sick: the route from Burgundy Gate to here has been a parade of wounded Frenchmen, from knights holding their armor against smashed elbow joints to foot soldiers trying to give her a brave face that effaced their missing limbs. A tall farm boy who took an arrow in one eye trying not to cry through the other. Worse than their wounds their nightmares: images of cut flesh and their own arms splitting horses. She could have spent hours with each one, especially the ones who didn't weep "La Pucelle!" but the push to this place, the braided voice's imperative, never clearer. Now that she's here, she shakes her head to clear them from it. Her own nightmare, the desert city burning its children, still smolders under it all.

Jehanne nods curtly at the Batard, and tries not to let the

battle-stink unravel her entirely. She turns instead to stare at the men he's brought back.

They've come from all across Valois France, these men, muddy and tired, the volume of their accumulated voices drowning out her strongest cry. The men from Soule are huge-bodied: what do they feed them there? They make the skinny Orleannais she brings look like branches ready to be snapped. She's glad for her armor, and grateful for the hugeness of the black steed Alençon gave her. She puts her gorget on for safety, though she hates it. The clanking of armor, the screaming of steel. She tries to reach back for yesterday's glee, push away from the desert, but the stink pushes it back in.

Dunois has let his beard shadow his face while he was away; between that and the mud kicked up by all their horses he looks a goat-herder in iron, not a young count and protegé of the Dauphin. He nods with a grim satisfaction at an English scream.

" My lady has had quite the time while I was in Blois," he shouts, again not knowing if she's listening. "What did you think you were doing?"

She ignores him, her arms tensed. With the gorget down he can't see her face, those flat blue eyes.

"I've already had thrown at me that my bitch went to see Suffolk and tried to shout him down. At least I *think* that's what they said," he stops to take a draught from his bottle. "I don't know what corner of wretched *Angleterre* spawned those boys, but they're mangling both languages."

Jehanne drops her gorget to reply. "Of course I went to see Suffolk," she says. "If it were up to you, Orléans would be in cinders before I saw that man's face and gave him notice."

"Oh my lady!" The Bastard bends at the waist in a mock-bow. "You gave him notice, eh? No wonder de la Pole is so mortally frightened. It's well known, after all, that when English are terrified they can't stop laughing." He swallows and drops his shoulders, and a little of the pose. "Seriously," he tries again, "how are you finding our fair city?"

"Exhausted," she says quietly, keeping it under the rumble of the troops. "There's nothing left inside."

A shout as a column spits out of the fort toward them, jams against his men coming the other way. He looks up at the midafternoon sun: how long has it been? Has there been enough time for the supplies? Can they retreat now? He turns to Jehanne and points to the troops she's brought. "Those men have been fighting longer than you've been alive. Most of them. It would be a damn shame to lose them now."

She glances at his face as he turns away. The shape narrow, long, the eyes set deep. She wonders if he eats, with that bony jaw.

Then a stench she knows, hates: a man's bowels loosened in death. That smell on the road to Vaucouleurs, strong as blood. Her own bowels tighten in instinctive response. Armor doesn't clank when it's pierced, it sings: explosive. Stolid faces, young faces, English pulled from some whorehouse or church to fight her. Around her Frenchmen swarm, surge, coalesce on the way down. The old men flow behind them, toward the *bastide*. Auguste, she thinks, can't wait to be dead. The men living and dead like a moving sculpture around her, fluids green and red from their mouths

The Batard shouts orders as she freezes. Till France is whole, she reminds herself. Pierre, beside her, is transformed, his face as gleeful as hers yesterday imagining. Not her, now: death makes her skin cold. She tightens her jaw against her own response: the Batard is watching her. She can't flinch at the blood now. Can't let him know she's not seen battle before, even if such an admission womanizes her. She can't flinch at the soft cries, the guttural calls as men use daggers on the stairs, the sound of battered crockery. Such sounds need become music to her, some kind of demented harpsichord issuing multiple tones.

She makes herself look at the bodies underfoot, the ones being more tenderly dragged to the side of the field by their squires. Will Pierre be one of them by the time the day's over? Her heart starts to beat faster, finally. It feels like three o'clock in the morning. Including that itchy insect feeling, the girls and boys muttering: unintelligible.

They try to remind her that this is the enemy, even if the old knights crashing out of there look like scared children in their big metal suits. Remember: they speak flattened words, tear open small girls, slice her horse in two, scream *hoo-er, wiche* at her. She can't see them now to know. But.

Amid the battle noise a shout from the Batard. Is that word *retraite*? Now? Already? With the mounds not yet cool, and the fortress still standing? She flicks her horse in the Batard's direction. "Did I hear right? You'll leave French blood here, and the bastide hardly breached?"

He acts like he doesn't hear her. Half-standing on his horse, his body is coiled, his lance an extension of his right arm. She looks at the city's low walls and thinks she sees a camp follower. The girl's hair exposed, she opens her mouth wide, looking down. Is she spitting at Jehanne, or asking for rescue? If she's calling something, Jehanne's ears are blocked against it.

Her blood heats. The braided voice is silent, mustering forces. Jehanne watches the Batard's strange troops mass beside her. She wonders if she's imagining the figures sitting behind each one, as if each had another rider. Angels on horseback, like in Revelations. One has skin the color of agate or new onyx. The phantom army is in place and about to move.

Jehan Pasquerel tries to shut his ears against the war-sounds, while he searches for Jehanne. And he tries to ignore the burning, howling pain in his foot.

He's not sure how it happened: some piece of Orléans stone

working its way into his well-worn shoe, or a wrong step on the damp spring ground. Now even on his horse, when it supports no weight, the pad of his foot is shrieking at him, demanding poultices, heated water, silence. Perhaps his foot is simply the first in his body to grow impatient: why *am* I here on this battle-field, instead of in my cool corridors at Tours? when the girl we've been sent to attend wants less than nothing to do with us? When Pierre came for him just now he nearly said to the boy, *you must have me confused with someone else.* his head hurts too, from lack of clarity: his prayers these days unanswered. met with silence and sadness.

Now he's just a little sick. All these years sheltering broken boys, girls made mute by soldiers, and he's never seen a dead body till now. The padding under their armor sticks out in strands where the blow hit, making of them bloodied dolls. Their stillness that absolute. Their smells also foreign to him. In a cloister since age eight, he's never even seen a farm animal killed, unlike Jehanne.

He can't see from here if she's exulting, the way she did at vespers: her body is rigid, her armor lined perfectly erect, but her face looks more panicked. He wishes there had been time to get a response from Isabelle to the letter he just wrote. *I'm useless to her,* he wrote. *Perhaps because you sent me, she's reminded of what soldiers did to her, at a time when she needs to lead them. I think I am going back to Tours when it's safe to do so* though who knows when *that* will be? Tours' dark halls and bustling convent a slice of heaven to him now. He's almost knocked down by a convoy of footmen retreating.

Jehanne looks behind her, looking for Alençon, and sees instead that priest. His figure seems for the first time comforting, like Father Guillaume, who knew this moment was in her skin. Now Isabelle is with her, at least, in the person of this long-bodied baby faced priest. *Maman I'm scared,* that's what the heartbeat means this time. She turns her horse to face him. Finally.

She wishes she could make him feel the crackling under her skin, the boys and girls in motion nearly as riotous as the soldiers around them. "Good afternoon, Father," she calls. Her voice comes out shakier than she'd expected, while half her attention is still behind her, trying to listen to the men at the *bastide.*

Pasquerel looks at her, trying to judge the métier of that voice as well. A teenage girl who's whelped cows, she's no stranger to blood but still. "Good afternoon —" he doesn't even have an address for her, *mademoiselle? pucelle? le petite Jehan-nelle?* "You asked for me?"

"Every battle should have —" An arrow flies over her head, crazily mis-aimed, and lands in the soft spring mud. "A priest to bless failed arrows," she finishes the sentence. They share a small laugh, breaking the surface of their not-shared rage.

Pasquerel watches her neck, her shoulders tighten. Isabelle's child, his petit generale. Awkward movements of their hands: she wants to embrace him like a father. He wants to touch her like a lover. They want neither of these things but only for the sound of steel against steel to finally wind down to quiet. Iron against wood. Blade softly sinking into flesh. The birds try valiantly to drown the noise: useless.

Then another noise, a high-pitched wail: the old man, waving his ancient lance like a talisman. "Mademoisellepucelle!" he seems to combine it all in one address, the color high in two or three points in his wrinkled face, competing with his liver spots for supremacy. "They're going! You should have seen it!"

"They're what?" She lifts herself on her horse, fruitlessly: as if she could see on the other side of the walls. Auguste waves, exultant. "Come!"

And before she can make an active decision they have surrounded her, the town militia, urging her forward through the now—breached gates. They surround Pasquerel, too, as her confessor, carry them both into the heart of St.-Loup, where they can see only the slightest flash of English armor. The iron sculpture now pushing in the other direction, away from her troops the Batard's, as if melted by the emerging sun.

"Mon dieu compattisant!" Auguste shouts as they proceed forward. "One by one they were stilled by Him. I saw them stop and look aside, as if stricken by His rage. You brought his terrible swift source, mademoiselle, I knew it would happen."

Le dé mentir, less so now? She looks down at the bodies yet un-swept, begs the braided voice for clarity. Like in the public house back in Domrémy: that stillness, just long enough to strike. What did they see? Who in her phantom army accomplished this so quickly? Her skin feels clammy, cold. She fights not to pass out, wants to ask Auguste for more details but he's forged ahead without her. He's the true happy *petite generale*. Where is her happiness? lost in the smell. She just wants to know how it happened. Then, maybe, she can enjoy their revenge.

Finally: Pierre, taking Auguste's place by her side. "Your victory, *ma soeur*." His exhilaration replaced by something quieter, darker, he keeps his tone level. She bows her head in reply.

They watch the English embankments burn for a while, then turn back toward Orléans before the populace finds out she's here and she has to endure a volley of "pucelle!" hosannas and requests for help. She doesn't know where the Batard is, and doesn't care. She only wants to do two things. She wants to confess to Pasquerel, for the first time: confess her confusion, confess her desire to know how this army she's molded is helping the other. She wants as hot a bath as can be drawn in this place. And she wants to write a letter to Yolande, a letter no scribe will dare pen. Perhaps Pasquerel will do it, for she can't herself yet. Only read and make cryptic notes in the corners of maps.

Pasquerel looks at his victorious young mistress. She looks exhausted, as if the English have been defeated by physical effort of her small body. But just as he's thinking that a grin begins to gather itself at one end of her toothy mouth and settle, half-unfurled, at the other. "*Quelle miracle?*" she murmurs, he doesn't know whether to herself or to him.

He watches her from behind, as the convoy winds its way toward the river. Her brother's face enough like hers, unhelmeted, to split Pasquerel's focus; behind them the old man, who may or may not have lost another limb, keeps up a chatter that may or may not bore her. She's the miracle, he thinks. Whether or not this victory is hers. A girl crawling home from the sheep meadow onto a horse and into white armor.

He feels a sensation in his chest usually reserved for flowers, and well-woven tapestries, and good mead. A desire not to kneel to her but tend her. He suspects he's not going back to Tours just yet. That Isabelle is right, and he needs to muddy his skirts a while longer. Even his foot has calmed, as if properly chilled by cold blood.

nine

YOLANDE IS GOING to bite her nails to bleeding, waiting for word from Orléans.

Not from Alençon, who has already written her of his safe arrival. Not from the Batard, whose last letter informed her that the girl seemed far too shrill, far too unsophisticated to be of any use, and that they should resume negotiations with Bedford. Not even from the army of scribes surrounding the girl, who cannot be trusted with more than routine battle announcements. A month now since she left Chinon and Yolande cannot believe how much she misses her. Her own daughter, wan queen in waiting, barely registers.

As the rainclouds finally lift from above Chinon, Yolande's spirits begin to follow them. Less rain means less talk, more battle, she and the girl agreed, huddled inside furs. And the bills from Tours attest that she went off well-appointed: fresh white iron, six horses, plenty of men. "There won't be anything left for my coronation!" her son wails over breakfast, as if he had expended any effort counting his fortune this past decade.

"What coronation?" she asks, dipping her bread into weak mulled wine and butter that despite all best efforts is already turning sour. "Remember who has promised you the coronation in the first place."

"You, madame," quietly, not without rancor but with truth.

Yolande drains her cup, quite as if she's trying to have a drunken night at eight in the morning. She bites down her own half of the truth, *when I wasn't busy trying to make sure you and I both stayed alive.* She points to the account-ledger that bothered him so. "Your best chance at that day," she says, "may be seeded there."

She tries to imagine him receiving the crown from the bishop as he is right now, his hair flat from grease, his skin still recovering from whatever insect recently laid waste to his left cheek. At least he's paying attention to what he's doing: this may be the best of him possible.

"La Tremoille," he then says pointedly, "thinks this La Pucelle adventure is simply a fruitless delay."

Yolande stands up then, leaving her cup on the table. *La Tremoille is a cockroach.* "We'll see who's proved right, shall we? In the meantime," she offers, "you might consider getting out of bed."

Though right now, of course, she can see his point. The castle still damp, her dress hangs heavy on her shoulders, tiring her out. And her rings feel one more pointless distraction: maybe she should gnaw at them next.

Jehanne can't stop her hands from shaking, no matter how hard she tries.

At Boucher's she kneels in a pool of wax light, watching them dance. The screaming of steel, the long spurt of blood after. Not tree-flesh but real. Her square hands with broken nails rest uneasily in her lap, make her hips shake instead. Her face is wet. The blood of France makes me weep, she told Louis de Cotes, the blood of English just applause. Did she mean it? Are her shaking hands just for her boys? All boys? Finally she braids her hands together, a classic prayer gesture, hoping it will lure any old angel to tell her how they did it.

Instead at dawn she gets screams outside her door, servants blockading a voice she knows. A young girl-voice, tart and un-quiet: a *ribaude*, one of those from the church, held back by Louis de Cotes. Jehanne opens the door and sees who it is: Marcelline, one of the youngest from that night. Jehanne tells Louis to go away, drawing the girl into the room.

Marcelline's mouth is bleeding. Victory gave her boy fire, she says. And broke her teeth. She sinks to her feet at Jehanne's skirt, and bows her head.

Jehanne finds her own bathing cloths and begins slowly to bathe Marcelline, as she remembers Durand's wife doing for her. The girl can't be a year older than Jehanne was at the sheep meadow: her breasts in new bloom, her shoulders cushioned from good mead. In the church she was one of those most defi-ant: *how are you going to help him, and me?* Now bruises on her upper arms where the boy held her down, likely after slicing an English back. *He didn't mean it,* the girl sobs as Jehanne washes her, carefully. Jehanne moves the bath-cloth slowly over her legs. In the hall beyond the servants are already busy, soldiers' heavy footsteps in the cobbled street outside.

The Orléans dawn rises over a city not much changed, despite the unexpected English retreat from their camp at St.-Loup. Suffolk easily batted away the Batard's men who swarmed at Pouair, near his Rouen *bastide,* while St.-Loup was being taken, despite the extra forces from the north and south that have shown up this week. None of the *bastides,* the wooden cities from London to Rouen, with their boulevards full of men and arms, have been touched, let alone the worst insult: the city's convent at St. Agustin, now infested with English armor. The elderly Glasdale, who Jehanne calls Classidas, late of Azincort, now glowers from the Tourelles, the city's slender guard towers The gamble endorsed by the Poitiers bishops has not paid off yet, and everyone involved knows it.

But St. Loup, that dual assault from the new infusion of soldiers and Jehanne's hailing of the local men, is the first victory in a long time, and enabled the food from Blois to arrive safely. The night after is filled with soldiers' mutterings, in English and Frankish and local marble-mouths, while mothers seize at the millet and fish-heads just arrived. Babies and old men feed, able to feast before dawn breaks on the Feast of the Ascension, when combat is proscribed. Still generals' torches stay lit, in and outside the city.

Jehan d'Orléans, the Batard, spends the night in his own bed —stealing a few hours of fitful sleep with his youngest mistress, Celié, her belly just beginning to bulge with her first child. But he's up long before dawn, trying to induce himself to go out into the still-chilly air.

He should be back out sleeping beside his men at the Tourelles, with the foreign armies. He has to get over being afraid of them, first.

Hard to admit to himself, but it's true: these Scottish giants and hairy southerners vomit his language out their toothy mouths, slap heavier armor than his around like it's nothing, and remind him too much of the English. Did they understand his orders yesterday? The Scots might as well *be* English and the ones from Soule spit out Latin, their skin already brown before the sun hits it. Yolande would know what to say to them, all of them would kneel to the Queen of Sicily. Or would they? Would they bow to her little protégée—who, they say, brought in that little ridiculous town militia and burnt St.-Loup, as surely as any conqueror?

He couldn't see what made the English bolt, but knows she did it. Small, stolid, neither girl nor boy, goddess nor witch—he saw his town militia follow her, others mill around her. Could she help with these foreigners counting their money, wondering why they should fight for Orléans?

Celié turns beside him, reaching a catlike arm to pull him back down. His baby shudders under his hand. They should fight for Orléans so it doesn't burn. Can she make them want to? Can he?

His side starts to ache again. He begins to slide out of bed, letting Celié curl around a sack instead of him. His cheeks have dried before the sky is fully light.

As dawn glimmers, Jehanne has dressed to greet the day, letting Marcelline sleep in her bed. Later she will give the girl enough *derniers* to melt away safely. *Tell them La Pucelle sent you.*

She's deeply grateful for Ascension Day, when all armies will retreat to conspire. She needs the time—not least to pull her forces into better order. To pull herself into better order too. Perhaps Marcelline's boy held her down to stop his own hands from shaking.

Jehan Pasquerel is waiting outside the Boucher house, as he promised.

The priest looks better than he has since they arrived: perhaps battle invigorates him after all. She's beginning to feel that too, feel the adrenalin again, even if the victory is mysterious. The braided voice, despite its refusal to explain, still pushes: *no time to waste.* Now a different push, spurred by Marcelline. Feast days are peace days, she reminded Pasquerel last night after she confessed to him. Now something more. *Time to clean house.*

"Do we have time before Mass, to talk a moment?"

They move into a chapel of Notre Dame des Miracles, not the big hall but a smaller, homelier one, where the altar-tableaux remind her of St.-Rémy. She starts by asking him what he knows about the Peace of God. About *chevalerie.* Father Guillaume told her stories about it when she tired of scripture, she tells him. Now that she leads an army she needs to know.

Pasquerel starts: the last place he expected her to start. She sits expectantly before him as if they have all day, her narrow jaw set tight, her blue eyes unwavering. The only sign of her sleeplessness is a slight redness in the highest part of her cheeks. From scorn to this? Tell me a story that will shape my army? He looks down at the tight fists that still her hands.

Are those fists dictated by the voice she told him about last night, at her first confession?

Like her, he's not gotten a lot of sleep. The volley of talk that slid from her, as he helped her disarm, had him praying as hard as he has since he was ten years old and decided to devote himself to God. After having to ask her, over and over, to repeat herself, for fear he was translating her words to the voices inside his convent walls, his heart began to beat a little faster, as if catching a fever. He then spent much of the night: in this chapel, asking that same God if He truly has manifested to a young girl in such a way. If the hum of dead girls and raped boys under Jehanne's skin is truly His word, or not. If He has given Jehanne a divine force in their shape, able to somehow mysteriously divert the English so her soldiers can move forward to create a new France.

Of course, to expect an immediate answer is the worst arrogance, and has gone un-satisfied. Now here she is, looking not for the Batard but for him. Declaring simply: "France's army needs a new Peace of God."

He searches for what seminary taught him, about a time much like this one, when rapine and looting marked warfare—even that in the name of God. About the knights that declared instead a code of honor, one that included leaving women and children alone and declining to torture your enemy. *The peace of God* meant dedication to God and to your king, fighting for the glory of both fighting only enemies as strong as you.

He wishes he knew the exact dictates, but it wasn't nearly as important to his order as to the Benedictines, like Jehanne's old pastor Guillaume. They held closer in their hands the councils at the millennium, the declarations by lords and bishops that swore local knights to forgo assault, pillage, and theft. As a young priest he most heard of their proscription on violating churches —and most especially about the declaration that all churches were sanctuaries where the vulnerable would be protected (thus his crammed Tours sacred space).

He looks at her, wondering where to begin: finally she prompts him, "One day the sky darkened . . ." Oh god, the Bourges story, of course, a divine eclipse inspiring the council. Something for priests to tell their foot soldier flock. Each bishop, issuing his own declarations to local knights, sometimes speaking of divine warnings: eclipses, showers of stars, hurricanes speeding their path. Each requiring quite a different pledge.

Why is Jehanne asking for this, on today of all days, when they've just shed their first blood in some time? When he himself knows that the Bastard of Orléans, among others, is looking for her and only Ascension Day is granting them a reprieve?

Finally she tells him—about Marcelline, crawling into her room with bruised hands and a bloody mouth. Her breaths grow faster, like last night. "So I cleansed her, and put her to bed. My advice pushes at me harder now—to end this. This is why —" Her face crinkles, her eyes bright, her words unusually slow. She holds up her hands, still finally. "France's army needs a new Peace of God. A new *chevalerie*."

The youth in the sentence makes him smile: an acolyte's faith, that a code derived by men, once broken, can still be fixed. The sentence itself makes him nervous. "When it was new," he says carefully, "knights talking about the Peace of God burned women and children too, if they were unbelievers—when the Church was spreading its cloak across all of Europe;" Pasquerel says quietly. "The Peace of God sent people to die in far-off foreign lands."

"Like this one?" that shattering laugh, the kind most try to hide in a box. "Good." As the word exits Jehanne's mouth her eyes widen: she didn't expect such a thing. She also can't think who said it: it doesn't feel like the braided voice. She knows she's decided that, for now, *dé dié diéu* will do well enough as a name for what pushes her. Isabelle and Father Guillaume use it, so does Pasquerel; she will too, and try not to feel it as a *de mentir.* "Still, my men need a code of conduct," she says. "And someone who will work them even harder at victory."

Pasquerel smiles again. She says this about men two or three times her age. "Who will you enlist at this?"

Jehanne smiles again. "Who will say no, to such good news?" She sits up straighter, her hands uncurling finally. She extends each arm before her, as if offering a harvest. "Perhaps the Batard will do it. Or Pierre's friend, the one who's won every battle—de Rais." She stands up then, nearly dancing from one foot to the other with her glee. "Let's find Pierre. He'll help us find the right one."

Pasquerel's still uneasy. He follows Jehanne out of the chapel, tasting transgression. "I should be preparing for Mass."

Jehanne's grin fades abruptly: a slammed door. "You're not the celebrant. Let the old Orléans priests and their faded ladies have their turn. We'll come, of course, but only after we've marched in a dozen commanders with us. This new *chevalerie* must begin with greeting our Lord properly." Another sentence she hadn't planned out of her mouth. From barely getting *dé* through her lips to this? What's false now?

The braided voice silent: she's the one deciding to weave a new world, a new order, to get this done. Her power alone. Let her angels sulk while she builds the not-phantom core. Her blood heats, keeping her awake. As Dolon and Louis hurry to catch up with her, she feels her spine snap just a bit erect.

. . .

The morning sun, when dawn finally sighs her last rose exhale, is merciless in the muddy field between the city walls and the English barricades. Men pull their capellines over their heads and wrap bandages around their red-rimmed eyes: the wounded yell against the sting of it. "It cannot be morning yet!"

Foot soldiers run like sandpipers between tents, carrying the boots of their commanders and averting their ears when clashing orders come down on them. The simple act of that many men getting up all at once to urinate is noisy enough to drown out childbirth.

The act itself, Gilles de Laval tells Pierre Darc, "might bolt the Loire."

Pierre giggles. He can't help it: it's funny enough that the day after a battle, in the midst of all this hairy stink and blood, Gilles can crack jokes at the expense of their wounded. Ever since they rode together in the entourage from Tours, Gilles has found ways to make Pierre laugh, which hasn't always been easy. He does it by making fun of his boss, Baron de la Tremoille, "who fights with the dauphin's mother-in-law like a slow, hissing cat." He does it by teasing Pierre about his quiet conquests behind his sister's back. And he does it with a use of language that makes Pierre weep, fearing his own vocabulary consists mainly of "stink" and "dig." Pierre also admires his tenacity with the long knife and the crossbow: he was the last one out at St.-Loup, pushing their advantage, once they had it, so that English blood washed what was left of the floors.

Gilles had also decided not to return to Chinon with his commander, but to stay loaned to Jehanne: a half-spy, if he chose to report. He basks in the admiration from the boy, and doesn't want to tell him why he fights so hard—because after all these years it's the only thing that makes him feel half alive. Instead he crams stale bread down his mouth and listens, with

Pierre, to the hoofbeats. On this feast day, at least they don't inspire fear.

"My sister!" Pierre scrambles, quite as if the Pope had dipped his velvet shoes in their mud. Not just Jehanne, of course; besides her is the Batard, Alençon, and their respective footmen, as well as that skinny priest Pierre thought she hated. They dismount quickly, Jehanne actually grinning as she embraces her brother. "Did you get any sleep?" he asks her.

She shakes her head slowly. "Too busy listening for voices, *mon frére.* And figuring out what we must do to prepare ourselves for the next battles."

Pierre looks over at the Batard, who clearly has had as little sleep as his sister and who's already scanning the horizon for English spies. "And what you've concocted is nice and holy, Mademoiselle Pucelle," the Batard says coolly, as if he's not paying attention. "But we need these men. And chasing away their women is not going to endear you to these soldiers one iota."

Jehanne shakes her head. "I know. But they'll do it. They'll agree to our new *chevalerie.*"

And somehow, unaccountably even to her, Jehanne goes troop to troop and obtains their agreement. She doesn't always use the word *"chevalerie"* but she always uses the word "France," a word that for many of them belongs to the past: to Charlemagne and the Capetian dynasty before the land dissolved. She tells them their women are going away for a while. And she tells them, these foreign armies, that they're fat and lazy, "too liable to drop over the edge of an English broadsword." And no one laughs at her, or leaves the field, though some of them do seem a bit stunned.

Pierre's mouth drops open: what has his sister been drinking? thinking? She was sitting with the *ribaudes* only a few days ago, now wants to drive them away? What has her voice told her? He follows her at a distance, watches her calm almost-cheer as she speaks to each group, her voice growing hoarse. Jean Pasquerel, beside him, says quietly, "So this is how you make an army."

"Not any I've led," says the irrepressible Gilles.

Finally she rejoins them, her eyes clearer than before, her breath moist. "Shall we to Mass? Our Lady ascended to heaven today—let's make a good showing before Orléans' nobles, eh?"

She doesn't get to talk to the *ribaudes* until the sun is nearly set, until she is beginning, just a little, to sleep on her feet. Her angels returned to her at Mass, slipping in between Alençon and the Batard, breathing down Pasquerel's unsuspecting neck. They kissed their approval of her new plan, to create order, to make of such disparate groups of men one smooth scythe to harvest a new France. The plan calms her stomach, stops her hands from shaking quite so much.

She also felt them in the high hall of the Batard's quarters, sharp-edged reflections in the dark wood of the Duc d'Orléans' best table. The Duc himself "in an English prison writing poems," the Batard barked as he rolled a map across the table. In addition to her, de Rais, and Alençon all the local commanders line the table's sides: de Gaucourt, de Xantrailles, La Hire. The strategies shot back and forth across that map like play-balls or painless arrows, like her and Pierre interrupting each other, words and places new to Jehanne as well as the familiar ones. "Not Agustin, yet," de Xantrailles growled. "St.-Loup was a piddling outpost. Agustin is another story."

"I remember taking communion at St. Agustin," the Batard murmured to no one in particular, bending to the map.

"But Agustin first, before we can hope to take on their wooden towers," de Rais murmurs, his fingers on the fading *A* bearing heavy, ancient rings. The *A* is her newest letter. Sometimes curved, an open mouth, like the sound it makes: some-times a castle's point. She traced it on her knee.

"De La Pole will definitely make an appearance," de Gaucourt shakes his head. "I fear it will take more mettle than our men yet have—including me."

Jehanne nodded, a proper acolyte of war; then she pulled her cape closer, trying to look as tall as she felt on a horse. A heavy angel in split armor helped her stiffen her back, project her voice, and remind them both of two assets they'd not had last fall. The first: the new *chevalerie* they were striking like hot iron. The other spoken by the heavy angel, lifting her voice louder and stronger: "La Pucelle is here. My advice will tell us when to strike." It seemed to help, but she's never felt so small as when she said that to de Rais' belt buckle. And the elder commanders still glanced away from her curved armor. Sometimes she just wants to cut off her breasts.

And now, after the Batard has hosted supper and the last mass been said, she stands in the courtyard of Jacques Boucher's home, trying not to let her eyes close. The courtyard is filling with women, seen more clearly in this twilight than in church a few nights ago. They're shy with her at first, and mistake her looking in the distance for a vision. But every few minutes, her eyes glue closed, and. another *desért* dream steals in: no dry sand but wet green, a deep forest dream, with louder noises than she knows: like huge cannons punctuating the night.

It takes all her strength to open them again, take a deep breath, and begin. She holds tight to her angels as she tells the girls they have to leave: Alençon and Pasquerel bar the door, at the ready to escort the *ribaudes* away one by one. She tells them about Marcelline, and promises they'll be safe.

"That lying puppy!" The voice is of one of the oldest of them, a woman with a bearing not unlike Regine's. She never came to the church: Jehanne would surely otherwise know her crusted voice and still-red graying hair. She turns Marcelline's name to a curse, quickly. "That black liar! She'd rather wheedle a cut of bread from you than cut it herself. She waves that tight little ass in front of the most well-fed man in the room. And now she's ruined it for all of us!" The woman's gesture a half-fist.

Soon Jehanne is surrounded by tears and curses, a number of dialects incomprehensible to her, so she has to keep checking these are human voices.

"You don't know what you're doing," says Katerin, the blond waif who reminds Jehanne of her sister. "This won't help you win this war. The English have their girls, and they stay strong."

Jehanne takes her hands, swallowing hard. Could Katerin be right? But she feels, from no source but her own gut, that to forge this weapon she needs to keep all things soft apart, in some other, safer place: her men need to be hard. The clanking of armor and screaming of steel: *pure,* calm. She breathes in the braided voice, affirming, but tears still wet her cheeks. "Till France is whole," she says, like an incantation. She reaches for her sword, the one with the five crosses, and raises it as if rousing troops to battle. She knows it's dangerous when she's this tired.

The sword heats, it almost glows. She knows what's happening and so do the women, who draws back just a little. "That fire in her hands," one *ribaude* hisses to another.

As night falls, the courtyard empties: slowly. Like a migration. She's frightened for them too but she has to swallow it. She embraces the ones who will let her do it, who don't spit in her face when she speaks of France. But most of her mind is already on her next task: to write her next letter to the English and tell them that the world has changed. Her fingers itch. She cannot wait to sign her name: the only word she can yet write.

The Tourelles fortress, across the Loire from the Bridge Gate, is an odd spot for an occupying force. Its delicate towers, built before Azincort rendered France moot, were built for pealing church bells as well as a city's defense: likely also for the Duke's spies, which is why they are the perfect spot to have been rendered ugly by forts of earth and stone. These twin *boulevards* are each crammed full of soldiers and artillery, mirror armies snarling at each other not a mile apart. High above, the fortress also offers a real bed to elder soldiers like Sir William Glasdale, who since Azincort has nearly always slept on worse.

The early dawn softens the city, Glasdale thinks; it gives even the sloppy *bastides* a certain grace, and makes the river huger, more mysterious. From the top of the towers, Glasdale can also see the shards of the bridge the Orleannais destroyed themselves, to stop the English from crossing the bridge into the city. Early sunlight makes the gray stone purple.

Behind the Tourelles fortress another *bastide,* larger and more full of gunpowder and footmen, separates them from St. Agustin itself, the former convent and monastery at St Agustin, now eviscerated, housing even more men.

Ever since the defeat at St.-Loup, the convent and the Tourelles have filled even more with English soldiers, evacuated from *bastides* far smaller than 'Paris' or 'Rouen.' If the Orleannais will persist in defying their true rulers, will raise this ridiculous army led by a witch, they will pool their far superior forces just across the river from the walled city. From these towers he will give the order, as soon as Bedford grants it, to end this charade.

Meanwhile from the towers he can watch the fort they've planted by the river. He's seen the witch as she raises Satan's cross, ensnaring men like puppies in weak armor.

His wet nurse told him about witches, whispered in his ear, repeated so he wouldn't forget. *Goblins and gremlins: they'll catch you in your sleep if you don't say your prayers.* The nurse's cheek against his, her hair falling against his eyes before sleep. In his dreams she's nubile, available to his small penis, overshadowing the girls he actually bedded. Let alone his wife, the sad shy Gretchen, whose green face after he entered her made him think of goblins indeed

After the priests took over from his wetnurse, over the years goblins and gremlins were succeeded by demons and devils, by images of hell that sure enough resembled the blood of battle. But these muddy sieges, Paris Orléans, weaponed by hunger and stink, still feel more like goblins' work. Complete with the crazy woman in men's clothes and fool's armor—now presiding, it seems, over slaughter.

She's shouted to him in a flat Frankish whose vowels lay so low under her mouth that he couldn't understand her, then put her gorget down when his footmen called her out for a whore.

He turns to Poole, earl of Suffolk, who's journeyed over from 'Rouen' to enjoy a meal not stuck in mud. "But now her witchcraft has eviscerated St.-Loup—how?"

"I'm not sure it's witchcraft," offers Suffolk. "A girl in armor is such a surprising thing." He cranes his neck to get a good look. "She gives them hope, so they push on."

Glasdale swallows. "And murders our good men." The men at that small fortress all so young. not yet ready for real battle. "Did their whores burn too? Is there anyone left, or did they kill them all?"

Jehanne nudges Arielle, her favorite filly, into a gallop. Once on, she's so happy to be on a horse that she wants to just keep riding. Ride till the houses blur; till the smell of dried blood and human feces is submerged by horse-smell, by her own sweat. Behind her ride Pierre and Gilles de Laval; four footmen and an archer; Louis de Coutes and Dolon. She ignores them all for the moment, this too-brief ride.

She's gone from sleepy to shaking again, the angels pushing harder at her now, their *oui* a silvery hiss in her ear: yes oh yes. Yes this *chevalerie.* Yes oh yes getting the girls to safety, yes oh yes making the boys pray every day and practice fighting. For the day when France is whole. The push vague, uncertain as to the details: just as they left her to breed the *chevalerie,* they're leading her to learn to command. Not a cow's teats but artillery, not pulling weeds but taming men. Her throat constricts. The clanking of armor and screaming of steel. Her face still wet with it.

Pasquerel her midnight confessor, her early morning teacher: her hand on his while he wrote. Curving the J line. Tracing the word *Dieu,* feeling it in her fingers. She giggled as she wove the words, whispering in the priest's ear like a lover's. *Ask for our couriers back, offer him some of those we captured from St.-Loup, who he thinks are still lying somewhere. Most of all, tell him he's doomed unless:* the threat a drug in her exhausted veins.

The gallop has got her to the shoreline quicker than she expected. The bastides by the Loire taunt her, as the meaningless shouts begin. She stops and waits for the rest to catch up and then nods to the archer, who extracts the arrow that holds her words. She takes a deep breath, to make her voice as loud as she can. As he shoots the arrow up to the Tourelles, she cries out: "This is news for you!" The words back loud, loose, understood if not heeded. *Armagnac,* they will never say France. *France,* her magic word. *Pour le jour où la France est entière.* when France is whole.

The old man the one hissing the words to her now. She cranes to see his wrinkled face. Classidas: he butchered French at Azincort. Rage cold inside: tight like her breath. The tower seems to tremble in her sleepless eyes.

Glasdale tosses the scroll, unread, to the younger man who can still stand to read their Frankish scrawl. "More words from the whore."

Suffolk uncoils the scroll, squints at it briefly. "Jesus Mary—her usual solicitation. Surrender, surrender, la la la . Oh! She tells you if we free her heralds, they'll return some prisoners." He suppresses a laugh: her words arch, playful, *for they are not all dead.* "She's charming on paper—she's made of herself a sun." He sighs, rolls the scroll tightly. "No wonder they adore her."

The old man nods. They kill for love, for hope. He was older than his young king fourteen years ago, when they marched first on Harfleur. Flaxen hair, that Henry: twenty-seven years old, soft eyes that turned steely when he gave the order. Knights wept in his presence, women collapsed at his feet, footmen embraced him and called his name out when they loosed the longbow: "Henry, my good king!" Agincourt won for love of him, the archers joyous in their exhaustion. Arrogant gilded French nobles crushing their own fields in shattered armor, blood pooled under them like jelly. Glasdale held one of their breastplates in his hand and imagined he could see it breathe. For love of a young king. A king who charmed another into disinheriting his own son, the one the bitch fights for now; a king then stolen from him, from all England by this pusbag of a country and its witchy sicknesses. He probably still kills for love of that young king, though not deeply felt anymore: just an ache in his rheumy eyes, a dead weight in his left side.

Maybe his young king was struck down by a curse from some witch, like the girl in long pants—the one who now makes Frenchmen kill for love of *her*, it seems. Glasdale shakes his head. "I don't doubt she bleeds small animals to buy her victories. And that banner—sacrilege!" He sends a volley of spittle out the window, though the bitch is long gone. The breastplate breathes its last.

Suffolk sighs. He's never fought so closely beside Glasdale, not separated by legions of men or court wall: he heard of his glory at Agincourt only by words. The old man seems bound by it now, nearly blinded: he keeps expecting the same, over-laden and clumsy Frenchmen they defeated there. Not this younger, hungrier crew. And the appearance of the boygirl has the old man completely bollixed, it seems.

"We'll crush them," Suffolk promises reflexively. "Think of the girl as that shudder after death, when the body delivers a hard kick just before dying entirely. A whore can't do that much damage."

Glasdale looks sourly out the window. He doesn't answer Suffolk: the younger man's assurances slide down his armor to the floor, nearly un-heard. He sees the witch's brother across the river, following a much larger man whose curls touch his shoulders, arrogant without him. The curly-haired giant raises a muscular arm and points: he sees him. "Look at that," Glasdale turns to Suffolk. "How long are we to put up with insults like that? I'm near as starved as them. Perhaps we *should* raise a bridge and burn them." He can almost hear the *pop!* of the young man's bones as they catch fire.

Why did he do that? Gilles thinks as he lowers his arm. The old Englishman Classidas, a vague shape in the half-darkened window, grew still after he pointed; for all Gilles knows he may be giving orders to cut his throat. He'd almost welcome it: he might feel it. Yesterday he cut himself on his own armor and welcomed the sharpness of the sensation.

"You can smell their horses!" Pierre exclaims, pointing himself to the masses of men crammed into the towers. "They're readying for a fight. They know we're coming."

"As long as *we* know," Gilles says tartly. "Come on—the mass they're leading the soldiers in will be over any minute. Then it's our turn." Jehanne has assigned them to lead these disparate armies in some form of training exercise, to test strength and communication, to ensure smooth transitions from one army to the next. It keeps Gilles testing all his language skills parsing dialect after dialect, and remembering the failed battle for Verneuil as he plans what they should do in the morning fields. Jehanne, the Batard, and the other commanders will decide, within the hour, what they should do for real.

Meanwhile Gilles, Pierre, and the others will charge at trees, share the controls of bombards, and supply one another with arrows all morning: And they are under strict instructions: as they do this, the soldiers are to recite the name of France and that of God in equal measure. "*France* is a word rarely used in Brittany, in Marseilles, along the Côte d'Azur,." she says hotly, "I want to hear it from every mouth. *pour le jour où la France est entière Pour France, e pour Dieu.*"

Gilles whips his horse, hard. He hopes the old commander can see it. Together, he and Pierre shout the new prayer across the river.

The messengers' packets to Chinon have always been delivered to Yolande: it's easier for her to go through the dross, the merchants begging for payment and tiresome university dons complaining about the coarseness of it all, in case something secret slipped in—a bribe accepted, a marriage disgraced. The ones from Orléans don't even go through her dependable *chatelain,* Gérard: she receives them direct from the courier's rainy hands, as if opening a bouquet of flowers. Even the university dons speak of La Pucelle, even if sneering.

Fleet-footed couriers have already come just to bear news from the Batard—last night's first victory in over a year, at St.-Loup. "A miracle!" they cried. *Not much,* she thought, knowing the Tourelles still burst with Englishmen. And the young man's words barely mentioned Yolande's gift to him. The queen of Jerusalem stood at vespers, that Ascension Day, and wondered if the girl was even there.

Her answer in this morning's packet, nearly-hidden under

some knight's vast complaint. Jehan Pasquerel's hand is even, scriptural, with more capitals than she is used to. The missive itself is brief, coded. It speaks of *chevalerie,* and the Bouchers' hospitality, and tells Yolande to "tell the Dauphin to ready for Reims." Yes, she was there, yes her madness is still live: even more so on the page, in the letters in it that waver, whether from dampness or something else that reveals itself at the bottom. A tall extravagant *J,* the slightly reversed *e,* the *n*'s that clump together and spill over onto the final *e.* And underneath, crudely drawn, crudely said: *"Les enfants son ici, et il est terrible."* The terrible swift sword of her boys and girls. Then: *You know what to do with this letter.*

Yolande holds up the letter closer to the light of the fire and reads it again. She knows better than to feel anything like the warmth in her chest, the dampness along one softly wrinkled cheek. Is she some girl, overheated by war? some boy aroused by a girl's voice, even on paper? Her growling stomach can't decide. Maybe she's just hungry.

Or maybe she's sorry that he's left already—the furry-chested Spaniard who climbs her back stairs every fortnight or so, on his way to his fields near Marseilles. She could use some physical comfort, even from another woman's husband—to replace the phantom warmth from another woman's daughter? Yolande shakes her head, laughing at herself, and drops the letter into the fire. She watches the girl's name melt.

Robert di Baudricort, commander of Vaucouleurs, has not been this far from home in a very, very long time. Compared to Orléans, his fortress seems like a hut, a collection of stones inhabited by young roughnecks and protected at the point of a needle. His crew, including the youngest son of Henri Le Royer, who hosted Jehanne at Vaucouleurs, has been swallowed up inside the militias of Alençon, de Rais, and even Jehanne's own:

tens of thousands of men and horses. He hasn't yet seen "La Pucelle," as all the soldiers who don't know her call her. Only a small, royal-looking figure in the distance, only from behind: Just her back, in that white armor; the banner with JHESUS MARIA and the fleur-de-lys. As far from the flat-booted girl in the red surcoat, holding her uncle's hand, as he could have imagined. Her steadfastness at St.-Loup sealed his original bet, taken in March: she's not a woman, she may well be sent by God.

The armies leave from Burgundy Gate en masse, a riot of metal and hoofbeats breaking the morning in two, and roar toward the shoreline, behind the Batard, Gilles de Laval, and the white-iron *generale*. The roar made up equally of human voices, commands shouted, confusion cried out, and wood striking metal, as the boatmen on the shore push back the knights who thought their boats capable of anything. Separate boats carry the artillery: the bombard, the cannons, the gunpowder array and long heavy gunrows.

Di Baudricort can't stop grinning, and wants to suppress a laugh: it's been far too long since he was part of such theatrics. The Loire is far grander than the spit called the Meuse, too: it feels a lake. And he admires the evidence of the Batard's work, bits of the main bridge peeking their heads out above the water like stone corpses.

When he reaches the south shore of the Loire, behind the Agustin boulevard, there she is: as if she has waited till now to greet him.

Off her horse, her gorget set aside and her hood thrown back, she looks young again, and her eyes have the same directness. "Commander," she bows to him. "Finally I can welcome you, though we are all"—she bites her lip—"a little busy."

Di Baudricort has to fight off an odd urge to kneel at her feet, as if she were a sovereign or saint instead of a former peasant girl. What he sees instead is the straight shoulders, the easy hand on her sword, not the one he gave her. "Your voices tell us we'll have victory here?" he decides to answer her directness with his own.

"Against the desires of some," she spits, for the first time nasty. "I won't bore you with my arguments—you'll just notice who is not here." And she doesn't mean old Auguste, who she's ordered stay in his pub, or her dear Alençon, who's returned by stealth to his family estates, before a major battle risks his return to prison. She means the commanders like de Gaucourt, who would have delayed this day forever.

She turns then, with him, to face the *boulevard,* the wall of weaponry and edgy archers. The boats' landing has brought them all to attention, and the odd silence awaits only her call. Her hands tight in her gloves: this far huger than any fortress she's seen, this military machine, this wall of men and guns. The clanking of armor and screaming of steel as it explodes.

But before she can do anything, say anything, the wall molts, knights flooding out of the Tourelles and the Agustin boulevard toward them. For most of the rest of the day she knows only calling to her men, signaling to di Baudricort and Gilles and the others. kneeling to help a cannoneer and trying to deafen herself and not die. Her horse braver than her. Hours of it. Five times more men than St.-Loup, blood streaming along the narrows between cobblestones. Her blood heats. Where is the braided voice? Is her phantom army working elsewhere? Her form of prayer: *show me what you can do. teach me how.* Their lance, their sword in her hand.

Then she forgets them amid the burning powder: is this what charred her village? She finds herself staring at the base of a bombard as if it were a tiny altar, and hears herself cheering when its projectile launches. Peace of God indeed, these bombs could burn them all. Why is she cheering? The bombardier hears her and grins, before loosing another. The fire comes in their direction too, followed by arrows from longbows, that English poison.

Then she sees it: an English archer pauses, looking behind him as if struck, though no fire or sword has yet come near. Like the public house. Like at St.-Loup? The pause is a fraction of a second, as if a cramp in the leg or a fierce need to shit had moved him—but his face looks like he's been seized by a nightmare. A day nightmare. Like her, milking the cows. She lets herself separate, like back then: watches herself talk to di Baudricort, watches Gilles and Pierre guard her back. But she's separated, off inside the *boulevard.* where she sees a small but important number of knights do exactly the same.

Her skin is damp. What nightmare? Were they all raped too? Too many for that, what do they see, what pulls them away? For the first time since she was twelve she wonders if they are devils after all, this phantom army, pushing men to defeat with black art and story. She watches de la Pole, that fat man who taunted her last week, tremble and recover himself. She wants to ask him: *what happened to you?* Another, not much older than her or Pierre, is crying openly, just before a *couleivrin* sends a rock into his temple. The blood races his tears down his face.

The braided voice tells her she's seen enough now, and returns her to the shoreline, where Dolon and Gilles and Pierre all surround her like a phalanx, trying to force water through her lips. The noise is beginning to die down as the remains of the English retreat. Di Baudricort, among others, is forcing the shackled into boats headed to their prison. She pushes Gilles' hand away. "Get it to one of our wounded." Then she looks over their heads. "Where's the Father? Who can write the news, that the Convent of St.-Agustin is returned to the hands of God?" Her own tears stop the laugh that wants to come, at the thought of the commanders who ran from this work. They didn't yet believe what she has. And she still can't tell them—especially when she still only knows part of the answer. But even that part would have her burned as a witch as surely as the walls of the boulevard burn now.

. . .

Pasquerel's too busy administering last rites to be any sort of a scribe. The words of extreme unction fall from his lips like a child's Hail Mary, like the opening paternoster of a rosary, till they become near-meaningless. Jehanne's insisted on this, "the peace of God doesn't let them go unshrived." He's developed a rhythm: When he sees a young or old knight climb a barricade, swinging a pickax or hefting a crossbow, he tries to remember the man's last confession. If the man is mortally injured, he's ready; he meets the litter as the dying man is carried to him and begins. "Per istam sanctam unctionem et suam piissinan misericordiam," *through this holy ritual and the great goodness of His mercy,* "indulgeat tibi Dominus" *may God forgive you for sins of the flesh, or the word* or some vague muttering that he hopes will be understood as an encompassing cry for mercy. The whole process tiring and soothing in its way: he didn't have to watch the fighting, or try to understand what was going on. Just oil them with his long-cloistered bottle and throw toneless words over the body, trying to race the stopping of breath.

The end of the battle finds him empty, though, as if all those Latin words had sucked the rest from him. It's Gilles who finds him, still knelt by a burly knight from Bourges, who wept for his grandchild and his whore and whose beard is soaked with drool. "Pater," the Latin falls smoothly off his tongue. "Come, they're waiting for you."

Pasquerel looks up from his damp palms. For a moment he forgets who this is, the handsome mustachioed young man whose eyebrows seem to move independent of his eyes. They only met two days ago, after all, and he's mostly seen the commander from Rais in the company of Jehanne's brother. But then the other man kneels and pulls him to standing by his elbows, gently, like a father getting his son to stand on two feet. Pasquerel hadn't realized how much taller Gilles is.

"Is she all right?" Pasquerel remembers to ask, astonished that it's taken this long.

Gilles nods. "She's led us to victory when no one expected it. How do you think she feels?" He reaches out and dabs at the priest's face: Pasquerel starts when he sees what's on de Rais' hands. "Someone spit blood on you, father?"

"I suppose," Pasquerel says, as tartly as he ever has. He steps back from Gilles and begins to walk beside him. The last battle he'd seen from the periphery, and anyway it felt like a court theatre compared with today. Now he feels flayed, overstimulated. Too many bulging eyes and tongues gone loose, still. When they get to a stand of plane trees, flush with the fullness of spring, Pasquerel veers under one and throws up.

Gilles stands, impassive, as the priest stands and rights himself. Priests either shake with glory or dissolve: why he's never quite understood the point of bringing them to the battlefield. And isn't this one for La Pucelle? Why did he veer so far from her? Still, he holds out his hand when Pasquerel rejoins him, and says the only thing he has to offer. "It gets easier, Father. You likely won't throw up again."

"Because my heart will harden?" Pasquerel feels righted, now: able to look more closely at the young man, even if it hurts his neck to do it. "How can I stand the memory?"

"You swallow them, Father. Like bile. Then you forget, except. They become the bile you fight with." Gilles lets a smile play on his lips then: the best revenge.

"I'm not sure God would approve."

"God makes it happen! Who makes us forget but Him?" Gilles sighs. 'Listen—a soft wood makes a terrible tool. . . . If we want to be useful to her, to God—how can we be soft? I'm not saying you will become dead, Father. But you will feel a little less —and it will enable you to help her more, not less." And anyway you don't have a choice, he thinks. If this war goes on many more years you may feel as little pain as I, and have no memory of pleasure. But then, what is pleasure to a priest anyway? "What do you enjoy, Father?" he asks the somber man as they approach the shoreline. "In moments not taken up in prayer."

Pasquerel looks up at him, startled by the sweetness of the question. "Good food," he says, though his thinness belies it. "The sound of a choir warming up before Mass. A fire roaring during dinner, in winter." He looks over and realizes he's lost the young man's attention. Just as well: he's a little too young to be such a doddering sentimentalist.

"She's gone ahead, to the other bank," Gilles tells him, helping him balance as he places one foot, than the other in the rickety boat, and sits next to a sleeping footman. Pasquerel wonders if he'll sleep tonight, and if he can stand to dream.

When William Poole thinks he's finished vomiting, it starts up again: as surely as if he'd eaten sour meat atop St. Agustin. He can't even find a place more comfortable than the back of the boat that brought him across the Loire; every time he stands up, the pain in his midsection shoots hard, threatening diarrhea. At this point there's nothing left: he has only bits of tooth and his own snot to hack into the bad water.

"My lord!" his manservant keeps offering cloths, and urging him to get up and inside toward warmth. "Take my shoulder, sir. It's not far."

He doesn't want a cloth, or to get back on a horse toward the boulevard. He wants his stomach to stop heaving: he wants to stop seeing her body by the side of the wall. Seeing all of them. Rouen is English now, her face ten years dead, why now why this defeat? piles of useless mouths and child bones. The smell of piled cunts. Not now: the Tourelles choked with the smell of their own defeat. Suffolk groans and lets his servant help him out of the boat, and onto an old nag kept at the Tourelles for that purpose.

"Maybe she is a witch after all," he tells Glasdale, who remained behind while younger men massed to defend the Augustinian fortress. "They fought bravely and well, with her name in their mouths." The word haunts him. "*Poo-cell, poo-cell,* they call her Virgin like some recreation of the blessed Mother."

"Sacrilege," Glasdale murmurs, but his heart doesn't seem in it. It's late, and despite the pandemonium he mostly wants to sleep. "Are you all right?" he asks Suffolk. "You're a bit green."

"I've never been beaten by a woman before," Suffolk says, despite himself. Does he really think it's due to her?

"Well, get yourself right, son!" Glasdale suddenly the senior commander directing a new recruit. "Go find a woman to bruise. Practice defeating her." He starts to laugh, loosely, almost obscenely. "Smash the cunt by all means necessary."

"Oh, we will, no doubt!" Suffolk picks up Glasdale's laugh, until his stomach heaves again. Rouen dead cunt smell. Gnawing on child bones. His own pickax across a French throat. Memory as pickax: dangerous. He still accepts the fatherly slap on his back as he says his goodbye; then he gets back on his horse to go sleep at 'Paris,' before Glasdale makes him throw up again.

Glasdale watches Suffolk ride off from the window; he can also see the twin opposing boulevards stuffed with soldiers, though depleted from the battle on both sides. He's not as confident as Suffolk about their prospects here. They should have overrun the city walls last fall, after they nearly killed the Batard and sent the others fleeing, when they still had Burgundy firmly with them. Now, he may be deceiving himself but the lights still lingering in the French boulevard seem brighter, with more noise coming from it, as if victory were keeping them awake. His men, in the other boulevard, already deep in sleep. He wonders if they're gathering what they need for the next battle, or already practicing for their final rest.

ten

"WHY ARE WOMEN SO BLOODTHIRSTY?" Georges de la Tremoille leans to the floor and picks up a broken arrow from the pile he keeps there. He leans back and hurls its tip toward the wash-tub in the corner of his bedroom—a game he learned from the young soldiers in his company, a dozen years past. When it sinks into the water, he laughs and hands the next one to the young man beside him, who is also the young dauphin of France.

"You mean my wife, or your mistress?" Charles holds the arrow in the palm of his hand like a gift.

"I mean these women pushing more war at us."

Charles sighs. Like Yolande, the man means?

"Or the one she's sponsored, who claims to come from God." He reaches over and holds the young king's hand, manipulating the arrowhead till it points out, toward the washtub. "Like this!" He pushes Charles' hand forward, but the arrowhead falls far short of its goal. "Women like to let men bleed, for the glory of some idea; they're not the ones who end up with nightmares. Oh sure, they'll weep for their sons, but I've never seen a woman happier than when she hears of a battlefield victory she didn't have to earn." He throws the next arrowhead. "Did you see Yolande, when she heard of that one piddling rout at Orléans? You'd think someone just impregnated her." Together, they watch the half-arrow crash against the side of the tub. "She's not the one thrown in prison, or worse."

Charles retrieves the arrow, before raising his eyes to meet the older man's. At forty-four, the man *has* been imprisoned by the English, some the same Englishmen now holding Orléans. "You fear Classidas is about to slaughter everyone?"

The older man sighs, and shifts in his chair. His massive bulk seems huger in this small and highly layered room, with soft cloths and thick-woven bedclothes occupying much of the empty space, his bejeweled wine goblet a ghost of his own rooms, back in Bourges. "Not exactly. . . . Perhaps we even need to do this. But *only* this," he throws another arrowhead. It pierces the side of the washtub, ever so slightly. "My people can begin negotiating immediately. We'll be a united front soon enough." He hands Charles another arrowhead.

Charles' throw is surer now, though not as sure as his mentor's. De Tremoille does seem to have a powerful vision—even if it directly contradicts that of de Richemont and Yolande. *Front uni*: a joining of Armagnac and Burgundian, Capetian France indeed. Hands joined in peace—*then* to expel the English. Not until. Yolande thinks it's all a fanciful story. to cover his spin from Dijon to Chinon, from the Duke to the Dauphin. "So he doesn't think it's treason, just strategy." He watches the old man gather up his next arrow, and tries to imagine him subject to English taunts.

The next arrowhead never reaches the tub, stopped instead by a gloved hand.

De Tremoille looks up, startled, and bursts out laughing. "I thought it was your Sicilian boyfriend!" He half-stands, gesturing to his chair. "Your Majesty, I am humbled by your arrival—with me in my dressing gown."

Yolande gestures dismissively. "My lord, you are more in need than I of its support." Her hip tells her otherwise, but she won't admit that to him or Le Brat. "I do apologize for interrupting this important conference. . . ." She waits a second for their demurs, then raises her right hand and gives a scroll to her son. 'I thought you'd be impressed," she says to La Tremoille, "what she had the soldiers chanting today, as they took St.-Agustin."

The two men rise to their feet, involuntarily. Is she really telling them that—but before they can ask she's barreling forward, before the Dauphin can unroll the parchment. "*Pour le jour où la France est entière.* Your idea?"

The older man reaches toward the scroll, until he and Charles pull at it from opposite ends. It's hard to tell, from the expression on his face, what the revelation means to him. Either revelation: if St Agustin is really theirs, and if Jehanne has had soldiers chanting for a united France. "She thinks to unite us in blood," he says finally. "As blood-filled as the Scripture. I prefer, as you know," he says to Charles pointedly ignoring Yolande, "more peaceful means."

Charles stays bent to the scroll, and doesn't reply. The list of dead as daunting as the other words from the unfamiliar scribe. He reaches over and takes one of the arrowheads in his fingers, starts to use it as a pointer as he looks at the small map drawn in its center. He wishes it could speak. And that both of them would stop, and leave him to work on the proclamation he keeps trying to write, to inform his people of what has happened. He looks for the name of Jehan d'Orléans in the scroll and finds him, thankfully not dead. "Jehan will know," he says carefully. "Who cares more about Orléans?"

"The Batard is being kept a little busy, by your pet," la Tremoille says to Yolande. "Perhaps too busy to know what will most serve Orléans."

Charles raises his voice louder, against being ignored again.

"But if it's your way," to la Tremoille, "I'll never be crowned!'
He hurls two arrowheads toward the tub at once, and cracks its
side. As manservants rush to absorb the water seeping to the
floor, La Tremoille has one of them lift his feet and put them on
a stool. Charles blushes deep, mortified; Yolande covers her
mouth, to stuff back in the laughter.

Jehanne watches the moon rise from her tent, and tries to let a
strange man inspect her right breast.

The roof over her is heavy cloth, the room inside crammed
with the familiar and unfamiliar; the Batard, Louis, Pierre,
Pasquerel and even Gilles de Laval. This day a blur of fighting, of
men climbing pieces of the Tourelles, even men like de
Gaucourt, who'd argued against the speed her angels demanded.
Somewhere, in there, her standard—the flag she's carried since
Blois, Christ on one side a dove on the other—went missing, so
she grabbed her banner instead and howled louder so they still
know where she is.

And over and over the same: English cannoneers and archers
momentarily blinded, so her men can cut their throats. Until she
saw, and was distracted herself. The tent smells of olive oil and
bacon.

'We'll have to have a real surgeon on this wound when all
this is over," the shy barber murmurs as he dabs at her breast to
clean it. She winces at the sting of bacon fat. She told Pasquerel
this would happen. She'd begged her angels last night to tell her
how they did it: what they made the English see. A vision of
apocalypse? Their own death? The destruction of their homes?
In reply, they'd slammed her with a presentiment of an arrow in
her flesh.

Finally Jehanne nods to the barber, who retreats. The
Batard, who has waited patiently through it all, clears his throat
as she begins to re-arm. She lifts her head to his report, and meets

his tired exhilarated eyes. Many English captured, though "not de la Pole or Classidas."

"I know," Jehanne says quietly.

The Batard starts. Though her words aren't smug or chiding, his pride is hurt. His men died well, he personally put shackles on de la Pole's closest lieutenant: why is she not surprised? "Your voices told you this?"

She shakes her head. It was when her eyes locked with de la Pole's that she got her wish, she saw what he saw. Her hand still clenches with it, four hours later. A city all dark red-brown stone, a proud fortress: siege walls thicker and closer than these. Only the tiniest of quarter-seconds, of the other city surrounding her, a death-stench worse than here. A memory full force, smells and breeze and sound. No ghosts or apocalypse. Only memory, a canny weapon indeed.

And it was while she was looking at the red-brown fortress, instead of the battle before her, that it happened: a pain unexpected, almost unimaginable, as the arrow tore just above her breast and teased its slope. A burning pain, not drowned by the slick fluid that stains her surcoat, dissolved the Rouen in her eyes —for Rouen it was, she gasped aware. Dissolved into the circlet of men who pulled her down, her own forming a protective arc and moving her out of the line of battle. How did they find a barber so quickly? She doesn't remember what she said then, only that she urged her men to fight on, that she yelled herself hoarse from just outside this tent. More hours of it, her men pulling the one empty tower apart like so much bread. Once-elegant stone now squashed under boots.

Now the Batard is telling her what the commanders have decided, yet again: yes, it is time to retreat. The exhaustion as clear as the exhilaration. "Two long days of fighting . . ."

She shakes her head again, to sweep Rouen out from under her eyelashes, and tries to concentrate on what the man is saying. In her throat and chest a different yearning, for affirmation from her braided voice. She needs to know that they approve of her speed. Of her men of *chevalerie* pounding at the Tourelles before anyone thought themselves ready.

In the tower still standing, Glasdale stares out, stunned. How many of his men are lost? Can that witch have truly returned, after the Augustine, to slaughter another day? He waits while his man tightens his tunic, nearly snapping the aged string pulled hard against too many feasts. He hasn't felt the need of full armor until now: but now is their last chance to hold this city. to hold off the supernaturally strong whoreson army. To fight for his young blond king's vision. Not just the dead Henry V, for whom so many died and killed at Agincourt, but also the new one, the seven-year-old monarch who has already presided over sessions of his cabinet; whose flaxen hair recalls his father and who believes, with all his infant heart, that France is English ground. They fight for love.

And Thomas Glasdale, veteran of Agincourt and Verneuil. has a plan. When the sun's fully down, as they retreat for the night—this is the time to descend in full fury, make a bridge across the Loire, and burn their cathedral. He'll take on the witch personally if need be.

He holds out his arms so the servant can put on his breastplate. It's older than he is, the young servant thinks, as he holds up the battered metal. The evening wraps the towers in quiet, but it's more like the whole war is holding its breath.

As Jehanne finishes dressing, Jehan d'Orléans keeps looking at the bridge half-destroyed by his own command last fall.

The thought frightens, soothes, impels. *His* work, his war, his city. As pleased as he is with how all this has gone, he wonders if anyone will remember him when this is all over, or only the magic boygirl with the loud voice and the priests' heart. His own men are saying it: *la pucelle. le béni pucelle*—even, God help them all for the temerity, *la saint pucelle,* as if she'll next birth a new messiah. He can't think of anyone less motherly than this squat soldier-figure. squeezing out of a tent that can barely hold so much armor. She must know that. Instead of her standard she holds a small torch, and for a moment he wonders if it's her hand that's aflame. He's still hoping he can trust her.

"Every time I see you," she says softly, "you're calling retreat. Even now."

"Only for time to gain strength, mademoiselle," he says formally. "In the morning we'll finish the task." He can't any more hope to curb the fanatic energy in those eyes, which has only grown bolder with this week's victories. He reaches out and dares touch the patch of bloodstained surcoat still visible.

Jehanne looks down at his hand as if at a small cockroach. "Start preparing them to retreat," she says softly. "I'll go consult my advice, and tell you what we are to do." She turns away without waiting for assent, Pasquerel following her out of the tent.

The priest is still a little drawn about the face, as if yesterday's festival of extreme unction had doused his lights. He can't believe this girl, whose face grows rosier, it seems, with each battle. Now it's as if the wound in her breast sent blood to her face, like fresh winter air or new love. Her eyes still as distracted as when it hit.

She leads him to a small vineyard by the river, tentative green spurts of vine and a battered bower. Pasquerel finds himself watching the mass of soldiers nearby for familiar faces—looking in particular for Pierre and Gilles, the faux brethren who helped nurse him back to shore yesterday. The knight from Rais makes him feel safe somehow, he told Isabelle when he last wrote her (coaching the courier in the Lorraine pronunciations. *your son has chosen well.*) He stops when she does, along with her

footman and a couple of trusted archers, and watches her drop
to her knees. Her eyes closed, her shaking hands press together
on a vertical. The vines like rough-hewn lace.

Gilles de Laval hasn't finished pulling a *gisarme* out of an
English body when he hears Pierre's voice calling for help. He
turns at the voice—the young man who feels more like his
brother than La Pucelle's—and roars *"Moment!"* He rears back
to gain more leverage and the forked weapon emerges, bits of
flesh on each blade. One blade half-curls, like a demented garden
implement.

Pierre comes round the side of the curved tower, his face
flushed. "I can't get up to the second window!" He points to his
boots, as cracked and torn as the Englishman's skin.

"Your sister," Gilles says pointedly, "will kill me if I help you
do it. Don't think she makes you immortal." He makes the sign
of the cross over the Englishman and moves away, letting the
thick body fall against the wall. As night begins to fall the soft
light makes all of them sculptural, live and corpse alike.

"Is she going to keep us fighting in this darkness?"

"Hasn't she told you?" Gilles watches the moon rise over the
young man's shoulder. His back aches and his cock hurts. He
knows he'll have a good beer when this is over, if not relief from
the girl Jehanne sent away. "Why on earth did she chase off good
pussy?" he asks for the tenth time.

Pierre hesitates. Can he tell his friend? would she forgive him
if he did? His reverie is interrupted when Gilles points, and he
sees his sister kneeling in the vineyard. He knows that face. It
means she's remembering, in pieces.

Jehanne blinks against the onslaught of angel-faces. She's no
longer used to seeing or hearing them, grown used to their pres-

ence as only a touch or a breath, or that elusive maddening braided voice. Less disorienting, to be sure—but now, when the delivery of Orléans trembles on the vine, there they are. The boy from Tunis. The pregnant girl from Sicily who rode on Yolande's shoulder. Women swathed in black from the *desért* dream. A new headless girl with black skin, one of hundreds who were left with those heads inserted between their legs by miffed soldiers: and in case she missed the connection a quick flash of the one who broke her apart, fumbling as he pulled at twelve-year-old legs. Old men with yellowish faces and queer narrowed eyes.

It's like the very beginning, in her Domrémy bedroom, and she understands why: it's not to disable her, like then, but to do the opposite and light her rage. The clanking of her armor the screaming of her steel. The headless girl's hand clasped in hers.

And from the corner of her eye she sees it: her standard, rescued by one of the local Orleannais from whatever swamp it had gotten stuck in. The words "Jhesus Maria," the angel Gabriel and an avuncular God, the silver dove with more words out its mouth. All images not hers and suddenly hers, now that this dumpy little knight has found it, and her angels clearing her vision enough for her to see it. The Batard's retreat has to stop.

Jehanne takes Pasquerel's hand. "Look!" and bolts from the vineyard.

So the armies follow her standard now that it's more visible —while the Batard, at her sign, sets his men on the task they've so long perfected, destroying their beloved city in order to save it. Just as when they burned the suburbs, and hacked the bridge in two. Now they set fire to one of the city barges, send it roaring in the direction of the last drawbridge to the towers.

Glasdale finishes making his way down the stairs, cursing his bad knees all the way. Pride coursing through nonetheless, his men under orders to charge at his signal. But by the time he gets there the sounds of retreat have turned into something else: flames and battle cries. He throws his arm up to signal attack, even though they've lost the initiative. The witch, and those who kill for love of her, won't win this time.

She's only a few yards away, now, howling with fishwife rage. The name of the Savior spit foully from her sickened mouth. She's calling on him to surrender *du Roy de ciel,* as if she knows anything of God. His armor feels a thousand pounds heavy as he turns to her. She lifts her visor and he does the same: what do Satan's eyes reveal? Blue. merciless blue, tears like his wife's. *You lie.* For the love of a young king he will take her down. He roars in her direction, hand on his sword.

Then: his skin cold suddenly, a feeling of rain: instead of night full day, mid-morning. Body not so heavy now, he moves agilely between troops. No Loire here but mud-streaked autumn leaves, and his body a hundred times stronger: Instead of this trembling tower a flat field. His glaive, his long knife, is deep in a Frenchman's throat but not an Orleannais: he holds the trembling bloodied plate of his memory and can't breathe. Laughter and tears and the memory that has pushed at him the hardest these fifteen years, now not in pieces but full color.

When his vision clears and returns him to Orléans, the Loire is streaming into his eyes and his struggles to breathe are not for fear or memory.

In the roar of cannon fire and men's shouts, in the blur of the dark, the splash of the fully armored old man sinking into the Loire is barely felt. The noise Pasquerel hears the most is Jehanne's involuntary scream. He turns and sees her double over, quite as if she's about to plunge herself. He's stopped giving last rites, for this moment: and runs to lift her into his arms.

By the time he's at her side she's standing again, but she's hysterical—crying one second and laughing the next—all of it deep in her chest. Around them the battle shifts—the English are in retreat, those that haven't drowned with their commander —and she won't stop crying. She only quietens when Dolon and Louis join them, but doesn't stop.

When Pasquerel prompts her, she says plainly that she's weeping for the souls of Glasdale and the others, dying un-confessed before God. An answer that brooks no questioning, even if he doesn't believe it for a minute. She won't admit to what sounds like laughter, and wraps her arms around herself in some sort of private language. "Do you need time alone, again?" They all pull away from the huge tower as the barge, the Batard's burning cannon, does its fine work.

By the time the Batard joins them, exultant, her eyes are dry and her voice calm. The only thing that betrays her is the white-ness of her fingers on the pole of her standard. Her eyes meet the Batard's. and she extends her hand. "Thank you for the barge," she says, *and for turning the retreat on itself, at my terrible order.* "Your men are brave and work well." She looks down, in what only looks like shyness. Right now she's afraid to meet any warrior's eyes.

Jehan d'Orléans sees the tears on her cheeks: she might be human after all. He looks anxiously over her shoulder a moment, before he accepts the Maid's gesture.

Then he takes her hand in both of his and inclines his head. "I've set them now to build us a bridge," *to put new wood over the shattered arches and fuel our way home.* He points to the younger soldiers swimming in the river as the English melt away. "They're happy to build again," instead of burning. Jehanne looks up. then, and her smile broadens into a crooked grin, one they've seen mostly when she's riding.

"Building new—the best part of *chevalerie,*" she says softly. An odd-feeling word in her mouth just now. A shadow still of the bleeding armor in Classidas' memory: *Egencor-teh.* Was there *chevalerie* at Azincort?

Part of her isn't watching the seal-like soldiers building their rough-hewn, temporary bridge, poor substitute for the nineteen arches they destroyed. She's trying to understand what she has just learned—from what filled her mind as completely as the angels do.

Her body still holds the sweat and mud of that other place, the young Classidas' body light, strong, his arm sure as he drove his weapon into flesh. The fleur-de-lys bleeding in his hands. That same memory blinding the old Classidas to drowning, long-delayed wages of the worst sin. It makes her chest lift, finally, her grin open wider. Vengeance in her mouth like one of Isabelle' saint cakes. It's so delicious she wishes she could shout it out to the new moon, to her confessor, to the Batard and di Baudricort. *You may be brave but my armeé fantome has turned chevalerie's enforcer.* The clanking of their armor become nightmare, and her victory.

She almost shouts it to Pierre, when he shows up, mud covering his face, but instead accepts as much of an embrace as is possible in full armor, both their mouths tracing the same word. *"Sûreté,"* thanks for the other's safety as the rocks stop flying. She doesn't know if she'll tell him, anyway: the knowledge too exhausting. Instead, she lets Pierre fuss over her shoulder, its smelly dressing. "I don't know if we should tell *maman* about this," he says again. She hopes he doesn't notice her foot tapping with angels' glee.

When the wooden faux-bridge is complete she cheers the loudest, nearly kissing the mud-strewn squires who jammed its stones and wood into place. Louis de Cotes holds her standard as she waves to the mob behind her. All their armored feet, crossing over to the other side, make a bass rumble so tremendous that one might take it for the opening of Hell.

· · ·

Jacquot Darc is deep in his cherry orchard when he hears the hoofbeats, and shouts that tell him there's news.

The Meuse Valley in May is a festival of young greens, not yet the lush variants of summer but a newer wave of shoots, excitable and pleased with themselves. The grove where Jehanne first conceived of going to Vaucouleurs is a flowering riot, past buds to voluptuary, and her father's fruit orchards are beginning to call for their first picking. There's very little, besides the absence of a few young people, to mark the war a day's ride away.

The summer harvest is in a few weeks and the cherry trees have been plagued by a particularly virulent crop of blackflies this spring, due to the luxuriant rain. With his younger children, including his odd daughter, off fighting the endless war and his field hands of dubious reliability, he's taken the time after church to give them one more feeding of lamb-dung and river water. He decides to wait, and not to join the tiny festival that attends the arrival of each herald.

Darc has never much liked couriers anyway, especially during planting and harvest season. They arrive at inconvenient times, their horses muddy up the fields and they always want to eat as soon as they arrive. Isabelle has taken to baking extra slabs of bread so that there won't be too much delay in the news they carry. Jacquot thinks that any useful communication can come later, directly from the person one's doing business with—or else it's not business worth doing. Like telling bad news. Isabelle's friend Aurelie has still not recovered from hearing her son's name on the list of the dead.

Let the others greet the courier, hand them bread and wine, and listen as the comical man wears himself out telling stories to the town. If it's good news, it can wait even longer. He bends under another tree, ducking to let the blackflies whiz past his ear.

He's about two-thirds of the way down the row when he hears the old church bell being struck—not the hesitant little stroke of Father Guillaume but something faster, either alarm or celebration. His feet seem to have heard it before he did, because he's out of the orchard before he knows it. And he can see from some distance away that even more of a crowd than usual has gathered. Now he's anxious. "What's the news?" he calls even before he gets there. He can see one woman is crying, men praying, others craning at the herald's scroll as if they could make out the marks on it. "Where's Isabelle?"

When Joubert, the carter, gestures to the church door, Jacquot's heart drops to his stomach. Is she having to pray for their daughter's soul? Did Orléans burn? By the time he gets to the church, he's pushing his way past the excited group, not bothering to stop and ask for details. And thus it is that Jacquot Darc, village doyen, interrupts Father Guillaume's ceremonial Mass celebrating the liberation of Orléans.

Father Guillaume's whispery voice stops a moment, and meets his eyes; Isabelle nearly yanks him into a pew before she returns to her prayer. The smile on her face tells him what he needs to know most—that their children are safe. He folds his muddy hands in his lap, waiting for the Latin to be over. He hates this church, has since his wife began her pilgrimages, hating it even more when his daughter began to spend hours here. "*Laudeamus dei per il returnam Johannam. . . .*" Where? where? Jacquot feels his own eyes mist a little. Jehanne's return to where? Not to his farm, to the sheep meadow where she was first defeated.

The service is over soon enough, devolved into the chatterfest the villagers really want: suddenly it's Isabelle to one side and Jehanne's friend Mengette on the other. "Bertrand says she was magnificent," Isabelle burbles. "She chased away the women of ill repute, and made a new *chevalerie*. She led a battle when all the generals said it was hopeless. And today, the English bowed down and left—just like that!"

Mengette listens carefully, saying nothing. Her belly glints another pregnancy, just a shy half-moon under her waist; little Xavier now walks gingerly beside her. She wonders about Jehanne's angel-children, and wishes she could ask her about them. As they leave the bells begin again.

The bells of Notre Dame des Miracles ring firmly, then furiously, after the English begin retreating from even St. Pouer ('Paris') or 'Rouen.' Sunday, the 8th of May, is an extraordinarily clear day, and the gentle hills surrounding Orléans carry the sound further. To William Poole, leading the retreat, each bell may as well be another blast of gunpowder, out to burst his eardrums once and for all.

Suffolk knows he'll have to answer to Bedford for this: perhaps to the history-books. *why didn't you stand and fight? Fastolf is on his way, and we'll send more reinforcements soon. Were you in mourning for Glasdale?* The old man's death has thrown him a little, to be sure—but his order came more from a need to re-group. To leave these wooden boulevards for the safety of stone walls, of fortified towns fully occupied and thus fully theirs, like Meung, Jargeau, Beaugency. To have a few days without fighting—to better understand what has just happened to them.

His neck hurts. He's afraid to ask his men if they had memory-flashes like his, fearful that they did and will break down—and equally fearful that they did not and he's the rare one who didn't die of it. Glasdale's squire has told him how his master stood frozen, whirling, unable to get to safer ground. Frozen, trapped, distracted, like him, like men in his company at St. Augustin who didn't survive that moment. He now fears the girl as much as Glasdale did. He wonders if she's the witch the old man feared. What he fears more: that she's not. She was not lying or deluded in her claims, her high-sounding letters. If that Rouen memory was a visitation straight from God.

He knows he feared to meet her eyes this morning, when her army assembled before the wreckage of the Tourelles. No words issued, but no attack issued either: a silent willingness to fight, should the English violate the Sabbath truce. Tall Spaniards and white-haired Scots adding to the elderly Orleannais and the hotshot knight from Rais, whose slim shoulders belie his power. All of them ready to charge forward, to slaughter another day, but for the smallest armed figure, her battered standard firmly in a herald's grip, whose confessor leads them instead in prayer. The two armies in battered standoff.

If he's not mistaken, she refused to meet his eyes also: is whatever she follows too huge to be shared? *Pater noster, qui es in caelis, sanctificetur nomen tuum.*

All prayer then drowned by the furious clatter of the English retreat, hundreds of armored feet and heavy wagons pulling further from the Loire. Suffolk loses himself in the mechanics of it, in evacuating the boulevards and taking at least some of their ammunition; of making sure their whores are safe; of shouting far too loudly for his advanced age, perhaps to drown out those damn celebratory bells.

It's after Mass and after Jehanne is safely secreted that some members of the town militia, encouraged by the Batard, set to give the enemy chase—to capture their artillery, in case the retreat be a feint and they plan on charging back over the river. "Don't come back," Jehan d'Orléans says slowly, "without English crossbows and bombards. Get that sleek cannon from the bottom of the Tourelles, too." Old man Auguste insists on playing, his wounded arm barely fitting in the armor he's not worn since St. Loup; Robert di Baudricort and La Hire, discomfited by too much prayer, take refuge in sword and shield. They will drag home enemy gunpowder like treats on Easter, like wedding gifts for the newly reunited

Orléans. And (it's understood) they'll kick any lingering English into dust, the more valuable being already held for ransom.

Gilles and Pierre are laden down with bows. Pierre, newly schooled in their use, is fascinated by the lightness of the long-bow, embracing it like a lover; he slips it on in its harness, ignoring the stink of its previous owner. In his arms a Germanic crossbow that kills, Gilles says. "purely by intimidation." They circle outside the city's walls, passing Renard Gate and Bannier Gate, glimpsing the proud Dutch exterior of the home of Jacques Boucher, where Jehanne sleeps. The crossbow feels lighter to carry when he gets used to it.

It feels better to be in motion than frozen in standoff, Pierre thinks. Motion means you're still alive. They jump like colts over corpses, pausing only when there are weapons to be had; the footmen that join them then scour the bodies, stripping them of hand weapons. They move north and west, toward the bastides named for cities, toward the English asses. Three days of battle and Pierre's nerves are frayed and lit at the tip: he can't decide if he would rather fight or sleep.

A mile past Bannier Gate the group happens on a pair of English soldiers who first look dead, until Pierre sees one of them groan and turn over. The French group rears back, startled: Pierre looks at Gilles—Should they be trying to capture these men instead?—while the men, instead dead asleep, barely flinch at the noise, perhaps drunk on defeat.

"Or starved of French blood," Gilles says quietly. "*Cauchemare d'Angleterre.*" Calling them out for vampires, the way they call Jehanne a witch. Pierre feels his chest open, relax. Gilles will know what to do.

The footmen swoop down and start to strip their torpid bodies of weapons, pulling off side-swords and heavy flails with iron tips. When the large Englishmen stirs and raises his arm to fight back, Gilles steps in and runs a knife across his throat, calmly, staring into the spurt of blood as if it were a calming fountain.

Taking it as a signal the footmen descend further, tearing off their visors and battering faces with stolen flails. Their tensed shoulders loosening the longer they're at it: pouring pent-up rage into these vessels. Gilles lets himself smile, and stands calmly on the large man's ankles to make the assault easier. He looks over at Pierre, nods gently.

Pierre watches Gilles' face, the face of bravery, of victory. Jehanne has praised him. And after all, these are the invaders. *Rapist of Orléans, of France, of my sister, feel my wrath*, none of it necessary to say. The motion of muscle, the laughter of the footmen, like huntsmen slicing game. The deer on Jacquot's property, eyes not near as beautiful here.

Pierre's amazed at how little he feels, bending over the thrice-dead Englishmen.

By the time they leave the field , the bodies are barely recognizable as human, but for the man-shaped armor stomped into the soft ground.

Yolande loves the soft evening air more than mead. It warms her stiff bones in ways no fire can.

One of the joys of late spring is this warming of the night; she loves the ritual unblocking of the windows, the cloths jammed in for warmth each night sighing as they're shaken out like dancing veils. Now can see out into the jewel-forest, reading code in the proud new leaves. The girl-servant who sleeps in a corner of her room is off bedding someone, leaving her with her thoughts, and freeing her to leave one of those bright cloths hanging out the window, like a girl urging in a secret lover.

Charles has finally gone to bed, after he sat up half the night composing his letter to be read in town squares announcing the delivery of Orléans. She's proud of him: it's a beautifully written document, managing to incorporate all the late news that kept breaking as he wrote—*what, Agustin? what, the Tourelles? what, Classidas?* and mentioning the most important players, so the Spaniards and Bretons don't feel slighted. And he didn't even give away their stealth weapon, already honored more on villagers' lips than she wants enemies to know. Surprise is one of the girl's best weapons, though she doesn't seem to know it.

That thought interrupted by, in quick succession, the sound of a horse skidding to a stop; a howl of watchmen, and a quieting; and a small figure crawling headfirst through her window, trying to squeeze an un-armored body through. Wiggling furiously until Yolande reaches up and helps. She pulls off the figure's heavy sword and gloves and yanks the body out till it lands, ungracefully and forcefully, in the middle of the room, the muddy boots blackening the straw spread across the wooden floor. By this point Yolande has begun to giggle, like the girl she hasn't been in forty years.

"Do I still have knees?" Jehanne asks, as she does the best curtsey possible under the circumstances. "Your Majesty d'Anjou, Sicily, Jerusalem . . ." At which point her laugh joins Yolande's and she sinks to the floor, Yolande trying to have some modicum of dignity by sitting slowly, carefully on the muddy straw, trying not to break her hip. She wants nothing more than to embrace the muddy girl, still laughing; part of her wants to strip her and clean her wound, which by rights should be seen and bled properly.

"You just couldn't let anyone else break your news," Yolande says softly, reaching for and taking the girl's damp hands. The sweat smells salty, vinegary.

"I had to ride," Jehanne says softly. She lets her eyes meet Yolande's; hers are clear, reddened, exhausted. "I can only think on a horse. My girls and boys come most freely there."

Yolande watches the quivering chin: an unlikely face of victory. Whether God or delusion, her words have weight no paternoster can offer. "Do they . . . Does your advice approve, of what happened in Orléans?"

"Approve!" Jehanne stops, swallows. Something she's not saying, replacing it only with, "They thank everyone who's done this. The Batard, La Hire, *mon frére* Pierre. His bravest of friends, the lord from Rais. My old mentor di Baudricort. They . . ." She closes her eyes, as if someone's just tossed acid in them. "They tell us to clear the way for Reims." She shakes her head, speaks more normally, the laughter returning. "I have to be back before dawn. My brother is waiting for me, for us all to travel together with Father Pasquerel. To his place."

"I know, I know, we also go to Tours next. Where your confessor—"

"Keeps his sanctuary. With more girls and boys . . ." Jehanne's voice trails off, and Yolande puts a shoulder under one of her arms. They walk together lopsidedly, like a puppet theatre or royal litter.

Together they move slowly to the bed, and Yolande helps Jehanne to lie down. She pulls the hard boots off the girl's calloused feet and loosens the strings of her undertunic, whispering nonsense syllables. Within minutes, the girl's crashed precipitously into that hard generals' sleep. Yolande remembers it from her husband, who could sink from drowse to stone sleep without a pause, who just as quickly would be up hurling a sword. Jehanne's hands uncurl, and her mouth loosens; a drip of saliva slowly travels across her cheek, cleansing and softening. Her lips are still moving, perhaps in dialogue with her girls and boys; perhaps issuing orders. Her breasts rise and fall more slowly now.

Yolande groans softly, as she lets herself lie on the edge of the bed. Her own eyes close, her arm still around the girl's shoulders. She thinks it possible that she might sleep herself, more peacefully than she has for a long time. Maybe since Azincort.

acknowledgments

My first exposure to Joan of Arc came from a Catholic children's book, a present from a beloved aunt and uncle. I must have been about ten years old, and attracted to her strength and rebellious voice; generations of former kids remember her that way. So the first acknowledgment should be to Uncle Joe and Aunt Carol, who have been my boosters through many trials and many books.

Including in the 1990s when I went to work for a peace organization that co-founded the G.I. Rights Hotline, and ended up writing a book about that work called *I Ain't Marching Anymore: Dissenters, Deserters and Objectors to America's Wars.* This book, in its way, is as much about war and dissent as my nonfiction, both woven into a hallucinatory tale about the most famous female soldier in history. That's why *Kirkus Reviews* began their summary with "The Maid of Orleans rises from the trauma of war in Lombardi's historical novel."

It then mentions one core trauma, the only one that's most obviously fictional -- the rape of young Jehanne Darc by English soldiers, something that doesn't exist in the wealth of historical sources that otherwise anchor the story. But they also know—not least from Christina Lamb's epochal *Our Bodies, Their Battlefields*—that such a rape is the opposite of inconceivable. And that it might explain the visions that drove young Joan to war. After all, in her time--150 years earlier than Shakespeare, toward the end of the Hundred Years' War--Europe was made up less of nations than atomistic states, riven by warlords and their militias. Families were still losing children to the plague, as well as the war's accompanying violence against women and children.

I first began to write *Jehanne Darc* when I was in grad school for creative writing. I'd moved back to New York to train better as a writer. But I never forgot the callers to the GI Rights Hotline—many of whom were survivors of military sexual trauma — long before it had that name. Before the Emmy-winning documentary and historic changes in the Uniform Code of Military Justice, changes that took jurisdiction in such cases away from the commands that had often ignored them. So these acknowledgments need to include those who helped me think clearly about MST, including Kathy Gilberd of the Military Law Task Force; Bruce Shapiro, now the director of the DART Center on Journalism and Trauma, and ABC News' Kathleen Hendry-Fitzgerald, who let me shadow her investigation into "Rape in the Ranks."

None of whom were in my conscious mind at the City College of New York in 2001, when the great Frederic Tuten assigned my class a ghost story. But all of them would have been unsurprised by the ghost story's first line: "By the time the fourth soldier pulls her legs open, she can't feel anything below her throat." The book is dedicated to Fred, though I'm not sure I ever talked to him about the above, about why I came back from that assignment with a French teenager who sets her church afire and sees saints.

Before we leave CCNY behind, I need to thank everyone at that English and Creative Writing Department, especially Lindsay Abrams, who like Fred helped me make that story into my masters' thesis. I wish I knew the name of the CCNY person who awarded that masters' thesis the winner of the Geraldine Griffin Moore Award, who taught me what "completely unsentimental" could mean.

But the transformation of that thesis into the book you're

holding has different midwives. The first is Mike Karpa, whose Mumblers Press got me believing in myself as a novelist again (first with *blue: season,* another tale of trauma based on a historical figure.) Mike's careful custody of the story, contending with multiple languages and fact-checks, has been essential. Speaking of fact checks, next are the members of my "Freedmanite" writers group: founded to support the writing of nonfiction by graduates of Sam Freedman's book seminar at Columbia, it broadened last year to include members' fiction and provided *invaluable* guidance as I revised the old text and began Book Two. They also keep asking me how a peace activist became obsessed with Joan of Arc, who arguably invented my two least favorite things: nationalist war and the use of artillery therein. And the last of these midwives, but absolutely far from least, is my bride, Rachel McGregor Rawlings—who teaches me every day about love, bravery, and the importance of not taking yourself too seriously.

about the author

Chris Lombardi's fiction has been shortlisted for the Pushcart Prize and the Bellwether Prize, and won both the Lowell DeJur Prize and the Germaine Griffin Moore Prize at City College of New York. Lombardi's also a veteran journalist and advocate, and author of the nonfiction *I Ain't Marching Anymore: Deserters, Dissenters and Objectors to America's Wars* (New Press, 2020). Lombardi's fiction has been published in *minnesota review*, *Anything That Moves*, *Lurch*, *The Pearl*, *Living Room*, and assorted anthologies, including *Hey, Paesan! Lesbians and Gays of Italian Descent*. Her journalism has been published by *The Nation*, *Ms. Magazine*, *Poets & Writers*, *Women's Enews*, *ABA Journal*, *American Book Review* and *Inside MS*. Her novel *The Suicide Project* was one of 12 finalists for Barbara Kingsolver's Bellwether Prize.

also by chris lombardi

I Ain't Marching Anymore: Dissenters, Deserters, and Objectors to America's Wars

blue: season